Charles F. Dole

The American Citizen

Charles F. Dole

The American Citizen

ISBN/EAN: 9783337405953

Printed in Europe, USA, Canada, Australia, Japan

Cover: Foto ©Andreas Hilbeck / pixelio.de

More available books at **www.hansebooks.com**

THE
AMERICAN CITIZEN

BY

CHARLES F. DOLE.

———•o҉⚬҉o•———

BOSTON, U.S.A.
D. C. HEATH & CO., PUBLISHERS
1891

TO

AMERICAN CITIZENSHIP

after the type of

Washington, the Adamses, and Lincoln,

noble, devoted, disinterested, magnanimous, fearless, reverent,

this book is dedicated.

PREFACE.

THERE seems to be a growing demand for the more adequate teaching of morals in the schools, especially with reference to the making of good citizens. But it is difficult to teach morals directly, or apart from the concrete subjects about which moral questions grow. Neither can sound morals be taught at all, without the touch of enthusiasm.

We have, however, in the great and interesting subjects of the conduct of governments, business, and society, precisely the kind of material to furnish us indirectly with innumerable moral examples. The consideration of the public good, the welfare of the nation, or the interests of mankind, lies in the very region where patriotic emotion and moral enthusiasm are most naturally kindled.

The design of this book grew out of a smaller one, *The Citizen and the Neighbor*, which, though intended for a very limited use, was received with such kindly favor by teachers and others, as to encourage me to try to meet a larger need.

I have had specially in view the large class of boys and girls in the upper grades of grammar schools and in high schools, or academies, as well as many adults who may wish to make a beginning in the study of citizenship. Only a few scholars can be expected to go to college or to take a thorough course in Political Economy and Politics. But all must become citizens with the responsibility of acting in private or public upon various grave and difficult problems. They ought not, surely, to meet these problems without some intelligent and serious view of their meaning.

Every intelligent boy or girl, indeed, may be presumed to wish to know the facts about the government of our country and our social institutions. The object of this book, however, is not merely to state these facts, but also to illustrate the moral principles which underlie the life of civilized men. The thoughtful scholar asks to know why we establish and maintain certain methods and usages. He can much more willingly honor the usage or obey the law after he has seen that it is founded in justice. If he can perceive the purpose, namely, the good of the whole, which all useful methods or customs are meant to serve; if he can be helped to understand that respect and obedience for established rules and usages will distinctly enhance human welfare and happiness; if he can catch the spirit of friendliness, which ennobles social intercourse and public service; if meanwhile he can see what faults and perils threaten society and demand the patriotic effort of each generation, he will thus be prepared for that which is the aim of all education — to be a good citizen. For information alone is obviously of little value unless our boys and girls have acquired a decided moral impulse. We wish them to know that they are not at school merely to learn how to earn a living, or to be able to read many books, but to become men and women who shall help the state by their lives and work.

I have endeavored, therefore, to state with sufficient clearness and illustration the chief facts and principles which every good citizen ought to know. I have also wished to leave such a permanent impression of the character of the subjects treated, as to persuade the more thoughtful scholar or reader to take up a more thorough course of study.

Some may regret that the book does not trace government and ethics to a religious basis. I profoundly believe that there is such a basis. It is possible, too, that it might be so broadly and simply treated as to develop very general agreement. But there are at present too many differences about definitions and names to make this branch of our subject suitable for a book designed for use in public schools. Meanwhile the political and economic facts here presented, and the ethical laws which they suggest, will often, I hope, lead the student to ask deeper questions, and therefore to find the closer connection and unity of the various departments of thought and life.

I have not hesitated in the case of important subjects to accept the risk of some possible repetition. For the different branches of our study run into each other and cannot be sharply divided. Thus certain subjects belong at the same time under the head of both Politics and Economics.

It will be obvious to the intelligent teacher that the kind of study which this book is designed to serve must not be made mere task-work. The main hope of its usefulness is by awakening the interest of students and stimulating them to think and talk freely about the various subjects considered. One method of use in schools, which has been suggested by a grammar school master, is as a reading-book for the advanced pupils. The teacher should then have the class discuss with him the subjects covered by the reading.

A short list of books, such as may be of interest to teachers and the more thoughtful readers and suitable for school libraries, has been added.

Besides the helpful service of my wife in revising the proof-sheets, I have to express my obligation and thanks for the aid and encouragement of my friends, Mr. John G. Brooks, Instructor in Political Economy in Harvard University; Mr. Nicholas P. Gilman, the author of "Profit Sharing"; and Mr. George S. Merriam, the author of "The Life and Times of Samuel Bowles," and other works.

CHARLES F. DOLE.

JAMAICA PLAIN, MASS.,
    March, 1891.

TABLE OF CONTENTS.

PART FIRST.

THE BEGINNINGS OF CITIZENSHIP.

PART SECOND.

THE CITIZEN AND THE GOVERNMENT; OR THE RIGHTS AND DUTIES OF CITIZENS.

PART THIRD.

ECONOMIC DUTIES; OR THE RIGHTS AND DUTIES OF BUSINESS AND MONEY.

PART FOURTH.

SOCIAL RIGHTS AND DUTIES; OR THE DUTIES OF MEN AS THEY LIVE TOGETHER IN SOCIETY.

PAGE

prisonment. The death penalty. The rights of wrong-doers; what we ought to do. The indeterminate sentence. Prison reform. The power of pardon. The prevention of crime. The detection of crime. Lynch law. A final caution 263

PART FIFTH.

INTERNATIONAL DUTIES; OR THE RIGHTS AND DUTIES OF NATIONS.

PART FIRST.

THE BEGINNINGS OF CITIZENSHIP.

PART FIRST.

THE BEGINNINGS OF CITIZENSHIP.

CHAPTER I.

THE FAMILY AND ITS GOVERNMENT.

WE come under government as soon as we are born. It is the government of the family. One of our first lessons is to obey the authority of parents or guardians. We find at once that we cannot do as we please, but that others besides ourselves must be regarded. So with the property of the home, which must not be injured or wasted. If we disobey, if we hurt the others, if we injure the house and its furniture and try to do as we please, we immediately find ourselves liable to punishment.

Obedience. — We have to obey this family government whether we understand the reasons for it or not. If it were not always perfectly just, the children would still have to obey. But there must be some deep reasons why we ought to obey. One of these reasons is the welfare of the child. We all see this for young children; since they do not know what is good for them, there must be some authority to protect them from themselves. For the child's own good, it must not be suffered to do harm to itself. It is hard to tell precisely when the child knows what is good for him, so well that he does not need to obey the parents' authority any longer; but it has been found in the experience of many generations that on the whole, while the child is still growing, that is, to the age of twenty-one years, it is best for all concerned to continue the authority of the parents. The parent, if not always wise, is likely to know much better than the child what is good for him. There might be an exceptional child wiser than his parents; but we have to make rules in view of the best good of all children.

Another reason for the family government is plainly for the sake of justice to others. Suppose a boy hurts his brother, or disturbs the household with noise, it would not be right to allow him to continue to annoy others. Indeed, every intelligent child has a good and reasonable side; when you appeal to him on his fair side, he would not thank you for letting him do harm to the others. His true self would vote that he ought to be stopped, if necessary, by force. It might happen that a parent had ordered unwisely, and an older child might think that he knew better than the parent; nevertheless, the harm that disobedience does to the family is so great that the older child ought, for the good of all, still to obey.

A third reason why we should obey parents is that they have to bear the responsibility of the family, to provide a home and the means of support, and to take the blame and loss that might arise from an unruly household. They must therefore have power to enforce the rules that seem necessary in order to succeed with their charge. There is another reason why we ought to honor and obey our parents as long as we live — this is because they love us; but we do not like to be told that we ought to give them this kind of regard, since at our best we give it freely.

Punishments. — Since there has to be authority in the family both for the child's good and for the welfare of the home, and since there must be obedience to prevent disorder and mischief, it follows that there must be punishment or restraint in case of disobedience; in fact, there is an animal nature in us with its passions and greed which requires to be curbed. If the child is intelligent and strong enough, he will curb his own passions and appetites; but if he has not yet learned to do this, some one must help him till he is strong enough to need no help. Punishment, therefore, ought to be directed to give the child self-control. He should be made uncomfortable when he does injustice; he should find that falsehood will prevent his being trusted, that violence takes away his freedom, that by disorderliness he will have his privileges cut off, that if he behaves like a baby, he must continue to be treated accordingly; but punishment must always be for the good of the child and for the good of the home, in which case there will need to be very little of it.

The home a primary school for the state. — It will be seen that the home is the first school in which we learn to be citizens. As the home and its teachings are, so will the citizens of the state be later. Indeed, there are perhaps as many kinds of government in the home as there are in nations. There are homes in which the government is a form of despotism, though possibly firm and benevolent. There are homes like a little republic in which everything is discussed in family council, and where nothing is done without common consent; and there are unfortunately homes without thorough order, discipline, or authority, but where each member does as he likes. If now we can learn what the best kind of home is, we can see better how we should live together in the state.

A true family government. — Let us ask what kind of home we should like best to live in and to grow up in. There would certainly have to be authority in it, or there would be disorder and discomfort. The authority would be such that every one could have the largest freedom of action consistent with his own good and the comfort of all. When the freedom of any one made annoyance to others, or when freedom was abused, it would have to be curtailed. As fast as children grew to deserve more freedom, it would be given them; but on condition that they proved worthy of trust. We should like also to be gradually taken into our parents' confidence and consulted upon matters affecting ourselves or the home life; and so fast as our opinions came to be worth considering, they should have weight accordingly. On certain subjects, as we grew older, the decisions of the family should be taken by vote, and a majority should determine what was best; but we should always trust our parents as wiser and more experienced. They would have to bear the responsibility for the conduct of the family; they should therefore always hold the " veto power " to overrule the opinions or wishes of their children. Moreover, the father and mother, while each having his or her own office in which each should be supreme, should work together for the common happiness of the home. There would be some subjects, as for example in the care of the younger children, in which the mother alone would be responsible, as the father is responsible for the conduct of his business. The older children, also, after a while might be assigned certain duties, as for example the care of the grounds or of rooms in the house, for which they too should be responsible, subject only to the oversight of the parents.

Thus we have established a little state, with different departments in it, in which every one has a voice as soon as he deserves and as long as he is trustworthy, in which each has liberty as far as he uses it fairly, in which each also has duties and tasks for the good of all. In this government the parents are naturally the supreme authority, though influenced in many ways by the opinions of their children. This little state would change its character according to the members who made it up. If the children were very intelligent and good, there would be at the same time order and great liberty; if the children, however, were perverse and stupid, much authority would have to be exercised and many rules would have to be made, spoiling the liberty of each. If the mother were wise, but the father were foolish and incapable, some of his responsibility would have to be taken by the mother, and there might be conflicts of authority between the heads of the house. If, again, the father was tyrannical, he might take more power than was good for the home. Yet it would be a very bad government by the parents that was not better than to let the children grow up to do as they pleased.

An exception. — There is a law even higher than the command of a parent. It is the law of right. The parent must not require of the child what is not just or true or pure. In such a case it would not be doing real honor to the parent to obey. Indeed, the parent at his best would not wish the child to obey a command that violated right, or that injured others. To obey a wrongful or wicked command would therefore be not only an injury to one's own conscience, but to the person who, perhaps in a hasty mood, had given the command. To disobey, however, is to risk punishment. Whoever, then, for the sake of his conscience feels obliged to refuse a wrongful command must be willing to take the consequences. It will be better to be punished undeservedly than to do a wrong. Fortunately, it is a very unnatural parent or guardian who requires a child to do wrong, and the laws of the state can be invoked to protect or even to take away children who are thus abused by bad or intemperate parents.

CHAPTER II.

THE SCHOOLROOM AND ITS GOVERNMENT.

WE will suppose that one of the children from our good home is now sent to school. Here is another little state, with the teacher at the head of it. What is the teacher's government for? It is, as in the home, to secure the good of each and the greatest comfort of all. The school must therefore have certain simple rules or laws. These rules have been found necessary by many generations of schools. There must be regularity in attendance, punctuality, order and quiet, prompt obedience. Why? Because without all these conditions, not only the teacher cannot do his work well, but the scholars are robbed of their opportunity to learn. If a number of the scholars were late, the whole school would suffer. If every one could talk or whisper as each pleased, lessons would be interrupted. Whoever disobeys delays the school and robs the others' time. A certain measure of strictness is needed in the school, precisely as every part of an engine needs to be screwed to its place; for strictness, if it is good tempered, prevents friction and discomfort.

So when the teacher insists upon the right way of doing anything, getting a lesson or pronouncing a word, it is because the right way as a rule is the best and easiest. The scholar who comes from a good home will see this; he will know that the government of the school is not for the sake of the teacher, but that it is for the scholars.

He will have learned already to trust authority and to obey without always understanding the reason, for he will have found that there generally are reasons for every command.

Different kinds of school government. — If the children in a school are young, there must be more restraint and many rules. The teacher must simply command and teach, and the children must obey and learn their lessons: the school is a little monarchy. In an older school the government can be different. The scholars can be trusted as they become intelligent; they can be given greater liberties; their opinion can occasionally be taken by the judicious teacher; they can even by and by be taken into the confidence of the teacher; some of them can be appointed to assist in certain school offices. The scholars are put upon their honor as fast as they learn to know what honor is. The character of the government of the school grows to be more like a republic, the more mature the scholars become. There will be subjects on which the master takes the vote of the school and lets the majority decide. There will be occasions when the teacher can hear open discussion of a question and let the scholars express themselves. The more honorably liberty is used, the more liberty can be given; but the authority must always rest with the teacher to forbid whatever would injure the school, since the teacher is responsible for the welfare of all.

Co-operation in the school government. — Even in a primary school the teacher does not govern alone. The pupils also help govern; they help by their consent and obedience; they may help very much by their good temper towards each other and their teacher. In a school of older and intelligent scholars the teacher hardly governs at all.   There is little need of discipline or rules or punishments.   This is because the scholars have learned to govern themselves.   They now see that the school is not for the teacher, but for them.   The teacher is not an enemy to their happiness, but their friend.   To help make the school a success, to win and keep a good reputation for it, to free the teacher from watching the conduct of his school that he may use his strength the better to teach, — these are ways to serve themselves.   Thus the school becomes like a university of grown men and women.   The good school is now fitting boys and girls who will also govern themselves in the state, and who will therefore be able to use the largest liberty as citizens.

CHAPTER III.

THE PLAYGROUND: ITS LESSONS.

Boys and girls learn some of the most important things without knowing it, when they are at play. They learn to act together, to respect each other's rights, and to obey their own leaders and officers. We may call the playground a little democracy, like a little nation where all have equal rights. It may be a wild and lawless democracy, however, like savage tribes who have not learned to live together. There may be quarrels settled by fighting; there may be bullies who tease and oppress weaker children; there may be sulky ones who withdraw from the rest unless they can have their own way. If these things are so, it is because the children are still young or unintelligent. The playground is not well organized. We call the state of things *anarchy* where the members of any society pull apart instead of pulling together.

The organized playground. — As soon as children grow older, they begin to see that quarrelling and sulking spoil the sport. They learn that it is not only unfair for one to insist upon having his own way in spite of the wish of the others, but that the one who insists or else sulks by himself has an uncomfortable time; for no one likes to play with him. They learn that fighting is a poor and clumsy way to settle difficulties and that it is likely to leave ugly feelings after it is over. They agree therefore, for example, in a game of ball to choose a captain and to obey him.

They agree to go to play where the majority decide. Instead of stopping to quarrel over the questions of the game, they choose some fair boy as umpire and agree to abide by his decision. The playground now becomes a little republic, with its own officers and its rules. The boys find that they have a much better time as fast as they learn to govern themselves and respect each other's rights. Though they have to keep their rules, they have really more freedom so than when before they interfered with each other. They can give all their strength now to their play when before they had to be on the watch to protect themselves from bullies or tricksters. Even in contests of strength like wrestling, they find that the advantage is with him who keeps a cool head and controls his temper. Thus they discover that rules and government even in games make the game better sport. Good rules or laws, instead of restricting liberty, protect it.

Moreover, the same playground, when organized and fairly divided, will accommodate twice as many boys as could play on it before they had agreed which part each should have. Precisely as civilized men, who divide their land, get many times the product from it and enjoy it more freely than when wild and hostile tribes roamed over it.

Public opinion. — Besides the rules of the playground, there is a force which is always over the boys and girls to restrain or compel them. This is the common opinion of their companions. Thus, telling tales is generally held to be mean. This public opinion of a school or a playground may be right and just, but of course it is sometimes hasty and unfair. In this case it requires courage and independence to resist or question it. Whoever acts or speaks against the public opinion of playmates runs the risk of unpopularity and sometimes of mischief.

It is very desirable, however, that there should be those who are brave enough sometimes to take this risk and do the unpopular thing; for often one or' two independent boys or girls will carry influence enough to prevent an injustice or to hold back others from joining in a mean or cowardly act. It will be found that a considerable number were ready to agree with the independent fellow, but had not the courage to say so. At the worst, if one has to stand alone, opinion always comes around at last to support what is fair and honorable. Neither is the bold stand for justice, good order, or fair play likely to be really unpopular, if the independent person is also brave, outspoken, and good tempered.

Taking risks. — There are certain risks that have often to be taken in games or sports. There is risk of accident to the person, or of loss or injury to property or clothing, of one's own, or others'. There are certain times and places specially fit for the purposes of play, where risk is least. There are other places so unsuitable that the risk becomes excessive. In general, it is right to take the necessary risks of any sport which come within the rules of that sport. It is fair to take the risks of pain or loss which one can afford to meet, such as hurting one's fingers or losing one's ball, but it is foolish to take extra risks, like bathing in a dangerous undertow. It is wrong to take such risks, that if harm came, others would have to suffer or pay the expense. It is unfair to play baseball in front of one's neighbor's windows, which if broken one has not the money to repair, and it is unfair needlessly to risk clothing, or anything else which another must mend or replace. In short, the risks of play and sport begin to be hazardous and soon come to be wrong, as soon as they involve trouble, anxiety, loss or injury to others.

Playing to win. — It is natural to like to win in a game. But there is one thing better than to win. It is to play with skill and honor. Thus, it is better to play well and to be defeated by a worthy and superior antagonist than to play ill and only to beat an inferior. It is better to play honorably and be beaten than to win a game by foul means and tricks; for example, by maiming one's opponents at football. To play a dishonorable game is a confession of weakness.

Betting. — What harm is there in betting, for example, upon the result of a game? Or, in putting up marbles to win or lose? The trouble is that it forms a habit in a mischievous direction. Betting and gambling have done so much harm among men that laws are made to forbid them. Betting men and gamblers are apt therefore to be a dangerous class of citizens.

CHAPTER IV.

THE CLUB OR DEBATING SOCIETY.

WE will suppose that a set of boys or girls form a Tennis Club or a Debating Society. It is evident that there must be some order and certain simple rules.

The president or chairman. — In the first place there must be a chief or head. It will not do for several to speak at once, but some one whom all are agreed to regard shall keep order and require the members of the club to take their fair turn in speaking. The person who presides at a meeting is often called the chairman ; and he is said " to take the chair." When the club has been thoroughly formed, there will be a regular or permanent chairman, who may be called the president.

As soon as there is a chairman, whoever wishes to speak or to propose a plan must rise and address the chairman, who will call his name, unless another has the first claim to be heard. While one speaks, the chairman will not suffer others to interrupt, for no one else would wish to be interrupted when his turn comes.

The chairman must be impartial and give equal chance to every one, since he is the officer of the whole club. It would be unfair, for example, for him to let his particular friends have more than their share of the time, or, if there were two parties, to favor one of them and allow his favorites to interrupt the speakers of the other side. Indeed, a partial or one-sided chairman would soon break up a club, since it would not be worth while to attend meetings which were unfairly conducted. So important is it that the chairman should not needlessly take sides with one party or the other, that it is not customary for him while acting as chairman to speak on any question, or to vote unless there is a tie, that is, an equal division of the votes between *Yes* and *No*. In that case the chairman may throw the *casting-vote* and decide.

The constitution and rules. — It would not be well to expect any chairman to keep order without some instructions. He needs a plan which all shall understand and agree to. The club will therefore have a constitution and rules. Whoever joins the club agrees to live by these rules. But the rules must be framed so as to help the club and not to thwart it, or else they will have to be frequently altered.

The membership of the club. — Perhaps it will be agreed that any one can join the club who will agree to its rules; but some clubs are exclusive, and only allow such members to join as those already in ·the club permit. At any rate, there must be some rule to determine who the members of the club shall be, and there must be a list of the members, otherwise the president might not know who had a right to speak and to vote.

The quorum. — One of the rules of the club will provide how many members must be present before the meeting can begin to do business. For it would not be right for a very small number to decide a matter, like the spending of money, without waiting to see what the others wished. At the same time, it would not do to keep a considerable number waiting till all the tardy members arrived. If then the club numbered thirty, it might fix half its number, or fifteen, as the *quorum*.

Fair notice of meetings. — The rules will also provide that full notice of every meeting be given to all the members of the club. Thus it would not do for a few members to call a meeting and make up a quorum by themselves, or to call a meeting at a time when others either did not know of it, or could not conveniently attend. Notice should also be given of any important business to be discussed at a meeting, so that all who are interested can be present.

Changing the constitution. — Some of the rules for a club are merely for convenience (By-Laws), and are intended to be easily altered or set aside on occasion. But the plan of the club, or the constitution, ought not lightly to be set aside. If the club, for example, were started to play tennis, and certain members proposed to alter it to a boat club, there ought to be a thorough understanding of the new plan and a general agreement before a change was made, since many who had joined the club might be disappointed at the change. It is generally agreed, therefore, that the constitution must not be altered at any one meeting, or without the agreement of a large part, perhaps two-thirds, of the members.

Free discussion. — If any question is before the club, there ought to be ample time for every one to understand it, and for those who wish, to say what they think on both sides. Even when the larger number have made up their minds, they should be willing to hear the other side patiently, and be persuaded to change in case good reasons can be given. This is what each would wish for himself if he thought that his side had not had a fair hearing.

On the other hand, members must not be selfish and obstinate. It would not be fair that any one should speak twice on the same subject; at least, as long as others had not yet had an opportunity. It would not be fair for any one to speak for an unreasonable time, or in any case to speak for the mere satisfaction of hearing himself. Neither is it fair, unless for some very serious reason, to go on objecting after both sides have been heard and the larger number are ready to decide. Rules are therefore made, on one hand, to give the few their full rights to object and persuade the others, or to delay hasty action; and, on the other hand, to give the majority, or larger number, their rights also, and to prevent a few discontented or sulky members from blocking all the business. It needs to be said that rules are not enough, unless there is also a spirit of fair play. For good rules can be abused by mischievous persons, and even forced to work injustice, if members of a club are willing to wrong each other.

The method of business. — When a number of persons meet together, there is apt to be a great waste of time in talking. For nearly every one has something to say, often about subjects which are of no importance. The talking must therefore be confined to some subject which really belongs to the club to discuss. The rule is, if a member proposes anything or " makes a motion," that some one else must " second " it, before the chairman can allow talking about it. At least two persons ought to be interested in the subject before the attention of the club is asked to it.

One thing at a time. — When a subject has been proposed, it must be attended to before anything else is brought forward. If any one wishes to speak, he must speak to the subject, and not to something else. Whenever there has been talking enough about it, the members can call for the " Question "; and unless the larger number choose to hear more talking, the chairman must let it be decided at once. The club can, however, defer it, or "lay it upon the table," and then go on to other things.

Amendments. — It may happen that some one proposes a good plan, but another sees a better one. He can offer an "amendment" or improvement to the original motion, and if some one "seconds" him, the chairman must see that every one now talks about the amendment, till the club is ready to decide whether to accept it or not. There can be an amendment to an amendment, but business would become complicated if amendments could go any further.

How to decide questions. — If there were a few members of a club wiser than all the rest, it might do to ask them to decide for the rest. But it is often hard to tell who are wise, and the wisest sometimes make mistakes. Besides, no one would ever become wise without practice in thinking about questions and deciding them. Since, therefore, all have to share in the expenses and in the work, it is fairest that the larger number, the *majority*, shall decide. The smaller number, the *minority*, must yield, as they would wish to have the others do in case they had the choice. In particular cases, however, such as very knotty subjects, it would be fair for the club to refer the question to a select number of its best or oldest members (a *committee*), and either to abide by their decision, or at least to delay action till their committee should report. In a very large club or society, in order to save time, it might be necessary to refer almost every question to a committee, to find out whether it was worth while for the club to talk about it; as when a great ship is exploring, it sends a boat into a new harbor to find whether it is desirable for the ship to follow.

Voting. — The different modes of voting, or helping to decide a question, will be spoken of in another chapter.

It is enough to say here that it is evidently fair that each member shall have one vote and only one. To cast two votes on the same question is to steal a vote.

The reconsideration. — It is a pity for any one, after making up his mind, to have to change. But it is vastly better to change than to decide wrongly. If a member therefore thinks that the club ought to alter its decision, he can "move to reconsider" or bring up the question again. It must be some one who had before been in the majority, and has changed himself, who can fairly ask the others to change.

The secretary or clerk. — It is evident that there should be some one appointed to keep a copy of the constitution and rules, to have a correct list of all the members of the club, to give the proper notices to members, and to keep a record of all that is done at each meeting. For at the next meeting it will be necessary first to know what was done and what was left over at the meeting before. The secretary ought to be a careful and accurate person.

The treasurer. — It is likely that the club will have need of money. Perhaps the members will have to pay dues. In this case some one must be chosen to collect and keep the money and to pay it out as the club directs. It is not every one who means well who will make a good treasurer. He must be very exact in keeping his accounts or he will make bad mistakes; if he is heedless, he will forget to put down the names of those who pay him ; and he must be extremely careful not to mix the club money with his own. Of course he must not use the club money for himself or his friends, or borrow it for a day. All that he has a right to do is to keep it safe for the club. In short, he must not do anything with it that he would not wish every member of the club to know. He must also be ready to give account of his payments of the money, and the club ought to see that his accounts are regularly examined or audited. A faithful treasurer will always prefer to show his accounts. The treasurer should also have good manners, for otherwise he may offend those of whom he has to collect their dues.

Other officers. — There will often be matters of business, for which it would be inconvenient to call together the whole club. For example, it might be desirable to arrange for a picnic. A committee would therefore be appointed to take charge of the arrangements. Besides special committees, it saves trouble to have certain permanent committees, as, for example, to take care that the expenses of the club are proper and within its means, and to examine the treasurer's accounts. If the club had grounds, or bats and balls, there might be a person or a committee chosen to care for the good order and safety of the property of the club. For that which it is the special business of a few or of one person to care for is apt to be much better done than that which no one is responsible for.

Of course it is right that every one should be willing to take his turn in doing the work of the club. On the other hand, no one who cares for the success of the club should wish to have any office which another member could fill better. To scheme to get an office is almost as bad as to vote for one's self.

It will be seen that there are some places which any member would be useful in filling. It will be well to give as many as possible something to do. But there are other places, as the president's, where there is need of unusual fairness, judgment, and skill. The club must have one of its best members for president, as a boat's crew must have its most skilful man to steer.

It is well for every boy and girl to belong to some club, to help manage it in an orderly manner, to obey its rules, and to make it efficient and successful. For the club demands of its members, courtesy to one another, respect towards its officers, courage in speaking one's opinions, fairness to the other side — the same qualities of good citizenship which make the nation strong. It is because civilized men have these qualities that they are able to govern themselves. If in a legislature or congress many members are without these qualities, there will be friction, prejudice, faction, hatred, bad words, and insult, possibly blows and violence, and free government becomes impossible.

CHAPTER V.

PERSONAL HABITS. — THE CONDITIONS OF GOOD CITIZENSHIP.

ONE forms no habits which do not affect others, so as to increase happiness or else lessen it. If it were ever right to do harm to one's self, it would still be unfair to form habits which injured friends or neighbors. Moreover, the habits which are injurious in the home or the schoolroom are precisely those which hurt others in society, in business, or in the state.

Cleanliness and order. — One of the marks of barbarous men is that they do not know the use of water. They are unacquainted with soap, and their huts are dirty; their villages are untidy; they often therefore suffer terrible epidemics of disease; whereas the higher type of men find pleasure, comfort, and health in being clean. The more wealth they possess, and the more tools and appliances they have, the more necessary it is to keep things in place. The closer they live together in great towns, the greater the need is that every one shall co-operate to maintain wholesome and orderly premises and streets: for one badly kept house may poison a neighborhood; an unsightly yard may offend the eyes of hundreds of people; scraps of soiled paper thrown into the street and left there will give an ill look to a town.

Polite or civil manners. — The word *civil* means first what men do in cities, for civilization is the art of living together with many others. Rude or slovenly manners, speech, and habits, therefore, which might do less harm in the woods where men rarely meet a stranger, become very uncomfortable as soon as men meet in considerable numbers; precisely as a rude, selfish child, who has no brothers and sisters to be made unhappy, becomes disagreeable when he carries his bad manners to school.

The fact is, that every one naturally likes to have respect shown him : we would rather be met with a courteous greeting than with a scowl; we would wish our neighbors not to push or crowd against us. We therefore agree, in fairness to each other, to use the same respect to others which we like to have shown us. This is the root of good manners. We soon discover that life is far smoother and more pleasant so. Certain "rules of politeness," as they are called, are simply the ways which men have learned for best showing each other the respect and consideration which they like to have others give them; that is, there is generally some reason for the "polite rule." If we watch, we may discover what it is; as, for example, there is a reason why in crowded streets carriages are required to go to the right in passing each other.

If any rule or observance ever proved not to express respect or friendliness, we should be justified in giving it up; but we must be sure that we are right in our opinion about it, before we care to render ourselves singular; since it is unsocial to stand aloof from what our fellows do, without a good reason. We observe the rules of good manners, then, even when we cannot always quite see the reason for the rules, because on the whole they decidedly add to the convenience and happiness, — first, of the home or our school; and later, of the men and women who make up society, — and also because it is foolish, unsocial, and barbarous to disregard or despise what men and women generally do.

Examples. — It is a matter of very ancient custom for youth to pay respect to age. This is partly because we have a right to believe that older persons will have wisdom and character which deserve respect; it is partly because we should wish ourselves, when we come to greater age, to be treated with deference; it is partly because in advanced age there is often need of kindly help and consideration. It is also good for the young themselves to snow the marks of respect to their elders. It is part of the discipline in patience, gentleness, self-control, which goes to make manly or womanly character.

In barbarous times there was scant courtesy shown to woman. Then came the age of chivalry, when manners became more refined. It was held to be the mark of a gentleman to show special consideration and respect to womanhood. This is partly out of regard to the mothers, to whom true men recognize a debt of care and love which they can never repay. Respect is also due to women on the ground of their finer and more sensitive organization, as one handles delicate china more carefully. This respect to womanhood is not only for the advantage and happiness of women; it is equally for the advancement of men, who enjoy a high civilization in proportion as women are treated with honor. Certain outward marks of respect, like lifting the hat, are simply the tokens of such honorable feeling.

Money and its use. — Every one shows his character by the way he uses money. In some households an allowance · is given to the children to spend or save or give away. Almost every boy or girl has also means of earning money. One may soon see whether a young person is truthful or mean or generous, by his dealing with money. Does he keep account of his expenditures? Is he able to make his accounts balance, or does he forget to put items down? Is he willing or not that his father or mother shall see what he does with his money? Is he able to keep within his means, or does he fall into a habit of borrowing? Is he willing fairly to earn his money, or does he expect to be paid more than the market price? Is he sharp at a bargain? All these things determine and help make his character. By and by, when he takes his place as a citizen, we shall want to know how he uses his money, before we can trust him to take office and look out for the interests of others. If boys and girls cheat, or cannot live on their allowance, they will be likely to make bad or dangerous citizens.

Thoroughness. — The government of any country is certain to be like its people. It cannot be much, if any, better than they are. The scholars of to-day will soon be the people. Every thorough person then will help make the state strong, like a good stone in a wall; as every shiftless and slovenly person, like so much rubbish, weakens society and the state. Thoroughness is equally a condition of success in business. It is not, therefore, one's own affair merely, whether he is punctual in engagements and regular in his habits, or whether he gets his lessons. These things affect the state.

Honor. — Suppose, as soon as a scholar knows that the teacher's eye is not on him or that he will not be found out, he is always on the watch to break the rules: or suppose that a boy would steal or cheat if he were not afraid of punishment; or suppose that an umpire favors his own friends or the boys of his own school, — we say in every such case that the person has no sense of honor; in other words, we cannot depend upon such persons or trust them. There are schools in which the scholars would scorn to take any advantage of the absence of their teacher; there are boys whom you can trust to be as fair to the other party in a bargain as to themselves, and who would be equally fair if no one ever knew what they did. We call such conduct honor. If there were not at least some such men and women in every state and town, we could not maintain the republic.

Truth. — The story is that the early Persians, besides the use of the bow and the horse, trained their boys to speak the truth, and so their sons conquered the East. Lying is a mark of cowardice, as though the liar confessed that his forefathers had been wont to cringe as serfs or slaves, while truthfulness bespeaks noble and fearless blood.

Self-control. — There was a fabled creature called the Centaur. He was a man above and a beast below. Every human being may be likened to the Centaur. We call a man brutal whenever the beast is stronger than the man. We only call him a man when he rides the beast. The beast throws the man as often as he shows greed and gluttony, or pushes and snatches for more than his share. The man rides the beast when he says *no* to excess and holds appetite within bounds. No parent or teacher or master can do this for another, but each one has to learn to do it for himself.

The pure life. — There are many habits of life and speech which survive among men from barbarous or savage times. We easily and almost by instinct know them as low, base, and degrading. There are young persons, who perhaps from some weak strain in their ancestry, are specially liable to low habits and coarse speech. Others from ignorant homes or through thoughtless companions and bad books fall, if not into ruinous practices, menacing bodily health, at least into damaging habits of thought and conversation, spoiling the health of the mind; for there are things that soil and hurt the mind as pitch soils the hands, or dry-rot infects a tree. Whoever intelligently cares for happiness will therefore avoid the things that turn a man into a beast. Those unfortunate persons who lack self-control and moral vigor to outgrow the animal taint, become the most worthless and dangerous part of human society, who crowd the prisons and insane asylums in every state.

The narcotics and stimulants. — Whoever wishes to be strong, whoever wishes to keep health and vigor, whoever wishes a sound heart, a clear eye, and a steady hand, whoever wishes to render the most useful and patriotic service as a good citizen, will need to beware of the use of the alcoholic drinks and all narcotic stimulants and drugs. Especially in the period of growth, these things tend invariably to lower the health of body and mind. Tobacco has been found to be specially perilous to the life of growing youth. Wine and beer are conceded never to be useful for the young, and particularly in our bracing American climate to involve physical as well as moral peril.[1] The same, though in smaller measure, may be said of the frequently excessive use of candies and condiments which undermine the health, and threaten the vigor of the coming generation of citizens.

[1] This fact is now recognized by the laws of many of the States, which forbid the sale of intoxicating drinks or tobacco to minors.

CHAPTER VI.

THE PRINCIPLES THAT BIND MEN TOGETHER.

WE have now established a few principles which are at the foundation of human society. There is no one, fit to live with others, who is not able at once to understand these principles and to see the reason for them. Our consciences at once answer to them and tell us that they are right; at our best we mean to obey them. If we break them, it is because we are both wrong and stupid; we do ourselves harm, as if we had kicked against spikes. Let us briefly sum up these principles, which every human being who wants to live happily with others ought to make up his mind to heed.

Respect for others' rights. — We must treat another as we would wish to be treated. We must not hurt or defraud or annoy him. We must not injure his property. Why? Because like a brother, he is entitled to all the respect that we claim from him; because, also, every one is happier, richer, and more friendly, when all respect each other. This holds true even in our treatment of those who seem to be bad. We treat them as friends and not enemies, on the ground of our confidence that they are not altogether bad, but that they also have a good side like ourselves; in other words, we treat others as we should wish to be treated if ever we do wrong.

Authority and reverence. — We have also seen that there must be some one in the home and school, and sometimes on the playground, who shall direct or command the others, and who shall therefore exercise authority, for this is for the good of all. It is even for the good of the disobedient, who ought not to be allowed to hurt himself or others. Authority is meant to help him, as the harness helps the horse to pull more easily. But if there must be authority for the greater good of all, we owe it respect and loyalty. This is reverence, especially when we are loyal to truth, justice, or right.

Majority rights. — We have seen, too, that the only fair way to decide a question often is to see what the larger number want. This is another way of respecting others by respecting their wishes or their opinions. This is fairer to them and fairer to ourselves than to quarrel; that is, it is for the general good, always provided that the majority do not compel us to do wrong.

Responsibility. — We also find that each one has a share in whatever the others do. Each shares in the pleasure or in the losses of all. Even the minority share in what the majority decide. The minority must help pay the expense or bear the loss of all, as they will enjoy success if it comes. So if the majority do wrong, the minority have to suffer too, till they can persuade the majority to do right. This is responsibility. It could not be otherwise as long as we live together. It is fair, since we are perfectly willing to share in the gain that others bring us, that we should share together in the losses; for it would be evidently mean to take the credit that our club or our party wins, and not to be willing to take the blame which it incurs. We cannot shirk responsibility, then, except by living altogether alone, like Robinson Crusoe. Indeed, we should be responsible, if we deserted our fellows and left them to act alone.

The use of power.—We also see that power of any sort—ability, strength, skill—is not for the individual only. It is to share and to serve the others with, as the muscle of a good oarsman or the quickness of the cox-swain is for the whole crew. So the good scholar earns honors for the school. So the capable and trained man will make the town richer. The parent, teacher, or officer holds power for the sake of making all happier, and not for himself merely. This is fair in the family, because we there each belong to the other. It is fair, for the same reason, wherever we live together. It is fair in the great world, because the noblest way of considering human life is as a greater family of brothers. It is also fair, because, whenever we try this, it works better than any other way; besides, it is what the strong man would wish others to do with their power in case he became weak.

The public service. — It follows, therefore, that, besides obedience to authority, or doing as we are bidden, we owe something extra. We owe all that we can do for the common good. We evidently owe this in a home. We want there, besides doing what we must, to contribute something additional, as the parents, besides giving a bare living to their children, like to give them comforts and pleasures. So wherever we live together, we wish to add something to the good of the whole. This is fair and right, because we in our turn have received and inherited from those before us, who have left the world richer for their gifts and public service.

The two classes : the strong and the weak. — We see in every home and every school, and wherever men live, that there are two classes. One class are those who for some reason have to be helped and supported. The little children especially are in this class. So are the sick in body or mind.   The other class are those who do more for others than others do for them.   They therefore help support or take care of the weak.   It is necessary sometimes to belong to the first class and to have to be carried; but it is disgraceful, if one can help it, to stay in that class and to compel others to carry us.   It is like stealing, to be willing to do less for others than they do for us.   It is therefore ignoble to be idle; to receive and not to give; to inherit money or skill or the means of education, and then not to leave others richer for what we have had.   It is shameful to receive kindness and care, and at least not to give back thanks and cheerfulness'; for whoever is willing on the whole and through life to take more than he earns, takes out of what others earn.

Chivalry. — Since there are a multitude of persons in the world who have to be helped, and many others who, though able, are unwilling to do more than they are obliged, there is need always of some who will do more than their share.   While others will do their work, if praised and honored and paid, these will often serve without pay or thanks; as Washington would accept no compensation for commanding the American army, and even when his enemies critcised and abused him, cheerfully continued to serve.   We call such men as Washington chivalrous, like the knights in the old stories, who were pledged to help and defend the poor and weak.

We are prepared now to apply these principles in the large field of politics, business, and society.

CHAPTER VII.

THE DIFFERENT DUTIES THAT MEN OWE EACH OTHER.

As soon as we go outside the family or begin to read history, we find certain duties and obligations which bind people together as fellow-citizens or as employers and laborers. Thus the state furnishes protection and other services to her people; and the question arises, What ought the citizen to do in return? It oftens happens that there are present in a country an ignorant or a foreign class; and the question comes, how they should be treated. There are bad and shiftless people; and we want to know what should be done with them. There are people who work hard and have small wages, and others who do not work at all, and yet have great incomes; and the question rises, whether this is right. These and many other hard questions like them about right and wrong and duty arise whenever men live together in cities or nations, or when they buy and sell and employ labor. The same kind of questions apply to the duties of one nation to another, and to the important subjects of peace and war.

The divisions of our subject. — It is thus seen that there are: First, duties which the citizens of a state owe each other and the government, such as voting and obeying the laws. They depend upon the application of the principles of justice and friendliness, already perceived in the family, the schoolroom, and the playground, to the science of government. We call them *political* duties;

that is, citizens' duties. Secondly, there are duties which grow out of the earning and the possession of money. The wealth and comfort of a people ought in some way to be fairly apportioned; and no class must oppress or injure the trade and business, or subtract from the prosperity, of another class. We may call this second kind of rights and duties (from a Greek word which has been used to apply to wealth) *economic,* or the rights and duties of the fair management and distribution of money. They are the application of the principles of justice to the science of political economy.

Thirdly, we call the duties of the wealthier, better educated, and virtuous people of a community towards the ignorant, the vicious, and the poor, *social* duties, or the duties which men living together in society owe with regard to the evils of crime, pauperism, ignorance, and caste. These duties are the application of justice and humane principle to the questions of social science.

And, fourthly, we call the duties which one state owes to another *international.* The science of international law has its foundation in these duties. Obedience to these duties would forbid most, if not all, wars.

Examples. — More than a hundred years ago our forefathers rebelled against the British government. They believed that they were doing right; but their Tory neighbors conscientiously thought otherwise. This question of right or wrong falls under the head of *political,* or citizens' duties.

We frequently read of great strikes, in which workmen combine to compel railroads or manufacturing companies to pay higher wages. The question whether a strike is right, or what the companies ought to do, comes under the head of *economic* rights and duties, or the duties as to the management and distribution of money.

We have jails and prisons, in which criminals are confined, and often obliged to work without wages. What right have we to shut men up and punish them? The question of the treatment of criminals belongs' under the head of *social* duties; that is, the duties which grow out of the fact that different kinds of people who have to be treated differently live together in society.

The English have long held the government of India and compelled the natives to obey them. The question, What right have the English in India, falls under the head of international rights and duties, or the duties of one nation towards another; for example, a stronger towards a weaker. So, too, there has been much discussion about the use of the great fisheries off the coast of Newfoundland and our Alaskan seal fisheries. To whom do they rightly belong? And why? In the following lessons we shall study the duties which grow out of instances like these.

PART SECOND.

THE CITIZEN AND THE GOVERNMENT; OR, THE
RIGHTS AND DUTIES OF CITIZENS.

PART SECOND.

CHAPTER VIII.

THE PURPOSE OF GOVERNMENT.

AT a great seaport like Boston or New York one may see forts and ships of war which belong to the government, and soldiers whom the government pays; or one reads in the newspapers of troops fighting the Indians in the West. The iron-plated ships, the forts, the cannon, and the troops remind us that the government undertakes to defend its citizens from enemies.

The enemies of a country are not all in foreign lands, or barbarous tribes on the frontier. There is also a class of citizens who are enemies to the rest; they injure and rob property, and even take life; or they want to be idle, and live at others' expense; or they are unjust and selfish, and interfere with the rights of others. The government, therefore, undertakes to protect its people from enemies at home. The courts and the jails which the government supports; the judges, constables, and police whom it pays, — illustrate this second purpose of the government;

namely, to protect people from the wrong-doing of their fellow-citizens.

The government does not stop with defending the life and property of its people. It sends their letters over the world; it builds roads and keeps them in order; it bears the expense of schoolhouses and teachers; it owns the lighthouses; it pays vast sums to construct levees and breakwaters. Thus government undertakes many great works which individuals would not or could not do so well. A great army of surveyors, engineers, clerks, postmen, and laborers are under the pay of the government, and constitute the civil service.

What the government is. — When we in the United States speak of the government, we generally mean the President and the two houses of Congress at Washington. But, as we shall presently see, there is also a government or legislature in each state, as well as a government in every city or town. It is a government, for example, when at a town meeting the citizens decide how much money they will spend for roads and schools, and appoint a committee (the selectmen) and other officers who shall act in their name for the year. Congress is really a great committee of the whole people of the United States to make suitable rules or laws for carrying out the purposes of government; each state legislature is a similar committee of the people of that state. The government is thus the method by which the people of a country manage to defend themselves against their foes, to secure life and property from injustice, and to carry on necessary public works.

Examples of the duties of the government. — A colony of families who have established a new town in one of the territories are threatened by a tribe of Indians. It is the duty of the government to send an army, if necessary, to protect these colonists.

A man wants to build a high wooden house in a crowded city, or to keep a store of gunpowder. It is the duty of the government to forbid him from doing, even on his own premises, what would endanger the safety of his neighbors.

There are people who have violent prejudices against their colored fellow-citizens or those of foreign birth, as the Poles and Italians, whom they would perhaps like to prevent from getting work or from voting. It is the duty of the government, through its laws, to give exactly the same protection to all classes of its citizens.

It sometimes happens that a city or a corporation pollutes the water of a stream, and so injures the health of the residents of another town. It is the duty of the government, through the courts, to investigate such questions, and to order suitable redress.

In every closely built city it is the duty of its government to provide a fire department, and to make proper regulations for the health of the people, otherwise the ignorance or carelessness of a few would threaten the safety of all.

One of the dangers which threaten a government is ignorance. It is, therefore, a duty to provide at least a certain amount of instruction, and to require the attendance of children at school.

Two opposite ideas about government. — If all the citizens of a State were good and also wise, and if the people of other countries were well disposed, it is evident that there would be no need of government for the protection of its citizens from violence, or for supporting police, courts, or prisons. It might also be thought that the mails could be carried, roads could be built, lighthouses could be cared for, water pipes and sewers could be laid, and schools could be maintained by voluntary associations like express, railroad, water, and gas companies. There is so much that is well done by companies and also by individuals, that some are inclined to think that everything might be done without the intervention of government. If men were all fair and wise, a community might perhaps get on without any government, as a school in which every one was eager to learn might have no rules.

On the other hand, there are those who would like to have government assume the care and direction of nearly everything,— of the railroads and transportation, of the mines and manufactures, of the distribution of food and supplies; in fact, of all industry and business. The government should apportion to every one the work for which he was fitted, and should assign to every one his maintenance; as in a family the parents provide whatever each child needs.

This plan also might work, provided all men were fair minded, and if the wisest men were sure to be made the officers of the government.

The fact that men can hold two ideas as to the purpose of government, so far apart from each other, seems to show that the best government is that which unites both ideas; like a well-managed playground where, in order to secure the greatest liberty for every one to enjoy himself, all agree to sacrifice a little of their liberty, to keep rules and bounds, and to undertake some things, such as the care of the ground, together.

The trouble with the plans of those who would either get rid of government altogether, or, on the other hand, expect the government to do everything for them, is that the great body of men are not wise or perfectly fair. As in a school, therefore, not only the general happiness, but also kindness to the ignorant and vicious, demands the enforcement of order and obedience to laws. But the government is only the whole people acting together, like a group of boys on the playground. It can never then be trusted to be more wise or just than the people who make it. If the citizens are lazy, selfish, or grasping, the government which has such persons behind it can never be just or satisfactory.

Individual liberty. — As it is bad for children to depend upon older persons to help them get their lessons or do their tasks, so it is bad for a people to rely upon the government for what they can do for themselves. We know this, because it has often been tried, as when the imperial government of Rome provided the people with corn and made them beggars in consequence. On the other hand, when men are at liberty to try many experiments in their customs, in their business, and in their schools, and to make improvements if possible; when they are free to invent and apply new methods and machinery, and to make their own discoveries in science; when they are welcome to find fault if the government becomes negligent, — all this stimulates the curiosity, the inventiveness, the energy, and the quick-wittedness of the people. Even when individuals make mistakes and suffer losses, it is better than the gigantic mistakes and losses which a government that undertakes to do everything is liable to make. For the government, like an unwieldy vessel, has mostly to follow one fixed course; but the individual citizens, being many, if once they are free to try experiments, find shorter and easier ways.

As a matter of fact, all the progress that we know of in the world has come about through the thought and action of independent persons, like Galileo, John Hampden, and Samuel Adams, whom those in charge of government have frequently thwarted and opposed. The American way, therefore, is to allow as much liberty as possible to every citizen to think and to act for himself, because in this way the utmost energy is developed for the good of the whole people.

Two natural parties. — As we shall afterwards see, men often divide into parties on various subjects. But there are two great natural divisions that run among men as to the purpose of government. One party always seek to be as free of government as possible. They would prefer the utmost individual liberty consistent with the good of society. They would have little legislating or law-making; they would leave most kinds of work to individual enterprise. They think that energy and virtue are promoted by throwing all possible responsibility upon the individual citizen, and that if he sometimes abuses his freedom, he will thus learn faster the conduct of a true and intelligent man; as when a teacher trusts his scholars and leaves as many questions as possible for them to decide or to study out for themselves.

The other party would like to throw the responsibility from the individual upon the government, which shall accordingly regulate the details of conduct; as in a school, where every one's time was provided for by rule and each was told precisely what to do next. Thus it is hoped, at some increased sacrifice of each citizen's freedom, that certain abuses may be corrected and protection secured in favor of the poor, the weak, and the ignorant.

For example, one party would prohibit all use of intoxicating drinks throughout the country; but the other party maintains that it is better on the whole for men to learn to establish their own habits, than to have even good habits prescribed by the government. They think that it is better, likewise, to allow each locality to make its special rules than to establish rules for all by a central government.

So with the taxes or public expenses. One party might be willing to fix the taxes for the whole country by a great system with its central office at Washington. The other party would prefer, as far as possible, to permit each town or State to levy its taxes in its own way. The whole country thus gets the benefit of any wise experiments that may be tried in any part of it, but the whole does not suffer if a new plan works ill.

We need now to be told something of the forms and machinery of government, or how it works.

CHAPTER IX.

VARIOUS FORMS OF GOVERNMENT.

Despotism. — The study of geography has made us acquainted with various forms of government besides our own. Thus in Turkey the emperor, called the Sultan, has almost absolute power. He can appoint officers and make laws for his people, and if he pleases, can make war or enter into treaties with foreign nations. He can also hand down his throne to his son as successor. This is an absolute monarchy or despotism. Similar authority is often possessed by the chiefs of savage tribes. Nevertheless, such a ruler cannot generally do exactly as he pleases. There are old customs which he has to observe. The power is only his as his people allow it to him. If he utterly displeased them, or broke their ancient customs, or quite failed to defend them from their enemies, the people might take away his power; or, as often happens, some stronger or wiser man might seize his throne. It has sometimes also happened that such a king, like Charlemagne, has been just and patriotic, so that his people have enjoyed good government. But however good and enlightened the absolute monarch may be, his people, not having learned to act for themselves, but expecting the king to do everything for them, are usually helpless in case a weak or bad king succeeds to the throne. Neither have they learned to act together in times of public danger.

It is as though a father, instead of teaching his children

to serve themselves, had everything done for them, so that they at last became dependent upon others. So the kindest despotism hurts the people under it by its failure to train them to intelligent, independent, and watchful regard for the interests of their country.

The aristocratic government. — In many countries the rich or the heads of certain great families have contrived to get the power into their hands and to keep it, without consulting the rest of the people. Thus in nearly all the great countries of Europe for centuries the people were never asked to choose who should govern them or what laws they should live under. Sometimes, as in Venice, a ring of rich merchants managed the affairs of the city. More often, when a king ruled, the nobles who surrounded him got the great offices for themselves, so as to plunder the poor, or to have laws, such as game and land laws, made for their own advantage.

Ancient republics. — Even when the government was called a republic, as in ancient Athens, citizenship did not mean the same that it means with us; for only a limited number of the people could vote or hold office, and the great majority were slaves. So, too, foreigners coming to live in such a republic could hardly obtain the rights of citizens, for it was imagined that the interests of one class of men, the citizens, were hostile to the interests of slaves or foreigners. The latter were consequently treated with suspicion and even injustice.

Popular government. — In all civilized countries it is now held to be unjust for one class of men, merely because they are rich, to have authority, place, or office, or the exclusive power to make laws for others to obey. This change from the supremacy of one, or of a few, or of a class, to the acknowledgment of the equal rights of all, has come from the idea that men of every race or language are brothers, and that hence their interests are common. It is seen that whatever hurts or oppresses or degrades one class of a nation hurts the whole nation, precisely as that which hurts one part of the human body threatens the health of the whole. It has, therefore, become the custom to make the government rest upon the will of the whole body of citizens, who have to bear the burdens and expenses of the state; that is, instead of treating a part as citizens and the rest of the people as "outsiders," the rights of citizens, under certain rules and with some exceptions,[1] are conferred upon all.

In most European countries, even though a king or emperor is at the head of the state, he is now obliged to consult his parliament, that is, the delegates of the people. Neither could he long remain in power unless the majority of the nation choose to keep him. The rules or customs that restrain a king, the nobles, or the rich from oppressing a people are called the constitution. Thus while England is a monarchy, it is now a constitutional monarchy. The prime minister, like Mr. Gladstone or Lord Salisbury, who represents the majority in Parliament, enjoys more real power in directing the government than the king or queen; even the House of Lords or nobles can do nothing against the will of the chosen representatives, who constitute the House of Commons.

The modern republic. — A republic may be defined, as President Lincoln was fond of saying, as "a government of the people, by the people, and for the people." In this sense all the old world governments tend to become republican, but all republics are not alike. England, for exam-

---

[1] For example, a citizen who has become a criminal evidently forfeits his claim to be trusted with a citizen's duties.

ple, is substantially a republic, though without the name. Mexico, on the contrary, while called a republic and having a president at its head, is generally governed by a ring of rich men, who do not really consult the people, who on their part are unfortunately too ignorant to concern themselves about their government. Thus the names and the forms of a republic do not secure a true government of the people unless they have the will and intelligence to make their forms real.

The French republic. — France likewise is a republic, but not like our own; for during the period that France was an absolute monarchy it became the custom for the central government to administer the affairs and appoint the officers throughout the country, without immediately consulting the people themselves or expecting them to do anything but obey and pay the taxes; and so to this day, though the French people may elect the assembly who make their laws, the central government still undertakes much work which in America is left to the States and towns, or to the people themselves. Thus the French government pays the expenses of religion as well as for the police of the whole country. So, too, the French government appoints many officers, as the mayors of the cities, whom in the United States we choose directly ourselves.

A centralized government. — When the general government thus draws to itself under one great system the administration of all parts of the country, it is said to be *centralized*. If questions of local management or local expense, such as the salaries of the mayors, have to be referred for decision to some office or bureau at the capitol, it is called a bureaucracy; that is, a management through officials, instead of management through the people of the city or district. So far as the people of any town expect the central government to decide their questions for them, or to pay the expense of their public works out of the central treasury, they are in danger of losing their sense of responsibility. They may even permit lavish waste or fraud if they do not have to pay for it directly; whereas if the central government is efficient, the people forget that it needs to be watched and guarded lest it fall into negligence or corruption.

The American government, as distinguished from most governments abroad, is one which is designed to rest more directly upon the people themselves. We shall see that the great central administration only undertakes certain duties which concern the whole nation, but other public concerns are left to the people of each locality. The government most nearly like our own abroad is that of the Swiss.

The basis of the American system. — The old idea was that the people could not be trusted to know what was good for them. The American idea of government rests upon trust in the people. While many are ignorant, and many who ought to know better are selfish, there must be danger in any case; but Americans hold that it is safer to intrust men with power than to treat them with suspicion. Although they may often be wrong and may make mistakes, we believe that they are likely, on the whole and in the long run, to learn to act wisely and with justice. This is because there is a principle of fairness in almost every man, which, if appealed to, makes him wish to do right.

CHAPTER X.

LOCAL GOVERNMENT, OR, GOVERNMENT BY THE PEOPLE THEMSELVES.

WE can imagine that the people in each village or town might look to the great general government to do everything for them, — to appoint police or constables, to build their roads, to pay for their schools, and finally to collect money for the expenses. In such a case there would be no *local government*, neither would the people have to meet to discuss their affairs. By *local government* we mean the arrangement which the people of any place make for their own order, peace, and convenience. There is an old proverb, "If you wish anything done well, see to it yourself." This proverb contains the reason for local government.

The town meeting. — It is possible for the people of a small town or community to meet quite frequently and to consult as to what needs to be done for the common good; as, for example, to lay out a new road, to build a bridge, or to erect a schoolhouse, as well as to appoint proper officers, selectmen, constables, the school committee, and others. By common agreement and ancient usage, whatever reasonable action a majority of all present at a regular town meeting vote to take, all must acquiesce in. But what if the majority sometimes vote unwisely? It is nevertheless fairer for all, as a rule, to acquiesce for the time, than it would be to quarrel and resist like so many barbarians. There will soon be opportunity at another town meeting for the minority to persuade their fellow-citizens. Meanwhile, if the minority quarrelled and resisted, or refused to pay their share of the taxes, how could they expect the others to acquiesce in case they at last obtained the majority? "To do as you would wish that others should do to you," therefore, requires that the minority shall not resist the honest vote of the majority.

The origin of the town.—The town meeting is the simplest kind of government. Probably it is the survival of one of the most ancient forms, when all the freemen of a clan or a village of our Saxon or Aryan ancestors gathered to choose who should lead them to battle, or to say Yes or No to the proposal to make a foray against another tribe. The idea of the town was brought from old England by the early settlers who sought in the wilderness of New England the freedom to govern themselves. At first the towns were scattered, often of large extent, and of irregular area. As the population grew, old towns were subdivided and new towns were made to suit the convenience of their inhabitants. As a rule the town area is now five or six miles square. The meeting-place, or town hall, is near the centre of the population, or often in the largest village of the township. The name and idea of the town, being found convenient, spread from New England to most of the States where people from New England have settled.

The town meeting is sometimes called a pure democracy, that is, government by the people themselves, because all have an opportunity to express their opinion, and to vote upon all matters of public concern. The selectmen and other officers can only do as the people direct and carry out the people's votes. Whatever officer disobeys the will of the people is liable to be called to account immediately. The officers are also elected for short terms, and are only re-elected upon giving satisfaction and commanding respect.

The county. — A group of towns make a county. The name and the idea come from old England, and from the time when some great lord, an earl or *count*, had authority over a large district, often called a *shire*. For the purpose of justice, for maintaining a court and a jail and providing for public records, for keeping wills and deeds of land, as well as for the great highways, it is still convenient to group towns into counties. In some parts of the country, however, especially in the South, where the population is much scattered, the county, and not the town, is the unit of government.

The principal officers of a New England county are the Sheriff, who must preserve the public order and bring wrong-doers to justice, and who may, in case of serious disturbance like a riot, call upon the governor of the State to send troops to help him; the Commissioners, who look after the property of the county, its buildings, and its highways; the Treasurer; the Register of Deeds, whose books show to whom all the lands in the county belong, and whenever any land changes hands; and the Clerk, who keeps the records of the courts. These officers are chosen directly by the people. The towns contribute their share to the county expenses, according to the amount of property in each town. The public buildings for the use of the county are in the *shire town*.

In the Southern and some of the Western States, where there is no real town government, the county officers, viz., the Board of Commissioners or Supervisors, have charge of the business which in towns is managed by the selectmen.

Since the different States use several different systems of local government, it is possible to compare them and to find out whether the township or the county plan works best. It will be seen that local government cannot be as direct in the cŏunty as in the town. For on account of the greater size of the county, citizens cannot conveniently meet to discuss and to do the county business. Neither can they know each other as well as the men who live in a town. Since, then, they must leave more of their business to their officers, they cannot feel as much responsibility for good government as under the township plan. It is easier, too, for a few persons to get and keep the power and the offices, while the larger number stay at home and lose their interest. When men stop discussing their affairs and leave them to others, they soon become very unskilful. It appears, then, that the township plan is likely to be the favorite one. It is coming into use in many of the new States.

The school district. — The towns or the counties are subdivided into school districts, where people meet to consult and make necessary arrangements for the care of the schools. The district meeting is a sort of training-school in politics. For when neighbors meet to consult for the interests of their district, they are apt to consult also about town affairs and to observe what needs to be done.

Local patriotism. — We may suppose that the people of a town were resolved to make their town excel, to maintain the best roads and schools, to beautify their streets with trees, to prevent disorder, to secure efficient and honest service, and therefore to trust only their best men with office. This would be *local patriotism.* The more such towns there were, the better it would be for the State and the nation. We may suppose that the children were brought up like the children of the early Athenians, to be loyal to their native town and to help make it excel. They would be sure to be good citizens wherever they might afterwards live.

CHAPTER XI.

THE STATES, AND LEGISLATIVE GOVERNMENT.

States. — In the old days families joined into clans, and clans made up tribes, and finally tribes of kindred people were united for common defence into kingdoms and nations. So, somewhat after the old model, we have townships forming counties, and counties making States.

The sovereignty of the State. — Each State in some respects is like a separate nation. Thus, it can make laws for its people as though it were quite independent. The laws may differ from the laws of the adjoining State. It can make new towns and counties, and change the old towns. It can lay down the rules for local government, or alter them. The towns and cities get all their authority from the State. The State can also have a military force, its *militia*, for preserving order. And it provides courts and police for enforcing its laws.

Eminent domain. — The State has also the same right over the land as once belonged to a whole tribe or to a king. It can, therefore, take the land of any citizen in case it is needed for a public purpose, as for a railroad. This important right is called *eminent domain.* It would not be fair, however, for the State to exercise this right to take away property without compensation.

Why we have States. — A foreigner might wonder why we need to have States with many costly governments and different laws. Why would not one great State be enough, like France? The foreigner would also say that the map of our States looks like a checker-board, as if they had been made to order; unlike the states of the Old World, with their irregular boundaries, which grew through many centuries of change.

The answer is partly that the States are for the sake of convenience, in order not to load the great general government with too many duties. It would be cumbersome whenever the people in Chicago wanted to try the experiment of a new law to manage their city, to have to go to Washington to get permission, as it is now very vexatious for the British Parliament to be obliged to govern Ireland.

The old States. — The chief reason, however, why we have States, is because our forefathers settled this country in separate colonies and with different customs.

At the time when our forefathers asserted their independence from Great Britain, the thirteen separate colonies had each a government of its own, — a governor appointed by the king and an assembly or legislature chosen by the people of the colony. The people of a colony were not quite free to do as they pleased; for the royal governor might *veto* or forbid what the legislature voted. The governments of the colonies were also based upon charters or constitutions made for them in England, and which required them to act in obedience to the laws and government of Great Britain. Thus the British Parliament could make laws which might seriously affect the interests of the colonies, while the colonies had no delegates or representatives in Parliament to defend their rights; somewhat as the Dominion of Canada has no members of the Parliament in London. At the War of Independence, the colonies took the sovereignty, which had before been vested in the crown, into their own hands and became independent States; henceforth they each chose their governors themselves, who thus represented the will of the people. Instead of the royal charter, they made their own constitutions. There was, indeed, a period before 1789 when any State, as Massachusetts or South Carolina, had the right to establish a custom house, and to exclude goods from other States and hinder trade, and when it would have been possible for the different States to become quite separate from each other.

New States. — After the Federal Union was established, as the country filled up with people, new States were settled in what had before been the wilderness. Florida was bought of Spain. The vast region known as the Louisiana Purchase, comprising the Mississippi Valley and the Great Northwest, was bought of Napoleon, and later Texas, and a great portion of what had belonged to Mexico, including California, were added, by conquest and treaty, to the national domain. From time to time the new lands were made into divisions called Territories, with a temporary government, somewhat like the old colonies; and again, when the Territories grew populous, they became States, after the model of the original thirteen States.

Representative government. — It would of course be impossible for all the people of a State to come together, as in a town meeting, to consult or to make laws. They therefore choose their representatives at regular intervals, — in some States every year, in others once in two years, — to meet and discuss the business of the State. This is the legislature. Since the members have to give up considerable time and go to certain expense, it is thought fair to make them reasonable compensation. Thus the State claims the right to their faithful and disinterested service.

This makes it also possible for poor men as well as the rich to serve the State.

The beginning of legislatures. — It seems only just that the persons in charge of government should have the advice and consent of the people who must pay the expenses. But reasonable as this appears, it was not acknowledged in the fierce old times when " might made right." The famous story of King John and Magna Charta shows how hard it was for free men to win their rights.

Representative government and its methods have been slowly worked out by the bloody and glorious experiments of our fathers in old England through many centuries. For when the kings needed money and soldiers, they were accustomed to gather the leading men from all parts of the kingdom, including the great merchants of London and other towns. This was the beginning of Parliament.

How Parliament got power away from the king. — Although the king or his minister could propose any plans, such as a campaign against France, it was held necessary, after Magna Charta was granted, to have the consent of a majority of the Parliament, in order to provide the necessary means ; and since the king often wanted money, he was forced as often to summon his Parliament and ask its consent to levy the taxes. So it came to pass that bargains were made with the king, that if he would give Parliament what they wanted, if he would reform certain abuses or dismiss bad ministers, they in turn would grant his requests for money. Thus, while once the king used to propose and command, and the Parliament at most could only refuse to pay money to help him, now at last it has come to be the Parliament that proposes plans or makes laws, which the king or queen can hardly venture to veto or forbid. And whereas once the ministers and great officers were often made by the king's appointment, now they are practically the choice of the majority of Parliament. The Parliament, in the name of the people, has assumed not only the power to make laws, but also to carry out the laws.

American parliaments. — All our legislatures, including the National Congress, follow the model of Parliament. In old times, however, the rich and powerful came to Parliament, and the poor were not represented; but our legislatures are chosen by all the people. The legislature is thus a great town meeting made up, indeed, not of all the people, but of delegates or messengers whom their fellow-citizens have chosen to consult and to vote for them, and whom they pay for their services. Whatever, therefore, the legislature decides to do, all the people must acquiesce in; or, if they do not like the action of their representatives, they must wait till the next election, and then choose different men, who may act more wisely.

The legislature and the people. — It is also possible, in some cases, if the legislature do not wish to take the responsibility of any action, to refer it back to the people, who shall vote *Yes* or *No*. Thus laws to forbid the sale of intoxicating liquors are sometimes referred to the people either of the whole State, or, by *local option*, to the people of each city or town. As we have seen, each State has what is called a constitution, that is, a fixed body of rules for its government. This constitution binds and limits the legislature. Sometimes, especially in the new States, the constitution is very long, almost like a law-book, as though the people did not dare to trust their legislature to take important action without consulting them. For no change can be made in the constitution without a direct vote of all the people of the State, who, meeting in their accustomed voting-places, must say *Yes* or *No* to the proposed change. Sometimes, in order to make hasty changes difficult, the law requires as many as two-thirds of the votes before the change can be allowed.

Thus, although the legislature has many powers such as kings once wielded, yet it is always held close to the will of the people. Even if it passes acts which the people would disapprove, it is liable to have such acts soon reversed by a new legislature, or by a direct appeal to the people to change the constitution.

The English way. — So in England, if the Ministry, that is, the great officers who conduct the government, happen to propose measures which the Parliament disapprove, they must either give place to new ministers, or else, if they wish to insist on their own way, they can dissolve Parliament, which otherwise might hold through a term of seven years. They must then order a new election, to determine whether the people will vote for members favorable to their plans; but if the new Parliament still disapproves of their conduct, they must resign. In Switzerland, also, the laws require many subjects to be referred to the people directly, instead of trusting the legislature.

The two houses of the legislature. — As long as mankind was divided into two classes of people, Lords and Commons, the Parliament was divided also into an upper house where the nobles sat, and a lower house where were the representatives of all the rich people who were not noble; but though we have no longer two classes or castes of people in America, we still retain in our legislatures this old division of an upper house, commonly called the Senate, and a lower and larger House of Representatives. We do this partly from the force of ancient custom, but also because many think that subjects receive more careful consideration from the necessity of being discussed and voted upon by two different bodies, before any law can be finally passed. The Senate, or upper house, is generally much smaller than the other body. Thus there may be one or even more representatives from a town, but often several towns may be required to form a district to choose a senator. The legislature of Massachusetts, for example, has forty members in the Senate and two hundred and forty in the House of Representatives.

The duties of legislators. — There are two different ideas of the duty of members of a legislature. Some think that they are strictly bound to do whatever the majority of their constituents wish. According to this view, a member of the legislature ought to vote against his own judgment, if he believed that the people who elected him so desired. If he cannot conscientiously do this, he ought to resign and let some one be chosen who would vote as the people wish.

Others hold that a legislator ought to be trusted to act freely, according to his best judgment of the interests of the people. He may thus sometimes be obliged to vote against his party or to take the unpopular side. It is evident that it would be of little use to elect wise and conscientious legislators unless the people are willing to trust them.

State rights and State jealousy. — In the earlier days of the Republic the people of one State were often afraid and jealous of the people of other States, somewhat as in the ancient history of Greece the people of Sparta were jealous of Athens. It was feared that the strong and populous States might contrive to make laws to hurt the weaker States. The smaller States, as Delaware and

Rhode Island, would not come into the Union at all without being given the same number of senators in Congress as New York and Pennsylvania. The Southern States especially, where slaves were still held, were anxious not to be meddled with. When men become suspicious of each other, they are apt to think more of their *rights* than their *duties*. So it was with the States. Many persons thought that a citizen owed his duty to his State first and the Union afterwards; they cared more for the state flag than the national flag.

Our people, however, have learned that whatever is good for one State is good for the others. If the people of Alabama are poor, it is so much the worse for New York. As in a football team, the strength and skill of each member are necessary to win the game.

State patriotism.—If any State has had a memorable history, as Virginia or Massachusetts, if it has produced great men, if it has established good laws, and secured the freedom and happiness of the people, they naturally take a generous pride in their State.

By as much as it has made them happy, they are bound to do their loyal part to maintain its good laws and its prosperity. This is state patriotism, and like local patriotism, the more citizens possess it, the better for the whole country. Thus one can be a good patriot to his own State, and be glad also to see other States flourish.

CHAPTER XII.

THE PEOPLE ACTING IN CONGRESS.

The American idea. — The American idea of government is that the people shall hold the reins of power, so far as possible, in their own hands; that they themselves shall be responsible for their own error if ever they choose unworthy or incapable public servants; and that hence they must not turn over to others to do or to determine what they can do themselves. Thus the people of a town or city must not look to the legislature to build their roads or choose their school committee or provide water and light; but the people of each town must provide for their own local needs, or suffer the consequences of their neglect. So, too, each State, through its legislature, must consult and act in matters that touch the interests of all parts of the State, without expecting the nation to interfere to save the people of the State from the results of their mistakes or their negligence. The people of the State must be responsible for their own school system and for good order within their borders, and therefore for proper laws; but they should not without extraordinary reasons look to the government at Washington to vote money for their education or to provide national troops to enforce the laws of the State. The American plan therefore is, that we leave as much as we can to the honor and patriotism of the people of each town or State.

General government. — There are, however, as we have seen, many subjects which rest upon all the people of a

State together. No town or city must be suffered to do anything to the detriment of the health or the welfare of the people of other towns. Every town, therefore, must obey the laws of the State. Even if the laws do not seem wise for every town, its people must acquiesce till they can persuade the legislature to change the law. As each citizen must acquiesce in what the town meeting does, and pay his share of the expenses of his town accordingly, so the town or county must yield to the greater meeting of the State, that is, the legislature. So, too, between the State and the nation there are many subjects of common or general interest, for which, therefore, all the people in the United States are equally responsible. These subjects make the basis of our General or National Government. As a club of boys may have their own rules and officers and do what they please with their funds, but when many clubs are accustomed to play a common game, as base-ball, it becomes convenient to agree upon certain rules which all the clubs shall keep, so with the vast interests of millions of people.

The servants of the people. — When the government becomes general, it is not the less in the hands of the people. The people cannot, however, meet to hear and discuss the numerous questions that arise. They must, as in the case of the state legislature, choose men who shall give their time and attention to advise and act for them. These chosen men are accordingly paid a generous salary,[1] that they may be free to give up their private business and devote themselves to the public good. Their time and ability are thus in a special sense at the public service.

[1] In England, where the Parliament has usually consisted of rich men, no salary is paid its members, but the United States makes it possible for a poor man to serve the public in Congress.

The responsibility does not, however, cease to rest with the people, neither have they abandoned their power by choosing representatives to act for them. They must still watch their representatives; and if these fail to act wisely, they must send abler or more honest men in their place. Thus the power always rests with the people, who are themselves to blame if their national government is foolish or corrupt. If the government is extravagant, it must be because the people have chosen unfaithful servants; or if the government involved the nation in war, it would be because the people had chosen men who would vote for war in their name.

Congress. — The national Congress may be called the great "town meeting" for the country, or the legislature for all the States. Here, however, each member represents many thousands, or in the case of the senators of populous States, millions of his fellow-citizens.

The beginning of Congress. — While the colonies were fighting with Great Britain they had a kind of union among themselves and a congress to act for them. This union was called a confederation; but it had no power to raise troops or money, unless the States chose to heed its request. Its president was merely the chairman of its meetings; and it had no courts to settle disputes between the citizens of different States. However many delegates were present from a State in the old Continental Congress, they could cast but one vote. The smallest State had therefore as much power in deciding questions as the large States. The confederation was not, therefore, very strong, and the States repeatedly refused to do what Congress asked.

The Federal Union. — For a little while after the War of Independence, the States tried the experiment of acting almost independently of each other. It proved a bad and dangerous experiment. New York might make laws to hurt or to tax the commerce of the people of New Jersey or Connecticut. There was no sure way to provide for the common good or the defence of the States. There was no treasury with money in it, or the means to secure money, to provide for the large debt which the Confederacy had borrowed to carry on the war. A convention was therefore called, which met in Philadelphia in 1787. It included our greatest men, — Washington, Franklin, Hamilton, and Madison. It finally worked out the plan for our present Union, and recommended it to the people. According to the new plan the States agreed, by the vote of their people, to give up some of their independence, and to commit to Congress the charge of matters which concern all the people of the nation. No State now could do anything to injure the people of another State. No State could erect custom-houses on its boundaries to collect taxes from the commerce of the other States. The new Union could have a treasury and courts with the necessary authority to command obedience. No State could justly resist the authority of the general government; neither could any State withdraw from the others and set up an independent government. Since permanent union proved to be for the general good, it was not only unfair for any State selfishly to threaten the good of all by withdrawal from the Union, but the State which cut itself off from the rest would be likely to suffer in the long run.

What now, if Congress, which represents all the nation, is unwise and passes laws that seem to hurt any part of the people? The remedy is to send wiser and better delegates, or to persuade the mistaken majority; because it is a harm only to the few to acquiesce for the time in what the majority have unwisely decreed, whereas it would injure every one if any portion of the nation were to resist or break up the government. This was abundantly demonstrated in the Civil War.

How Congress is made up. The Senate. — Every State, however small, is entitled to choose two senators, who are elected by its legislature to serve for a term of six years. One third of the Senate are elected every two years, so that the senators' terms overlap each other. It is never possible, therefore, as it might be in the House of Representatives, to have a Senate of wholly new members. The senators are supposed to be the representatives of all the people of a State. If any bill or proposal for a law is passed by the House of Representatives, it must then obtain a majority in the Senate. So, likewise, the bills which are passed by the Senate must obtain the consent of the House. The Senate has the sole power with the President to make treaties with foreign nations. It may act as a court to try an officer, as for example the President, accused by vote of the House of Representatives of criminal abuse of his office. It also can confirm or reject the appointment of certain important officials, such as judges and custom-house collectors, made by the President. It is thus intended to serve as a check upon a hasty or wrong-headed President, who could do little harm against the will of the representatives of the people of the States. The Vice-President regularly presides over the Senate, without having a vote, unless there is a tie, that is, an equal vote on each side.

The House of Representatives. — Every State, however small, has at least one representative in Congress. The number of representatives which a State may send depends upon its population. The House of Representatives numbers over three hundred members, — a body somewhat large and awkward for the purpose of deliberation. The Speaker, chosen by the representatives, and usually from the political party which has the majority of congressmen, presides over the House. The House is chosen every two years, and directly by a vote of the people by districts. Since the senators are chosen for a longer term, and by the legislature of each State, it may happen that the majority of one body differs from the majority of the other. The House is supposed to represent the newest and freshest thought of the people, while the Senate represents the caution of the nation, which would hold the government back from hasty action.

The Territories in Congress. — A Territory may appoint a delegate who can speak on the floor of Congress, but may not vote. Congress passes laws for the Territories, and establishes courts until they are admitted as States, with constitutions of their own. The District of Columbia is governed by Congress like a Territory. The people of the Territories cannot take part in national elections. In the case of the District of Columbia, which can never become a State, this disfranchisement of its population seems to be a needless hardship.

Congressional districts. — The representatives are generally elected by *districts*, which must contain an equal population. The number of districts in a State is liable to be altered once in ten years after the census is taken. If the new States gain rapidly in numbers, while older States hardly gain at all, the latter may lose in congressmen. For the House of Representatives is large enough already, while the population of the country is increasing. It is therefore necessary to assign a larger number of people to each congressional district. At first thirty thousand made a district. Now more than one hundred and fifty thousand are required. There are States which have not so large a population as this, and which therefore have more than their due share of weight in Congress.

The representative usually resides in his district, but there is no law to prevent the people from choosing an able man from another part of the State.

Gerrymandering. — It is possible for the party which has the majority in a State to lay out the congressional district in such a way that the people of the opposite party shall not have the natural advantage of their numbers. If, for example, the opposite party would naturally carry three districts of a State, the division can be so made that the great bulk of its voters shall be thrown into two districts, or only one. Thus a district has been known as the " Shoe-string district," from its artificial shape.

It is not only wrong but foolish for a party to do what it would call unjust, in case the other party should come into power and attempt to do the same. For the same rule holds between parties as between men; namely, to treat each other as they would each wish to be treated. Otherwise injustice or fraud has to be paid for, sooner or later, with interest.

The powers of Congress. — The chief power of Congress is in laying taxes and spending money. The revenue of the United States amounts to upwards of four hundred millions of dollars. The method of raising this great sum rests with Congress, which by wisdom and fairness may distribute the burden equally, or for want of due care or honesty may annoy and oppress the people, out of whose labor the national expenses must be paid. A considerable part of the annual taxation has to be paid as interest upon the national debt, incurred in the Civil War.

Another enormous sum goes in the form of pensions, on account of wounded or disabled soldiers. Many millions are appropriated for the army and navy. Thus by far the largest part of the taxation is the cost of strife.

In all the appropriations, especially for improving harbors and the navigation of rivers, and for government buildings, such as post-offices and custom-houses, there is opportunity for lavish waste of the public money. Unless, then, the people send conscientious representatives to vote upon the expenditures, they must expect to pay heavy taxes.

Congress has power to pass important acts concerning the Territories and the great public lands; concerning the railways which pass from one State to another, and affecting the value of their property; concerning trade and intercourse with foreign nations, either to encourage or discourage trade, travel, and immigration. In all these ways, great interests and the rights of individuals are jeopardized by foolish, partisan, or dishonest congressmen.

Congress passes laws touching the Indians and votes the supplies of food, blankets, tools, and farming implements required by various treaties as well as the means for establishing and maintaining schools to educate and civilize them. Negligence or dilatory action in these votes may easily provoke trouble and war.

Congress has also the responsibility of sustaining and improving the service of government, as in the case of the post-office, the lighthouses, and the life-saving stations.

There are important subjects where the powers of Congress lie close to the rights reserved to the States, so that great wisdom may be required not to involve the general government in a quarrel with the people of a State. Thus, the Congress may pass acts in regard to federal elections, which might make it necessary to send troops into a State, in order to enforce the laws.

The House of Representatives must choose a President of the United States, if, as sometimes happens, the electors chosen by the people fail to choose one. The Senate must, in like manner, elect a Vice-President. But the choice for the President must be from the three highest names voted for by the people, for the Vice-President from the two highest.

The appeal to the country. — Once in two years a new House of Representatives must be elected. If, meanwhile, bad laws have been passed, or injurious taxes and wasteful expenses have been voted, the people can condemn the bad legislation by refusing to vote again for the men who were responsible. If the same men are returned to the new Congress, it will show that the people approve of their conduct.

CHAPTER XIII.

CITIES AND THEIR GOVERNMENT.

Cities. — When a town becomes quite populous, the whole body of its people cannot conveniently be assembled to consult for public matters. For while a small number can hear whatever may be said and can deliberate questions, careful deliberation becomes difficult in a crowd; the wisest man may not be able to make his voice heard. Neither is there needful time for all sides to be patiently discussed. Public business also becomes more complicated and extensive. New and often costly enterprises are required for the health, comfort, and safety of the inhabitants. Frequent meetings are necessary to provide for these enlarged needs. The old simple methods of the town meeting are therefore outgrown. In such cases the legislature, upon request of the people of the town, may give a charter; that is, a constitution with suitable rules, for the establishment of a city with new machinery of government. The city government is like a miniature legislature, or a town meeting of delegates. It generally follows the old fashion of the Parliament and has two branches, the smaller called the Board of Aldermen, and a larger one called the Common Council. As in the case of the legislature, both branches are elected by the people. A mayor is also chosen, who corresponds to the President or the governor of a State. His duties will be spoken of in another chapter. Since the people make their city government, they therefore agree to abide by whatever it votes to do, to obey the rules made for the city and to pay the taxes. The city government cannot do anything contrary to the laws of the State; neither can its charter be altered without the consent of the legislature.

Two modes of electing the aldermen. — Sometimes a city is divided into districts, each of which chooses its own alderman. The people of a district in this case do not choose the best man whom they could find in the whole city, but merely the candidate who can command the votes of his own district. It may be some one whom the voters of the other districts would disapprove. The alderman of a district also is likely to think it his duty to get appropriations of money for his own part of the city, rather than to consider the interests of all parts.

The other mode of electing aldermen is by a *general ticket*. In other words, all the voters may vote for all the aldermen. In this case the candidates are likely to be known outside their own wards. It is possible to choose a board with reference to their character, ability, and experience, who will seek to serve the whole city, and not merely one part of it.

By the latter method it might happen that the political party which had the most votes in the city would choose all the aldermen. If, for example, the Democrats elected the mayor, they might have the whole board of aldermen too. The first method would allow the smaller party the chance of winning a majority in some of the districts, and so of having part of the aldermen. On the other hand, if the majority of the voters are intelligent enough to wish good government for their city, they will agree to choose the best men of both parties for their aldermen. This plan has often been successfully tried.

The city government and the legislature. — The legislature is largely for the purpose of making laws for all the people of the State. It sometimes, also, undertakes public works. The great canals of Pennsylvania and New York were thus constructed by the State. It provides hospitals for the insane and prisons. It takes charge of such of the poor as can claim no home or residence in any town of the State. It pays the expenses of the militia, who may be called upon for the public safety. But the total amount of money expended by the State government is comparatively small, often smaller than the cost of managing certain great railways or manufacturing companies within its borders.

The duties of the city government, on the contrary, are largely in administering the expenditures of money. The city government has no laws to make except certain petty rules ; for example, about the public grounds, or the care of sidewalks and streets. But the amount of money to be expended for police, for lighting the streets, for water and sewerage, and many other purposes, is very great. The largest city of a State, as Boston or Chicago, may require much more money than the legislature has to dispose of. The cost of managing the city to each citizen may be many times the cost to each for managing the State, and much more than the cost to each inhabitant for carrying on the national government. Thus, while the State legislature chiefly makes or alters laws, the city legislature chiefly votes the expenditure of money. It is like the board of directors of a great mill. If it is wasteful or extravagant, it will increase the expense to each inhabitant or roll up great debt. It needs therefore, like the mill, the services of able, discreet, and honest men, On the other hand, since the city government has the expenditure of

money, it becomes an object of temptation to idle, designing, and unprincipled men, often unable to manage their
own affairs, who see in the great public treasury the
opportunity for plunder. Thus the notorious Tweed Ring
in New York City between 1860 and 1871, by various corrupt practices, by bad votes, and bad appointments to
office, and bribery and fraud, pillaged the people to the
extent of many millions of dollars and increased the debt
by eighty millions.

Where responsibility lies. — If the stockholders of a
company were to choose for directors worthless or incapable men, who ruined the company, we should not blame
the bad directors only, but the careless stockholders who
had chosen them and kept them in office. So when the
people, who are the stockholders in the vast public property of a city, choose men to be their directors in the
common council, whom they would not choose or trust
in any private charge of their own, the blame rests upon
the people; and since the less intelligent part of the
people would not willingly vote for bad men who make
it more costly to live in their city, the greater blame
rests on intelligent citizens for their carelessness in letting worthless directors expend the public money without
protest.

Village charters. — In the newer States, where the
people are sanguine in expecting marvellous increase in
numbers and prosperity, it is common to grant city government to a very small population, often to a few hundred.
In the older States a city means more than in the West.
In Massachusetts, for instance, the rule is, not to give a
city charter to less than twelve thousand people; there are
towns with a larger population which still prefer to govern
themselves in town meeting.

It sometimes happens that there is a large village within a town, which needs water, a fire department, and police, like a city. But it may not seem altogether just to tax the farmers outside the village for these increased needs of the villagers. The custom in some States, therefore, is to grant a charter to the village, as a corporation, to provide itself with such extra facilities as the larger and more scattered population of the town would be unwilling to pay for. In this case the villagers pay two taxes, one as their share of the town government, and the other tax for themselves.

The injustice to the farmers in helping to support a village within their borders is not so real as they are apt to think. For the increase of wealth in the village raises the value of the farms, provides better roads, and gives the farmers a good market for all that they can produce. Thus the good of one part of the town proves to be the good of the whole, and is consequently worth paying something for.

CHAPTER XIV.

THE MACHINERY OF GOVERNMENT.

THE EXECUTIVE.

THE first step in public business is to decide what to do. This is legislation; it is the work of the town meeting, or the legislature, or Congress. It still remains to accomplish the work. In a simple ancient village, indeed, as on the playground, the same persons might first consult and make rules, and then proceed to act together. Even then it becomes necessary to have leaders or chiefs to direct. But when much business has to be done, it is necessary to apportion it, and entrust certain persons with the care of it. This is the executive branch of the government. Sometimes a committee of three or more persons is given the charge of the public business, as in the case of the selectmen of towns, the school committee, the overseers of the poor, and various other commissions for public works. Thus in Switzerland an executive council of seven members is at the head of the government.

Undivided responsibility.—It has been generally found, when work of any sort needs to be done or important action carried out, that some one person should have the responsibility for it; for that which is the business of several to do, may more easily be neglected. In an army, therefore, there must be a commander-in-chief, who as long as he serves must have sole command; as in a ship there is one captain whom every one must obey. So it is wise to put the execution of the laws and the direction of the government into the hands of one man, the President; or in the State, the governor; or in the city, the mayor. As long as he serves, he shall be responsible for the faithful discharge of his office, as well as for the other officers appointed to assist him, who must therefore obey his orders. The less the responsibility of the mayor or President is divided with others, the freer he is, like the captain of the ship, to act promptly and with efficiency. But he cannot act contrary to the laws which the people or their representatives make. If he is unfaithful or incapable, or abuses his power, blame can be brought directly home to him, and he can be displaced. For this end, the executive officer is not commonly elected for a long term, often for only a year. The President is elected for only four years, and no President has ever been re-elected for more than a second term. No executive officer in this country can therefore long abuse his power, unless the people themselves become very negligent.

The veto power.— Besides the duty of the President, governor, or mayor to execute the laws, it has become the custom, following an ancient royal usage, to entrust him with the duty of forbidding the passage of an unwise law. Instead, therefore, of giving his official signature to such a law, which is the final step to make the law or vote valid, he can and ought to return it to the body which passed it, with his reasons for refusing to sign it. It would not be well, however, to give one man, even though he were the choice of all the people, the power entirely to thwart the will of their own representatives. Thus, if after further deliberation, as many as two-thirds of the representatives still continue to vote for the bill or law, it is passed, as it is said, "over the veto," and becomes law without the consent of the chief executive.[1] It often happens that legislative bodies pass a bill of appropriations, some of which are good while others are bad : it is therefore wisely permitted, in some constitutions and charters, to the governor or mayor to veto such items or parts of a bill as he may deem injurious.

The power of the President. — The President of the United States corresponds in some ways to the head of a monarchy. Thus he is the commander-in-chief of the army and navy : his consent or signature is necessary to the passage of laws ; he has the appointment, — with the consent of the Senate, who vote to confirm or reject his nomination, — of many important officers, who assist in the administration of the country, — judges, custom-house collectors, postmasters, and others, to the number of thousands. On the other hand, his power is very greatly limited. The king in an absolute monarchy could make laws or could even suspend laws. He could make peace or war of his own will. He could increase the taxes or levy a new tax, and use the money for his own purposes. As in the case of the father of a family, he had in his person both the law-making and the executive power. Matters of justice could also be referred to the king. The Czar of Russia has such powers to this day, as the " Father of his people." But our President cannot carry out any plan or public policy, however necessary it seems, unless the majority of both houses of Congress agree with him. He may recommend, but Congress may pay no heed to his advice. In many respects he has less freedom of action than the president of a great railroad, and less trust is placed in him. Moreover, the President is liable

---

[1] In some constitutions the rules make it less difficult to pass a bill over the veto. Four States do not give the governor the veto power.

to impeachment and removal from office, in case he violates the Constitution and laws. So fearful were the founders of our government lest the President might usurp the power of a tyrant, that it has now become a question whether he has power enough for best serving the interests of the people.

The governors of the States are also strictly limited in their power for good as well as evil. The legislature is not, indeed, bound to do anything that the wisest governor may recommend. Thus the office of governor, though one of honor, gives comparatively little opportunity for public usefulness. Its greatest duties, except in time of emergency, when the governor might have to act as commander-in-chief of the militia, consist in appointing honest and capable men for certain officers, as for example, in some States, the judges, and in vetoing bad bills that the legislature ought not to have passed. The mayors of cities likewise have been generally made mere figure-heads. They could perhaps prevent or veto bad plans, but they could not secure the passage of better plans. Thus throughout the machinery of our government we have cut down the powers of responsibility of the executive far more than would be well in the conduct of any other important business. We have acted like a club of boys, who, after choosing a captain, and making proper rules for his conduct, instead of following him, must stop and take a vote on every order that he gives, or even insist upon giving orders themselves.

The Cabinet. — Although it is wise to make one man responsible for the conduct of his office, it often happens that he wants advice, as a commander-in-chief must sometimes call a council of his officers. In the case of our President, the heads of the great departments of the government — the Secretary of State, who has charge of our relations to foreign governments; the Secretary of the Treasury; the Secretary of War, the Secretary of the Navy; the Secretary of the Interior, who has control of the business of government lands, the patent office, the pensions, the census, and the Indian tribes, the Postmaster-General; and the Attorney-General, who is the legal adviser for the government; with the head of a new department, the Commissioner of Agriculture — constitute the Cabinet, or the President's Council. These officers are appointed by the President, and generally from the party which elected him. He consults with them as to the course of his administration, but he is not bound to take their advice. They hold office during the pleasure of the President.

Each member of the Cabinet is responsible for the conduct of his department of the government: some of them have many thousands of clerks and other officers under them. Their responsibility is limited, however, and sometimes interfered with, and taken away by the action of Congress, who may refuse to do as the heads of departments recommend in their annual reports, or may fail to vote the money needed to carry on the work of any department. When, therefore, waste or loss occurs, or injustice is done (as, for instance, to the Indians), we cannot always be sure whether to blame the President and his secretary, or Congress, who may have neglected to do as the secretary wished.

In England the Ministry correspond somewhat to our Cabinet, but they must also be members of Parliament. On the contrary, our Cabinet have no voice in Congress. The English ministers hold power as long as they are supported by a majority in the House of Commons. If the majority changes and disapproves of their conduct, the custom is that they shall resign and let another set of ministers undertake the administration. It may easily happen that the sovereign does not approve of the Prime Minister in power. Nevertheless, if a majority of the House of Commons support him, he holds office in the name of the sovereign. In Germany, on the contrary, the chief minister must be acceptable to the Emperor.

The Governor's Council. — The governor of Massachusetts, and of two other States, has a sort of cabinet of advisers, who also act with him in making certain appointments to office, or in granting pardons to criminals; but his Council are elected by the people. He cannot, therefore, like the President, act independently of them. It is hard to see any reason for having such a council, except that it is an old custom. In many cities the charter or constitution makes the board of aldermen a sort of council for the mayor, who is so far hampered in his freedom of appointment of his officers, and in his conduct.

CHAPTER XV.

THE JUDICIAL BRANCH OF THE GOVERNMENT, OR THE COURTS AND THE LAWS.

THE legislative branch of the government represents the will of the people, determines what ought to be done, makes laws, and appropriates money. The executive branch of the government, assisted by an army of officers, carries out the laws that Congress or the legislature passes, and lays out the moneys appropriated. But frequent questions arise as to what is just or legal. Laws sometimes appear to conflict with each other, or not to be in accord with the Constitution. The laws of one State may be different from the laws of another, so as sometimes to conflict or work injury. Besides, there are those who, through ignorance or vice, break the laws or do injustice to others. The courts, or the judicial branch of the government, is intended to answer these questions and to pronounce what the law is. It is like the umpire on the playground.

The highest court is the Supreme Court of the United States, consisting of nine judges who are appointed for life. Only important questions come before this tribunal. If Massachusetts or Georgia were to pass a law which bore unequally on citizens of New York, travelling or doing business in the other State, the Supreme Court may declare such a law unconstitutional. For the Constitution of the United States guarantees the rights of the people of the different States. Part of the time the judges of the

Supreme Court hold session together in Washington. The country is also divided into nine circuits, each of which has a judge of its own, besides the judge of the Supreme Court who may for the time be assigned to attend upon the business comprised in the circuit. Below the circuit courts there are more than fifty district courts, each with its judge, its marshal or sheriff, and its district attorney. Appeal may be made in certain cases from one court to a higher or to the Supreme Court. If a ship rescued the cargo of another ship, and questions arose between the two owners, such a case would come before the United States court. So if any one were arrested for smuggling goods. If a question arose about a railroad which crossed several States, it might come before a United States judge. So with suits about patents upon inventions and the copyrights of books. If a question arose under any act or law of Congress; or between citizens of different States; in such cases the national courts may be asked to decide.

There are also Territorial courts, which are supported by the general government, till the Territories become States. The District of Columbia, as we have already seen, like a Territory, is under the laws made, not by its own people, but by Congress, who — since it is the seat of government — are obliged to control the District, and to take the charge of its expenses. A Court of Claims at Washington considers bills and disputed accounts urged against the national government; for differences sometimes arise between the treasury officers of the United States and the men who have furnished supplies or undertaken contracts of work for the government. There is much "red tape" or form required in the business of the government, so that mistakes and delays occur to the injury of individuals.

The State courts. — Each State has its own judicial system, with various grades of courts. There are magistrates in every locality, before whom criminals or petty questions can be brought. There are police courts for cities or for populous districts. The superior courts are held from time to time at the court-house or shire town of each county. Questions of law which cannot be satisfactorily settled in the lower courts may be referred to the Supreme Court, who, sitting together, make final decision, and if the meaning of the law is not clear, give it interpretation.

The election of judges. A bad method. — In some States the judges are elected by the people for a term of years. If the people are careless or ignorant, this practice furnishes inferior judges. A judge who, in aiming to be fair, renders an unpopular decision, is liable to be turned out of his office at the next election. Weak men may be tempted to use the office of judge, so as to secure a re-election rather than to administer strict justice. It is as though, not the players, but the bystanders, chose the umpire for a game. It ought, however, to be said, that judges have sometimes shown themselves thoroughly courageous under this system, and have risked their re-election in making honest decisions.

The better plan. The appointment of judges. — In some States the judges are appointed by the chief authority of the State, either by the governor and his Council, or in others, by the legislature. The judges of the United States are appointed by the President and approved by the Senate. The appointing power is thus made responsible for the high character of the judge. This is as though schoolboys were to trust their oldest fellows, or their captain, to name the umpire; lest the younger boys, instead of voting for the candidate who would make the fairest umpire, might vote for some one without experience. The judges of the United States, and of certain States also, are appointed for life. They are, therefore, independent of fear or favor. However unpopular their decision may be, provided it is honest, they cannot be turned out of their office. But there is a way provided, by which, if a judge should ever do gross wrong, he can be impeached and removed by the legislature, or by Congress. For the judge is still responsible to the people, through their representatives, like the umpire who should refuse to act fairly.

How far the courts have power. — In early times, one power, the king, like a father, might make laws and execute them, and decide disputes which arose under them. But each branch of our government is distinct from the other. Thus while the Supreme Court of the United States cannot send an army into a State to enforce the laws, the President, under certain conditions, might send a force. But it would be impossible for the President or the governor to carry out an unpopular decision of a court, if the Congress or the legislature were unwilling to make provision for the needful expense. Thus in a free country, all decisions of the courts must rest upon the general consent and the conscience of the people themselves. As boys, however, hold it dishonorable not to heed the umpire's decision, and since indeed no play could go on successfully without justice, so men generally agree in demanding of each other that all shall obey the decrees of the courts.

The machinery of the courts. — Besides judges, there are attorneys or lawyers employed in behalf of the people. The attorney-in-chief for each State is the legal adviser of the government. There are also attorneys or solicitors for counties or districts, whose duty it is to prosecute persons accused of breaking the laws. Each city, too, must have its attorney or solicitor, and perhaps, in a great city, a little staff of lawyers and clerks, who are constantly employed in defending the interests of the people. Thus the individual citizen may claim damages for loss or injury from the defect in a road, and the lawyer for the city must present the side of the people in the courts.

Besides the courts which try criminals or questions of business, there are probate courts, with their judges, which take care of the wills which men leave for the disposal of their property; or, if necessary, appoint guardians for orphan children. There must be some authority also, like the superior judge, who can decree a separation of husband and wife, or perhaps a divorce, in the case of a bad marriage. In such cases there may be suitable provision made, by the order of the court, for the children.

Sheriffs and constables also attend upon the courts, to serve their summons or to guard prisoners. Clerks and registers have the care of the records of the courts, or keep copies of the deeds and wills and other documents, without which there would be risk of frequent mistakes and disputes about property. Thus, if a man sells a piece of land, the sale is entered on record at the registry of deeds, and can at any time be consulted.

The police. — In large towns and cities it is necessary to have a body of police, sometimes numbering many hundreds, to watch the property and guard the safety of the citizens. The police are paid by the city and are at the command of the mayor. But in some cities they are under officers or a commission appointed, not by the mayor, but by the governor. This is because the people of the whole State do not trust the governments of the cities.

The jury. — It is an old custom that when a matter of justice has to be decided, twelve men are called in to act as a jury, and, after hearing the case, to vote which side should have the verdict. The early settlers brought this custom from England. It is indeed said to be traced far back to Germany. No one can be prosecuted for crime without a jury. The custom in most States is that the jury must be unanimous; that is, the twelve must agree, or else the accused cannot be convicted. The accused has the right to challenge, or decline to accept, a certain number of those offered as jurymen. The court may also set aside such men as he believes may have already formed an opinion about the case. This sometimes serves to narrow the jury down to the most ignorant men who do not read the newspapers; or, in some cases, to men who may be indulgent towards the offence; and since it is difficult always to bring quite conclusive evidence to compel twelve men to agree, it must sometimes happen that the jury system lets the guilty escape. On the other hand, it is thought better that some guilty persons should escape, than that any innocent person should run the risk of being punished.

The grand jury. — A charge might be carelessly brought against a person who would be put to great trouble and loss by having to stand a trial. Before a case is fairly brought into court, therefore, the *grand jury*, which may be as large as twenty-three men, examines the charge, and, if good reason is shown, finds a bill or indictment.

How jurymen are chosen. — Every man, with certain exceptions, such as lawyers and doctors, is liable to be drawn by lot to serve as a juryman. The duty is some-

what like that of serving in time of war as a soldier. For
if every one could shirk who did not enjoy the service, it
would make the work harder for others, and perhaps throw
it into ignorant hands.

The delay of justice. — The old custom of requiring
all the jury to agree may easily delay justice and render it
costly; for it may be necessary to try the same case repeatedly, before a jury will be found who can agree. If
then some fault is found in the decision, so that an appeal
may be taken to a higher court, the question may be kept
in the courts for years, not only to the cost of the parties
to the lawsuit, but also at great cost to the public, who
have to maintain the cumbrous machinery of justice, and
to pay for judges, sheriffs, and jurymen. Some think that
the laws should generally be changed so that, except in
criminal cases, the vote of two-thirds of a jury, or as in
the case of the Supreme Court, a majority, shall be enough
to decide.

The referee. — It is not uncommon for both parties to a
question or dispute, to agree to leave the decision to
capable referees. This is the method which good temper
would always dictate between honest and friendly men.

The judge and the jury. — In our system, except in
what are known as the equity courts, and in petty cases
before a police court, the judge does not himself decide,
for example, upon the question of the guilt of an accused
person, or a dispute about property; but the jury decide,
after hearing the witnesses and the evidence upon both
sides, with the arguments or statements of the lawyers.
The judge presides and sees that the trial is according to
law. He also gives the charge to the jury, or in other
words, instructs the jury as to the law and advises them
how to consider the question. He may also, in certain

cases, set the verdict of the jury aside and order a fresh trial. In the Supreme Court, however, where questions of *what the law is* are considered, the judges themselves decide.

Witnesses and the oath. — The usage is to require the witnesses, who bring evidence in the court, to take an oath or swear to the truth of what they testify. The breaking of the oath is called perjury and makes one liable to punishment. Important officers of government and clerks of corporations are also required to take the oath of office for the faithful performance of their duties. Those who favor the use of the oath hold that it adds the weight of religion to men's consciences, and urges them to be scrupulous and accurate.

On the other hand, it is said that no oath can make a promise or the statement of a witness more sacred than it is in itself. It is also objected that the oath is often administered in a slovenly and meaningless manner, and that a serious affirmation under the penalty of perjury is enough. The law already allows those who have conscientious objections to the oath to make such affirmation.

Habeas corpus. — In the days of tyrants, when often a great lord had power of life and death in his domain, it sometimes befell that a man was thrown into prison on some charge or suspicion and not brought to trial at once, but kept confined till he died. One of the ancient liberties, therefore, which the English people asserted, was that of a prompt trial in behalf of any person imprisoned on suspicion. A friend or neighbor could go in behalf of the prisoner before the proper court, and get what is called a writ of *habeas corpus* (Latin words, commanding the jailer to produce the body). Good cause must then be shown at once why the man ought to be confined, or else he is entitled to release. No king or enemy could, therefore, keep a man in jail without fair process of law.

Bail. — In most cases, unless the charges are very serious, the prisoner may procure *bail*, and go free till the trial comes off; that is, some person may agree to answer for his appearance when the trial is called, or to pay the forfeit of a sum of money.

Exceptions. — There are times of war or great public danger when the privileges of bail and *habeas corpus* may be suspended. It might happen that certain accused persons appeared to be very dangerous to the State,. or that popular excitement would not for the time allow a fair trial. Thus the laws themselves must yield to the public safety, as when in time of dangerous sickness, the ordinary rules of the house may be set aside.

The common law. — The early settlers brought with them the laws and systems of courts, which they had been used to in England. These laws had grown partly out of men's sense of right, as the laws against violence and crime; also out of men's dealings in trade, and in holding property. As new questions arose in the courts, the judges' decisions became precedents, or examples to help decide other similar cases. The *common law* is the accumulation of such decisions through many generations. It is possible that the old decision or custom was mistaken; some conscientious and independent court may then correct it, and make a new example to be followed by others.

The *common law* is like the rules of the games among schoolboys. The boys play according to custom, and their umpire tries to interpret the rules so as to do justice. In this way he will sometimes establish a new rule.

Statute laws. — It is also possible to make new laws or to set aside imperfect ones by the agreement of the people, or by their representatives. These are *statute laws*, such as the legislature or Congress makes.

The laws and the right. — Justice is often more than the laws. For the laws can only fix what the general sense of the people or their customs permit. The laws of a nation may thus allow wrong, like slavery. We may, therefore, keep within the laws and yet not do right. Neither do good laws profess to work perfect justice. The laws and the courts are like machinery, which will work wrong if men mismanage it. Hence the courts will frequently delay justice, because they are overworked. The laws must sometimes do justice for the sake of the whole, at the expense or loss of the individual. For the general rule may accidentally hurt the individual who falls in its way. The courts are also very costly, not only to the people who support them, but to the person who uses them, who must hire lawyers to defend his cause. Thus the actual working of the courts often discourages men from resorting to them, and tends to urge parties to settle their differences by friendly arbitration.

The tyranny of law. — In the old colony of Massachusetts Bay, and in Connecticut, the majority of the people made laws compelling every one to go to church; but even if it was good for all to go to church, it was wrong for the majority to use such laws to compel the minority. It is tyranny for one man to insist arbitrarily that others must do what he says; so it may be tyranny for many men to force others to obey their will.

The laws are merely instruments for the protection of all the people. Their proper use, therefore, like the rules of a club, depends upon the common consent. They fail to be useful as soon as any considerable number of citizens deem them unfair or oppressive, or especially, against their conscience. In this case, the laws may tempt to disorder, violence, and possibly to rebellion. Besides, a majority of men may for a time be mistaken about right, as a majority has often been mistaken about religion. The laws, therefore, which are made for all, ought not merely to enforce the opinions of one party, but to express the common agreement of intelligent and decent citizens. Whatever is right beyond the laws will thus come into vogue by persuasion, example, and enlightened public opinion, better than when forced through legislation.

Freedom of speech and the press. — The constitutions of our States generally secure to the people freedom to speak or publish whatever they think. They may speak and write against the government, and try to change it. They may publish gossip about the President and other officers. They may write or speak so as to shock the prejudices of their fellow-citizens. This liberty rests upon our trust in the people and in the soundness of our government. A timid or despotic government, like Russia, could not permit such freedom of discussion. Our laws only slightly restrict it. They forbid the publication of malicious or libellous matter designed to hurt a person's business or character. They also forbid low and immoral publications. On the whole, however, it is thought safe to allow men to speak their minds, since errors are most effectively answered when fairly brought to the light.

CHAPTER XVI.

THE TREASURY AND THE TAXES.

The public expenses. — The sum of money required for all the expenses of the town, city, state, and national government is several hundreds of millions of dollars a year. It is an average of more than ten dollars apiece for every man, woman, and child in the country. In the great cities of course the average is much greater, amounting in some cases to thirty dollars a year for each inhabitant. If all this money is wisely expended, it comes back to the people in various kind of service ; so that they are not only happier, but richer than they would be without it. For example, the whole country is richer and not poorer on account of the expense for lighthouses. So, too, with the fire department of a city. The amount needed for public expenses is collected in the form of taxes.

The taxes. — In every town or city there is a collector of taxes and a treasurer. There are also assessors; that is, officers who determine what property there is in the town, and what amount, therefore, each person ought to pay according to law. Each town must raise money enough for its own expenses and also its share of the expenses of the county and of the State government. Its share is determined by the proportion of the taxable property in it, such as land, houses, mills, railroads, compared with the whole amount in the county or the State. So with the share which each person pays. It depends upon the amount of taxable property which he or she has.

County treasurers take charge of the money which each county requires for its courts and other purposes. The county commissioners have authority to lay out the money of the county, according to law.

The State treasurer, with his clerks, keeps account of the moneys received from all the towns and cities (or counties) of the State. A board of officers or State assessors may determine the share that each town ought to pay for the common good.

Direct taxes: the income tax. — When a tax-bill is brought directly to each person, or to each business firm or company, it is called a direct tax. It is levied sometimes upon the value of the actual property that any one possesses, or again upon the amount of one's income or salary. The *income tax* would be a very fair method, if every one could be trusted to report his income to the assessors, but a very few dishonorable citizens who failed to report truthfully would at once throw an unfair burden upon all the rest.

Double taxation. — Besides the visible property which a man owns, such as houses and land (real estate), and movable articles, such as furniture, etc., he may have various certificates of the stock of corporations, or bonds or notes. A great amount of wealth is held in this form. It stands for the fact, as we shall see more fully later, that the holder owns a share of property which some other person or company manages. If it is a railway bond, it means that the holder really owns some part of the property of the railway company. If it is a note or mortgage, it means that the holder really owns so much of the property, perhaps a farm, that the man who gave the note works. This actual property, wherever it is, is assessed and taxed for all its value. If, besides, the man who holds shares in the property is taxed for those shares, the tax becomes twofold. This is thought by many to be unfair. For the man who owns the whole of a piece of property, a mill, or a block of buildings, has only to pay one tax upon it.

The property owned thus, in shares, goes under the name of personal property. Since the certificates, bonds, or notes are private papers, locked up out of sight, the assessors cannot determine how much property any one has in this form, unless each citizen makes a correct report. If any citizen fails to make such a report, the burden of taxation is thrown upon those who make a truthful report, who thus are obliged to pay more than their share. The laws about taxing such personal property vary in the different States. As a matter of fact, it has been found that such taxes are hard to collect, and tempt men either to be negligent or dishonorable about bearing their public burdens.

The single or land tax. — In some countries the government or the king has claimed to own all the land. This was the custom in many parts of India. The rent of the land was thus the government tax. In Russia, also, and in many half-civilized countries, the commune, or village, or tribe, own all the land in common. This was, perhaps, the most ancient form of possession. We can imagine that when the first settlers came to America, the royal government might likewise have kept the ownership of the land, and rented it to the settlers. When the government was changed and vested in the people, the nation would then have owned all the land; and every individual would have rented what he needed to use, of the nation. The taxes would thus have fallen in the form of rent. There are those who think that this way of raising the taxes would be easier and simpler than present methods; they therefore advocate a tax on land, and nothing else, precisely as though the nation owned and rented the land. No one would then be able to hold land without actually using it, or to buy great tracts of land, or house-lots, merely to make money by selling them again.

On the other hand, the same vast amount of money would still have to be raised. The people of the poorer country districts would perhaps need more money for schools and other expenses, than the amount of the rent of their lands. The management of the rents, and the fair division of the needed funds, would be likely, at last, to fall upon the central or national government. This would involve a change in the whole theory of our government, which, as we have seen, is desired to train the people of each State and town to responsibility about their own affairs.

Besides, if the government took all the rent, the present owners of the land would suffer the same loss, as though their property had been taken away from them. The truth is that the nation bearing the taxes is like a creature carrying a burden. You wish to fix the burden so equally as to make the least strain. If, then, you ever change the position of the burden, you must be careful not to bruise and injure the new set of muscles.

The duties of assessors. — It is impossible to tell exactly what different pieces of property in a town are worth. One man might set the value too high, and another too low. Several men, therefore, constitute the Board of Assessors, so that their different judgments shall correct each other. If, then, the assessors endeavored, as the law requires, to discover the true value of every one's property, the taxes would fall pretty fairly on every one;

as the prices of goods fall on all alike, although it is always harder for some to pay than for others. If, however, as often happens, the assessors fail to tax any piece of property for its true value, this brings an unjust burden on every one else. Thus, in many cities, men have been permitted by the assessors to hold lands at a lower tax than the real value. .The few have thus been enabled to grow rich by the rise of the lands, at the expense of the many. So, too, throughout the State, if every board of assessors did their duty, and told the true value of the property in each town, no town would have to pay more than its share for the expenses of the State. If, however, the assessors of any town deliberately tax their own townspeople for only one-half of the true value of their property, while more faithful assessors in another town tax the true value of their property, the latter town is made to bear an unfair proportion of the public burden.

The poll tax. — There is in many States a small tax which is levied equally upon all men from twenty years old, whether they have property or not, also upon women in case they are voters. This might be called the voter's tax. Since it often is not paid, and sometimes prevents poor citizens from voting, or again tempts candidates for office to pay it in behalf of their supporters; and since it is rather expensive in its collection, many think the poll tax unwise. On the other hand, it is held that every citizen who votes ought to be willing to pay something directly into the public treasury.

Licenses, fees, etc. — There are certain occupations, for example, that of a pedler or a pawnbroker, for which it is well that the persons enjoying them shall be registered and take out a license. They should therefore pay some fee to cover the expense of the registration office. Owners of dogs, also, are obliged to pay a fee. There are certain public privileges which may fairly demand a payment in return to the public. Thus, if a street railway enjoys the use of the public highways, it is just that it should pay for its franchise, that is, its right to use the streets. Since, however, the fares have to be sufficient to enable the company to pay their taxes, the amounts thus raised are apt to come out of the pockets of the people, and are a kind of indirect tax. Precisely as when the owner of a tenement house, after paying, we will suppose, a thousand dollars for the taxes, may fix his rents so that the occupants of the house share the tax, and pay each a few dollars a year on account of it. Thus no tax can be levied or increased without making itself felt somewhere in the expenses of the people.

Liquor licenses. — In many States the sale of intoxicating drinks requires a license, and since a large amount of crime and accident and public loss comes through these drinks, a fee — in some cities as high as a thousand dollars or more — is required to be paid for the purchase of the license. The liquor dealer, of course, pays the tax as he pays his rent, but he expects to get his money back from the people who buy of him. Of course, whenever a license is granted for any kind of business, the people are understood to authorize it as rightful. If the business is injurious, they then become responsible for it.

The taxes for the nation. — The taxes for the national government are separate from all others. They are usually indirect; that is, they are not assessed upon individuals according to the value of their property or their income. The government has a right to lay a direct tax, and in the Civil War actually levied an income tax upon all citizens whose salary or income was above a thousand dollars a year.

In ordinary times, however, the nation raises its moneys partly by taxes upon articles which are imported from foreign countries. In every seaport, therefore, there is a custom-house with a collector and other officers, if necessary, to levy these *duties*. The merchants who sell the goods then make the price high enough to repay them for the cost and trouble of the tax. Whoever uses the goods thus helps pay the tax according to the amount which he uses. If, for example, the duty on sugar were two cents a pound, and a man's family used one hundred pounds in a year, he would pay two dollars in taxes.

The internal revenue. — Another part of the revenue of the government comes from a tax upon various articles produced or manufactured in this country, such as tobacco and spirits. This is called the internal revenue. As before, the producer or manufacturer first pays this tax and puts a higher price upon the article when he sells it. Thus the people pay the indirect tax in the end, since each man who buys a pound of tobacco pays a tax as a part of the price. The manufacturer or producer only collects the tax for the government and assesses it when he sells his tobacco.

The government also has extensive lands from which, as they are sold, an income is derived. In some countries, as in Germany, the government derives a revenue from the mines and the timber in the forests. The money from these sources, however, must come in the end from the labor of the people, who have to pay for the land, the ores and coal, and the timber.

In the case of the post-office, or when, as in some European countries, the government manages the telegraph or railroads, the people evidently pay in postage, or fares, or freight, for what they use or enjoy. So in the water rates, when the city provides water, or the gas bills, if the city manufactures the gas. All the expenses of the government ought to go in some way towards procuring benefit, health, safety, or convenience.

The source of all taxes. — The cost of all the work of the government, national and local, throughout the country, may be roughly estimated as equal to the constant labor of a million workmen. All the produce of the nation may be likened to a vast pyramid of wealth which the labor and the skill of the people have brought together. This pyramid of produce is supposed to be greater for an honest government. The living of the million men and women who do the work for the government, that is, for all the people, must, therefore, come out of the common product. And while the average amount of (say) ten dollars a year seems at first to be deducted from the share of each inhabitant, the share left to each ought to be greater on account of the benefits that the government secures; as the amount that each spends for tools, so far from making him poorer, enables him to earn more money than if he had no tools.

Exemptions from taxes. — It is evident that the taxes ought to be shared by all. But it is fair, if the citizens generally agree, to free or exempt from taxation certain kinds of property, like colleges, hospitals, or churches, which are not for private gain. Such kinds of property, somewhat like parks or public libraries, are for the interest of the whole people and really add to the public wealth of a city or State. There would be no object, then, by taxing them to make them cost more, or to discourage persons from providing them. If, however, any such property ever ceased to be for the public interest, or was managed merely for private gain or pleasure, it ought to be taxed.

The public faith. — We hold every man to his promises, and especially to the honest payment of his debts. Even when he has been foolish in incurring debt or has wasted his money, we think it unfair that he should make others lose on his account. So with the promises or the debts of a city or nation. But a nation lives through hundreds of years. It may happen that a single generation makes difficult promises or incurs a great debt, as England did in the war with Napoleon. Perhaps the debt may have been foolish, and through the fault of bad government, as with some of the Southern States after the Civil War. In this case it may not at first seem to be just that the people of a new generation should be taxed to keep promises which others had wrongfully made. But when we think more carefully, we see that the people who have inherited the institutions and the public property of a state ought also to make good its promises and obligations; as one who inherited his grandfather's estate should be willing to pay his debts. This is not only right, but, as usual, what is right proves in the long run to be also wise. For a state that always keeps its promises and pays its debts has credit, or, in other words, is trusted, and can borrow money, if necessity arises, as France, England, and the United States easily can, at a very low rate; whereas a state which does not keep its promises loses its credit, and its citizens get a dishonest name.

CHAPTER XVII.

THE SCHOOL SYSTEM.

THE theory of our government is that, since the citizens are the rulers, every young person ought at least to be well enough educated to make an intelligent citizen, or, in other words, to be able, when summoned to vote, to know what he votes for. He ought at least to be able to read, or he might not be sure that he used the ballot which he intended. Neither unless he could inform himself upon the questions at issue, such as the tariff, free trade, etc., could he be expected to decide understandingly to which of the great political parties he wished to belong. Besides, the better educated and the more skilful people are, the more prosperous their nation becomes.

The common wealth. — There is another reason why we desire the education of all children. It is that every one may have equal access to that large part of the common wealth which consists in thoughts, ideas, inventions, and the arts, the discoveries of science, and the control over the forces of nature. This common wealth of knowledge, to which learning is the key, is worth more to the nation than all the goods and buildings in the land. It is through the wealth in thoughts and ideas that the other kinds of wealth are created and men learn the secrets of happiness. This larger and more precious part of the resources of the nation ought to be within the reach of the poor as well as the rich. The child who has knowledge without money will thus be better off than one who has money without knowledge.

Free schools. — Schools are, therefore, provided by law in every State, and children are usually required to attend for a certain term in each year, up to perhaps the age of fourteen years. They are also encouraged to continue at school longer, and high and normal schools are provided for them. These higher schools are expected to furnish teachers for the common schools, as well as to educate those who shall be leaders of public opinion and from whom we may obtain suitable officers for our government. The education is not only in books. Many of the States also encourage manual training, or the education of the hand and eye, so that boys and girls shall be skilled to take up trades and to understand the varied industries which the nation carries on. Most States support agricultural colleges, where the best methods of farming are taught. Grants of valuable public lands have been made by Congress to the States for the endowment of these colleges.

The higher education. — In some States, as Michigan, in addition to high schools in the larger places, education in the higher branches, including law and medicine, is provided by a state university. Many States, in order to encourage education, have made special grants to private academies or colleges ; somewhat as the national government, in order to secure education as fast as possible for the Indians, has voted appropriations to schools among them, under the care of private individuals or societies. But such schools are commonly sectarian ; and since it is unjust to help Methodist schools, for instance, and not to help Catholic schools equally, and since it is often hard to judge fairly between the claims of rival institutions, many hold that public money ought only to be given to public schools, and not at all to schools from the control of which any citizen could be excluded for his opinions.

What the public schools should not teach.—It is unfair that any teacher who is employed at the common expense should urge his religious opinions, or indeed any of his private opinions, upon the children of parents who may think differently; it would not be fair for a teacher who was supported by all the people to try to persuade the children of Democrats to become Republicans. Otherwise the public schools would become private, or sectarian, or partisan. There are some subjects, therefore, on which men differ widely, which are not well fitted for use in the public schools. But it is always right, upon such subjects as the schools consider, to teach the facts, since every right-minded person must wish to know the truth, and no one need fear that truth will do harm.

The teaching force.—Besides thousands of regular paid teachers, there are other officers whose business it is to look after the schools. There is thus a National Bureau of Education, which collects the facts about education throughout the country. The State also has its board of education appointed by the governor. Cities and towns or counties or groups of towns have their superintendents or supervisors of education, who are appointed to aid the teachers and inform them of the best methods. Committees, generally unpaid, and sometimes school agents, are elected in each locality to represent the people in the care of the schools, to appoint teachers, and to advise about the needful expenditures. The schools are also open for the public to visit. If they fail to serve their purpose, it must therefore be through the fault or neglect of the people themselves.

Women in the control of the schools. — In some States women, who do not otherwise vote, are invited to share in the election of the school committees. They are also made eligible for the various boards of education. This is not only because the majority of teachers are women, but because it is expected that women generally, and mothers especially, will take a deep and intelligent interest in education.

The cost of the schools. — It is estimated that more than one hundred and twenty-five millions of dollars, or about one-fifth of all the taxes, is expended upon schools. The schoolhouses are built and furnished by the town or district, but the State treasury assists poorer towns to pay for their teachers. The interest in education and the system pursued vary much in different States. Thus in Alabama, which has a large population of poor people, the amount appropriated gives an average of only one dollar and a quarter to each child in the State; or less than two dollars and a half for each scholar actually enrolled. In the city of Boston the average cost of each scholar is over twenty-eight dollars a year. This shows the cost which the community bears for the sake of having good citizens.

Public and private schools. — There are many schools, academies, and colleges supported by individuals, who pay for the tuition of their children; or supported by an endowment fund, under the care of trustees. Sometimes the private school is established by some church or religious denomination. Its teaching may or may not be as thorough as in public schools of the same grade. Since, however, in a republic all must live, act, and vote on equal terms as fellow-citizens, it seems desirable that, at least during some part of the course of instruction, all shall be educated together. The citizens will thus become better acquainted with each other, and will be likely to be more fair and tolerant.

The parents who pay for tuition in private schools are required also to pay their share of the taxes for the free schools. This is because it is for the good of all to support the schools rather than to allow children to grow up in ignorance ; precisely as it is for the general good to have police and courts, although some are rich enough to have private watchmen, and others may not need a policeman at all. In other words, it is believed that, upon the whole, the community is better off for providing free schools, and requiring the attendance at these schools, of all children who are not provided for in some other way.

CHAPTER XVIII.

THE CIVIL SERVICE AND THE OFFICES.

BESIDES the army and navy, of which the President is commander-in-chief, the administration of the country requires a large force of persons, men and women, who are employed in the various departments of the public service as postmasters, clerks, accountants, inspectors, and keepers of supplies of every sort. These persons constitute what is called the Civil Service. There is also a similar civil service in every State. In the cities and towns there is likewise a list of officials, — the police or constables, the fire department, the men who care for the streets, and the water supply, and many others. The public health and safety depend on the honesty and faithfulness of the persons who make up the civil service. While it is evident that the head of any department, who is responsible for its conduct, should be able to displace an inefficient subordinate, on the other hand, a good officer ought to keep his place as long as he remains faithful. It is therefore injurious to the public service when a President or mayor is able to turn out good officers, or to use the offices for rewarding his personal or political friends. It is as though the captain of a great steamer were to turn out good engineers and firemen for the sake of giving berths to inexperienced relations of his own.

Civil service reform. — Many years ago great abuses had arisen in England through the favoritism of the chief officers of the government. No one, however faithful and competent, could obtain a situation in government employ unless he had a friend in office. The heads of departments of business, like the post-office, sometimes appointed their own relations to fill places where they drew pay without doing work. Even in the army one had to pay money in order to get an office. Thus the men in power used the offices as if they were their own property instead of a public charge. This was called *patronage*. It meant that the great officers, such as the ministers of government, were allowed to give places away for their own benefit, or to reward services to their party, or even for money; whereas the places belonged to the people, to be filled by those only who would be the most faithful public servants.

The abuse of patronage led to such evils of waste, extravagance, and inefficiency, besides injustice to faithful men, that the Parliament at last made new and strict rules for the officers of the civil service. No official should be displaced as long as he did his duty. New appointments should be made on the ground of merit, and from a list of those who had passed a satisfactory examination for the place to be filled; and vacancies in the higher places should be filled so far as possible from those who had done well in the subordinate places. Thus the rules made it worth while for any officer to earn his promotion.

A bad civil service in America. — During the early administrations under Washington and his successors removals from office were rare. The founders of our republic regarded the government as a public trust. But after a while, and specially in the presidency of Jackson, the custom came in of using the offices to reward the political friends of the party in power. Meanwhile the number of offices grew, till the fortune and living of many thousands of people depended upon winning or losing a presidential election. For each great party came to believe that, though the officers must be paid by all the people, yet the places and the pay belonged only to themselves. As once in England, no faithful officer was sure of holding his place if the other party came into power; neither did useful service give promise of promotion. Moreover, it became the custom to assess office holders, and even letter-carriers and clerks, who are really the servants of all the people, to pay for the election expenses of their party. Thus the party in power sought to keep power in order to hold the patronage, rather than to carry out any serious policy in behalf of the nation.

The office-seekers. — The representatives or senators also came to feel that the offices in their State or district belonged to them to give away to their friends. Thus whenever the administration of government was changed or a new President was elected, old and experienced officials were turned out by wholesale that the party in power might have the offices and the salaries for their own men, who often had no experience. The time of the heads of government was largely occupied in filling vacancies from a horde of hungry and often incapable office-seekers. A class of dangerous men arose on each side, who lost sight of the real issues between parties as to the wise conduct of government, and merely plotted and struggled, either to keep the offices, or when the other party had captured them for a time, to recover their spoils. This involved great waste to the nation, extravagant expenditure, abuse of trust funds, as, for example, the funds held for the Indian tribes, and an unhealthy and feverish excitement over elections.

These abuses were not only in the conduct of the

national government, but they discovered themselves also in every State and city. Nowhere is there greater need of wisdom, fidelity, and experience, than in the management of the costly business of a city. And nowhere did patronage cause more frequent and injurious demoralization of public employees and workmen.

How reform came. — A true reform generally commends itself to the people as fast as they understand it. For they do not want to be taxed uselessly or to fail of good service. They also, like the boys on the playground, prefer to see justice done, and do not love those who play tricks and cheat them. When, therefore, a few patriotic men are willing to try together to carry any needed reform, they can usually depend upon persuading the people to support them. Especially is this the case when men of opposite parties will agree to let their party differences drop, in order to secure some public good.

So in the case of civil service reform. The best men of both parties accordingly agreed that rules ought to be made, such as had been necessary in other great countries, to give the civil service permanence, and to fill vacancies in it by promotion and by fair examinations. Few men would venture to vote against a plan so just. Suitable rules have therefore been made, and commissioners to enforce them have been appointed in some of the States, as well as for the national government, with the intent that the civil service may belong to the people, and not merely to the managers of the party which happens to hold the reins of power. Whereas once it often happened, that an official could be nominated by an irresponsible saloon-keeper, the new rules require candidates for a place, whether of a clerk, inspector, policeman, or laborer, to pass a just examination suited to the character of the place, and conducted under the care of the commissioner. No one can be appointed who does not get a reasonable number of marks; neither can he be removed without cause.

What remains to be done. — The larger number of offices in the country are still subject to the old abuses. A good Indian agent may still be turned out to give place to an unfit or dangerous man, who may involve a tribe in war. Thousands of postmasters are subject to removal every four years. The time of the President and the representatives in Congress is wasted by office-seekers. When the general government extends civil-service rules to all the offices, so as to protect every faithful employee; when it requires the appointments of postmasters and custom-house collectors to be made during good behavior, and not as now for only four years; and when all the States have established civil-service laws for the benefit of their cities, one great source of waste and injustice will be removed. Until this is done, certain kinds of work, which many think that the government ought to undertake, such as the manufacture of gas, and the control of street-railways by cities, and the ownership of the telegraphs and railroads by the nation, cannot even be thought of.

The consular and diplomatic service. — This is the branch of the civil service which concerns our relations with foreign nations. It is the custom of every civilized nation to maintain an agent, called an Embassador, or Minister, or Consul-General, at the capital of every friendly nation. This agent looks out for the interests of his government, has correspondence with the office of the Secretary of State in Washington, and represents the rights of his fellow-citizens abroad. It has never been the custom of our republic to send Embassadors, the ministers of the highest rank, such as kings appoint; foreign governments do not, therefore, send them to us.

There is, also, a consul or agent at most of the great ports or centres of trade, where commerce brings men of many nations together. For instance, if an American citizen were to be unjustly arrested in Liverpool, he would depend upon his consul for help; or, the consul would see that shipwrecked American sailors were cared for. The foreign ministers, consuls, and their various clerks make up the diplomatic service. This service needs men of experience, conversant with the laws and customs of the foreign nation, and able to speak its language. Such men are generally chosen by the governments of foreign countries, who often maintain a permanent force of trained men to manage this business. Our own government, however, for want of a sound civil service, has often suffered at the hands of incapable or negligent persons, ignorant of the language of the country to which they have been sent, who have owed their appointments in the consular service to partisan work in helping to get votes for some congressman.

Rotation in office. — There are two ideas in vogue about office. One idea is that it is a private perquisite or privilege, which ought to "go around" and be shared by as many persons as possible. Every boy in the class, for example, ought, if possible, to have a chance as the captain or president of the class. A new set of men should be made selectmen every year. So the representative or senator should not hold more than one term, or at most, not more than two terms. Even a judge should give place to another man. In short, the offices should be used for the pleasure or profit of as many individual citizens as possible. This is rotation in office. We have already seen the harm that it may do to the civil service. The winning of the offices becomes like a game of grab. The ancient Greek method of choosing officers by lot would be fairer and more decent than this.

The other and sound idea of office is to secure the best possible service of the people. What the office is for, is that the public business may be done most economically and efficiently. With this idea the people could not afford, if they had found a faithful officer, to let him go. If the present board of selectmen or the school committee worked well, they would prefer to keep them. If their senator had learned how to conduct the public business, they would return him to Washington, instead of sending an inexperienced man. If the mayor was capable and disinterested, they would re-elect him as long as he would serve them. This is what men do who wish their mill or their bank to be a success. They keep a good officer as long as he will stay. But they dismiss inefficient men, till they find one whom they can trust.

An exception. — The office of the President, as we have seen, has never been filled by any one for more than two terms. This is partly on account of the example of Washington, who refused to be re-elected to a third term. There is also a sense of distrust, lest supreme power become a means of temptation in the hands of a President who might hope for continued re-election. Neither is the nature of our government such that, in ordinary times, any one man would be likely to administer its affairs better than some other man who might be chosen.

Candidates and their place of residence. — There are two ideas in vogue about the candidate for an office. One idea is that he ought to be a resident in the town or city or district that chooses him to office. It is as though men, being about to erect a town hall, should decide that they must choose their architect from their own fellow-townsmen. This is like the idea that the office is for the sake of the individual. Men accordingly think that their town ought to take its turn in furnishing a representative to the legislature, or their ward of the city ought to have the mayor. With this idea the representative to Congress must reside in the district which elects him, even though a much abler man, who could serve the district better, could be found in another part of the State. Thus often a weak man is chosen because he is a resident of the district, who must shortly give way to another weak man, because he lives in the other end of the district.

The opposite idea is that, since the office is not for the man, but for the people, they wish the best and strongest man whom they can secure. The people will chose their fellow-citizen as architect, if he is a good architect. But they want the best possible town hall, and they will, therefore, send to New York or Boston for an architect, provided they can thus have a better building. So the people will choose a mayor from their own ward, if he will make the best mayor; but if the other ward will give them a more capable man, they will certainly choose him in preference. Or if they can find a disinterested and patriotic man from another part of the State to represent them in Washington, they will take care to get the best possible service. The law wisely allows liberty of choice within certain limits, although the politicians have so far established the contrary custom. For there is no one whom the small partisan managers more dread than a fearless public servant who only aims to serve the people.

CHAPTER XIX.

VOTING.

Viva voce. — The simplest and quickest form of voting, used sometimes in the schoolroom, is by the voice, or *viva voce;* when those in favor of a measure say Aye or Yes, and those opposed say Nay or No.   But it sometimes happens in this case that the smaller number seem to make more noise than the others, or the chairman may be charged with prejudice or unfairness in declaring the vote in favor of his own side.

The show of hands. — Another simple and more accurate mode of voting is to ask each side, the ayes and the noes in turn, to raise their right hands till they can be counted by the clerk or secretary ; or, if the numbers are large, by tellers; or, since hands are not always seen, and a dishonest person might raise both hands, each side may be asked to rise and stand till it is counted. If a vote of the voice is doubted by any one, it is usual to ask for the counting of the votes.   Sometimes, as in Congress, at the wish of a fifth of those present, the names of the voters are called in order so that it is known precisely how each one votes; or, whether any are absent so as not to be counted.   In the English Parliament the ayes go over to one side of the hall, and the noes go to the other side. This is the *division of the house.*

The ballot. — Men are sometimes timid and do not like to express their opinion openly, for fear that it may be unpopular, or lest some unfriendly person may resent their vote. Workmen do not always like to vote openly against their employers. It is often, indeed, a very delicate matter to choose among a number of candidates for an office, some of whom may be personal friends, and yet unfitted for the place. When many officers have to be chosen at once, it is also a matter of convenience to have their names written or printed. The *ballot* is the written or printed vote. The word means strictly a little ball, and in many clubs or societies black balls and white are still used to vote with; as the Greeks used shells on certain occasions. The ballot permits the secret expression of a voter's opinion, who might not otherwise like to have his vote known. It therefore protects timid persons and encourages them to vote as they really think.

The ballot is not so well fitted for a representative body like Congress, where it is desirable that every member shall be openly responsible to the people who choose him, and who wish, therefore, to know how he acts.

Fair election laws. — The written ballot is not enough to secure a fair vote. Various rules are necessary, especially if there are a multitude of voters, some of whom are ignorant, and some even dishonorable. Thus it must be provided that no one shall vote in two places, as for example, in two different wards of a city, and that no one shall bring in strangers to vote.

For this purpose the names of all the qualified voters of a town, a ward, or a district are printed beforehand on a list. As soon as any one votes, his name is "checked off" the list. It is necessary also that the ballots shall be carefully prepared; for example, if Mr. James S. Smith is the candidate, the name John Smith should not be printed instead; else the votes could not fairly be counted.

Candidates have often spent a great deal of money to be elected, and have paid their agents to put their own ballots into men's hands, or to try to persuade voters to change their votes at the polls or voting-place, and even worse, have sometimes bribed dishonest and careless citizens to give their vote for a present, a ride, a drink, a dinner, or money. Men have also been employed at the polls to watch the ballots and spy out what kind of vote each voter put into the box. Sometimes the officers in charge of the election have been false to their trust, and permitted fraud at the polls, and have contrived to count the votes wrong. Many laws have therefore been passed to protect the elections. For it is evident that if cheating at elections were permitted, or if any considerable number of citizens were willing either to cheat or to be bribed, popular government would become a farce.

The Australian ballot. — The fairest of the election laws is based upon methods already tried in England and Australia. It secures for each voter the privacy of a little stall or closet in preparing his ballot, as well as secrecy in voting. It also provides the votes at the expense of the government, so that no candidate or party can have excuse for spending money in an election, except for the perfectly proper purpose of holding meetings and informing the public. It allows any reasonable number of citizens to name candidates, besides the candidates of the great parties. It prints all the names on one ticket, so that the voter can choose freely for himself. The voter marks a cross (X) against the names which he chooses.

The elections. — The great election for President comes at a fixed time in November, once in four years. The elections for members of Congress in each district come once in two years. So with many of the State governments. Local elections, as of town officers, are apt to come once a year. Special elections of any sort must be appointed with due public notice, so that no one need to lose his right to be present and vote. In towns or counties voters meet in a common place. No one can send his vote by the hand of another. In cities, for convenience, there are many voting-places, and the great mass of the citizens never meet at the polls. There are various special election officers who serve at the polls, or take charge of the ballots and count them. They must be fair and intelligent, or else wrong will be done and the votes falsely counted. They are paid for their services. In a national election these officers, numbering many thousands, are paid by the United States.

Majority and plurality. — In some cases the law requires a majority to elect, that is, more than half of the votes cast. It is unfortunate that any important officer should be elected without the wish of at least half of the electors. In many cases, however, the candidate may be elected by a plurality of votes, that is, by more than any one else has, although the number who wish his election are not half of all the voters. When several candidates are in the field for the same office, this rule sometimes allows the election of a very insignificant man. On the other hand, it saves the trouble of repeating an election in order to secure a majority.

Who may vote. — In general, all the men twenty-one years of age may exercise the suffrage or the right to vote. But a foreigner must be naturalized, that is, take out certain papers showing that he will henceforth be an American citizen. One must also have been a resident in the country for a certain period, and also in the State, as well as in the town where he wishes to vote. Other·

wise, one might travel at election times, and vote in two or more States. Or a stranger might vote before he understood the questions upon which he was voting. The laws of the States differ about the conditions of voting. Most of them do not yet require the voter to be able to read and write. Others allow newcomers to vote on a very short residence. Whoever is recognized as a citizen to vote at a State election can also vote in the same State at a national election. But no one can vote in two places; even though a man owns a mill in Lowell, and pays a large tax, he can have no vote to decide how the money of Lowell shall be expended, unless he resides there.

Property suffrage and manhood suffrage. — That all men, wherever they are born, should have equal rights in the government under which they live, is a new idea in the world. For men of foreign birth used to be treated with suspicion, as outsiders. It was also thought that a man ought to have property in order to be a citizen. Many of our States once had laws requiring that a man should own a certain amount of property to entitle him to be a full citizen. There are those who still hold that, especially in town or city affairs, no man should be allowed to vote, at least on questions concerning property, or for the expenditure of money, except property-holders. But the prevailing American idea is, that every man has a stake or interest in the government; since every man, however poor, directly or indirectly helps pay the taxes, and is oppressed if the government is wasteful or extravagant. The American idea, therefore, is to trust every man to do his duty by the government, since a man, whether rich or poor, is a man still. The State does not fear the votes of men who are poor, but it fears the votes of dishonest or ignorant men.

Woman suffrage.—In barbarous or warlike times it was neither customary nor safe for women to come to public meetings of any sort. The business of government, as of war, was thought to be the affair of the men. Customs of such a sort are slow to change. It was therefore taken for granted, when our government was formed, that women were citizens to be protected, and to pay taxes, but not citizens to vote, or to bear arms. Meanwhile, with growing civilization, great changes have taken place in the purposes of government. As we have seen, government has come to be for many other peaceful ends besides defence against enemies. A large part of the functions of government interest all intelligent women as much as they interest men. For schools, for the public morals, for pure and patriotic officers, men and women are equally concerned. In matters of local expense, in towns and cities, women often pay large taxes. Many women, indeed, through the death of the husband or father, have the responsibility of a family. Moreover, the customs of a civilized country now permit men and women to go everywhere in public together. Many, therefore, see no valid reason why women should not exercise the suffrage equally with men. In England this is now allowed in the case of women owning property. Some steps have been taken towards it in the United States. It is at present one of the open questions upon which good women as well as men are divided. For some say that it will do no good for women to vote, that it will only double the number of voters, and that if ignorant women vote, it will do harm; besides, good women have great influence now without voting. But others reply that it is right, and, if so, that it cannot do harm. Moreover, it educates citizens to put responsibility upon them.

The purpose of voting. — The vote is the exercise of a right ; for it is not fair for the government to require the obedience or the support of any of its people without their consent or advice. If, then, a part of the people voted and the rest were obliged to obey, it would be a tyranny. The vote is thus a means of defence and protection. But the vote is not merely for the individual. It is also for the sake of the State. Thus, if on any question the vote Yes seemed to be good for the voter, but the vote No seemed to be best for all, he certainly ought to vote No. Or, again, if it were against the public interest that ignorant persons should vote until they could learn to read, it would be the duty of such persons to wait till they could really help the public by an intelligent vote ; precisely as it is fair, on the whole, that. children, however intelligent, should wait till they have grown up before they are given the ballot.

So, too, if it were true, on the whole, that it would not be for the good of the State for women to vote, it would be unfair for individual women to claim the right, merely for themselves, aside from the good of all. In fact, a "right" which is not good for all, is not likely to be good, or a real right, for any one. Those, therefore, who claim that it is time to give the suffrage to women endeavor to show that the change promises to be for the public good, and is a step towards the higher civilization of the people.

CHAPTER XX.

POLITICAL PARTIES.

Debate and discussion. — Men rarely work together for any time before honest differences arise as to the best methods of doing their work. It is so when men undertake the duties of government. There are such differences of opinion at the town meeting. Some want to expend more money for schools or for roads, while others think that the taxes are too high already. Some may want to borrow for the new expenditures, and others think that the town should live within its income, and "pay as it goes," like a wise householder. It generally happens that many of the citizens are not fully informed upon the questions that arise, or they know only one side, and have not yet heard the reasons to be given on the opposite side. It is therefore fair, before the vote is taken, to give opportunity for any who choose, to inform others why they deem one or the other course best. This is debate, or the discussion of the question to be decided. The more important the subject, the more needful it is to give ample time for discussion. For it is neither intelligent nor fair to vote without knowing the reasons on both sides; nor to defeat any proposed measure which others offer, without giving them the chance to explain fully why their measure ought to pass.

The purpose of debate. — It is thought by some that the purpose of debate is in order to get the victory for one's own side or party. On the contrary, the true object of all discussion is that the people may have the fullest understanding of the merits of the question. If a course of action — the building a new bridge or schoolhouse — cannot really be shown to be best, no good citizen wishes to urge it; as, when boys discuss how they shall spend a holiday, the object is not that any one shall have his own way, but that the whole company shall see which plan will give them the most pleasure. While it is fair, therefore, to try to persuade the others, it is not fair to be unwilling to be persuaded, in case the others' arguments are better. It is fair to give others as candid and respectful a hearing as we wish them to give us.

The broad or narrow view of public questions. — Sometimes in town meeting there is a plea for a road in another part of the town. A narrow or selfish view will oppose the expense, because it does not seem to benefit one's own district. Or men from the other end of the town refuse to vote for the new road, unless the town will vote an equal sum, and perhaps build an unnecessary road in their own neighborhood. But the true question that a broad-minded man asks is, whether the proposed road is desirable for the public good, in whatever part of the town it is. For if it will make one part of the town more prosperous or accessible, in the long run it will be good for the whole town.

Rules of debate. — In order to secure perfect fairness to all, there must be certain rules of discussion. For here, as everywhere else, order serves the comfort and convenience of all; and through the seeming sacrifice of a little liberty by each, all have the greater liberty. We have seen in Chapter IV. that there must be a president or chairman, whom every one agrees to obey, and who enforces the rules. There must be a secretary who keeps account of what is done. The rules will not permit any one to take an undue share of the time, or to speak too often. The rules allow only one to speak at a time. They also prescribe how, after discussion has gone far enough, it may be brought to an end, and the real business not delayed. It is an abuse if the rules are managed by any one or by a clique to obstruct business, or to obtain unfair advantage over the opposite party, or to silence a speaker. This is sometimes called *filibustering.* It is in debate what fighting would be on the playground; in which case arms and strength are withdrawn from their real use, — namely, to win honorable victory, — and are made to do harm instead.

National parties. — In the government of towns and cities the questions that divide the citizens are constantly shifting. There is, therefore, no good reason why parties should be permanent; but men who vote together on one subject will often differ upon another. So in the State government the chief things that any good citizen wants are wisdom, honesty, and economy. To a large extent this should be the same in the national government. Subjects and questions are constantly changing; men who unite for one course of action, as the conduct of the Indian department or civil service reform, differ upon another subject; as, for example, the voting of national aid to the public schools. There are, however, generally certain great subjects so difficult to settle, and needing so much time to be fairly discussed, that men divide upon them into national parties. For example, the question of the proper policy of the government in the treatment of slavery divided men into great parties. The question of the tariff, or how far it is wise to tax goods, wool, lumber, iron, clothes, etc., imported from foreign countries, is one of these national questions. New questions of this sort may arise from time to time which occasion the drawing of new party lines; or, again, great questions which agitate the whole people may not for a time appear, in which case the old parties struggle mainly to see which shall have the government and the offices. Each party then claims to be wiser and purer than the other.

There is no reason why there should be two parties only. There have often been two or three, or even more. But since it requires a majority of votes to secure the government, a small national party cannot permanently accomplish much, except by getting the balance of power, and thus influencing the larger parties.

Party organization. — It is the chief object of the national parties to get control of the government by the election of the President and a majority of Congress, so as to be able to carry out their policy. The great parties, being obliged to discuss and persuade voters, and, if successful, to determine what ought to be done, are in the habit of organizing throughout the country. In every town and State the citizens who belong to a particular party hold meetings called Caucuses and Conventions, in which they appoint their party officers and choose their candidates to be voted for at the next election, and pass " resolutions," or statements of what they think should be done. And since men become accustomed to working in party ranks for the great national elections, for example, as Republicans or Democrats, they are apt to vote largely on the same lines and with the same party organizations in State or municipal elections. Thus, although there is no good reason why Republicans or Democrats should not unite in choosing the same candidate for mayor or alderman, provided he will make an honest and efficient officer, as they would unite in choosing the best man as superintendent of a railroad, yet they often prefer to vote with their party for a less capable man rather than to elect a good man of the opposite party. The more ignorant voters are, the more likely they will be to vote without thinking, merely as their party leaders bid them. The watchword of such voters is, " My party, right or wrong."

Independents. — Among men, as in the schoolroom, there are always some who ask questions and want to know the reason of things. As on the playground, some do not care always to go with the crowd, or even prefer to be by themselves. Such as these, who think for themselves, and dare to stand alone, make the independents in politics. Sometimes they are wrong-headed, or unsympathetic, or unsocial. They may make mistakes, as the wisest men sometimes do. But it is important to have independent men in every community. They are likely to prefer the good of their country to the success of their party. They will not act with their party, or will leave it, if it is wrong. If the other party changes, as parties sometimes change, and advocates measures that they believe in; if they change their own minds as sensible men sometimes must; or if the other party puts forward better candidates; or if a new party arises, the independent voters are willing to act wherever they believe that they can best secure the public welfare. They therefore help to keep the great parties right.

It will be observed, however, that in a great country with millions of voters, no individual can effect much with his vote unless he joins somewhere with others who think with him. And although a few patriotic men, if banded together like the old Greek phalanx, may form a new party, or change the direction of the old party, or hold the balance of power between parties and accomplish a reform, yet the man who stands by himself and only finds fault or **votes alone, is in danger of throwing his vote away.**

CHAPTER XXI.

GOVERNMENT BY COMMITTEES, BY POLITICIANS, BY PUBLIC OPINION.

The work of committees. — In a large body like Congress or a State legislature it is difficult for every member to understand fully the merits of the many different subjects which have to be considered. It is therefore customary to appoint a number of committees, each consisting of a few members. Thus there will be a committee of Congress upon foreign relations, and another committee upon the Territories or the Indian tribes. In the city government likewise there will be a committee upon the police and another upon streets. Though the advice of committees need not be followed, it has great weight, both in making laws and in the appointment and the conduct of important officers. For example, the committee upon railways may further or thwart legislation affecting the value of millions of dollars and multitudes of people. Or, the committee upon streets may entertain or reject extravagant appropriations of public money. A committee may help or hinder an honest and efficient mayor or governor. Thus the power of committees for good or evil is enormous.

A grave difficulty. — When a single official is made responsible for any business, the citizens know whom to praise or blame. But when a number of men do a foolish or wrong thing together, it is difficult to fix the blame on the proper persons. Besides, in Congress or a legislature the newspapers report what is said, as well as the vote of every member, but the action of a committee is comparatively private, so that praise or blame cannot be rightly awarded by the people.

An example. — A bill in the interest of some great railway is brought before Congress by a member, who is the friend of the president of the railway. The bill is referred to the committee upon railroads. The railway president has another friend in this committee, who is able to persuade the members of the committee to report as he desires. The members of Congress, having left the subject to their committee, are prepared to vote as the committee recommends, especially if the advocates of the bill are of the party in power. Thus a bill possibly unwise, or even unjust, may be carried through Congress upon the report of a small committee.

However seriously the action proposed by the committees may injure the public interests, for example, the administration of the post-office department, custom does not allow the Postmaster-General, or any of the heads of departments, to come upon the floor of Congress and explain the difficulty. In fact, a bare majority of a committee, provided it is of the party in power, may recommend important action, which the same party will vote to carry through, while the officer who has the responsibility for executing the law may not even be consulted. This is government by committees instead of government by the people.

The appointment of committees. — Each branch of a legislature or of a city government chooses its own committees. A common method is to allow the chairman or president to " nominate " or select the members of these committees as he deems suitable. As the chairman is the choice of the majority of the body, he will be pretty sure to see that the committees are made up as the majority would approve. It is deemed fair always to appoint part of the members of the committees from the minority.

The committees of Congress, through whose hands all business passes, are chosen, in the Senate by its own members, that is, by the party who hold the majority, who put their own men at the head of each committee; and in the House of Representatives by the Speaker or Chairman. If the Speaker is a Republican or a Democrat, he therefore chooses so that the head of every important committee and the majority of its members shall be from his own party. This right to appoint committees makes the Speaker by far the most powerful man in Congress. He may appoint committees which shall thwart the will and defeat the purposes of the President.

The politicians. — The great number of the people have little time to spend in politics, that is, in the management of government. Beyond voting and occasionally attending a caucus or mass meeting to hear speeches, they are very apt to leave public business in the hands of a few persons. There comes, therefore, to be a class of men in every community who mostly manage the politics. They attend all the caucuses; they are put upon the party committees; they are chosen to go to the great state or national conventions which nominate candidates for office; they are ready and willing to take office themselves. They bring out their neighbors and friends to vote at elections, and work for their party. They are apt to think that they have earned the right to its honors and places if their party gets into power. Such men, who make politics their business, are called *politicians.* The name is given specially to those who make use of politics to serve or advance their own private interests. It is not usually given to those whose interest in public business is for the sake of the public welfare, and who do not seek place or office for themselves. The name, therefore, while it has not a positively bad meaning, is not one by which the most public-spirited men would choose to be called. The word *statesman* better describes the higher class of wise and faithful public servants.

Government by the politicians. — The politicians of any party make a strong organization among themselves, like the staff of an army. They meet often in committees and clubs. They know what they wish to secure for themselves through the aid of the government, while the people are often indifferent. They are able to bargain with each other, and to combine to carry out plans. They can usually contrive to nominate candidates of their own number. They can even trade votes with the opposite party, promising, if they are Republicans, to help elect a Democratic politician to some office, in exchange for help in electing one of themselves to another office, or *vice versa*. If they are chosen to Congress, or even to the highest office, they may be under obligation or promise to serve some of their fellow-politicians who helped to elect them, and to get places for them.

Wherever, therefore, men manage the public business for themselves or for their party friends, and nominate candidates, or appoint officers, or carry votes to serve each other, it becomes a government by the politicians.

Rings. — It may happen in a republic as in an aristocratic government, that a clique of men contrive to get the affairs of a city or a state, or even of the national government into their own hands. It was in this way that the notorious Tweed ring usurped the government of the city of New York. They managed the party caucuses, and named themselves and their friends for office, and brought ignorant or indifferent voters to do their bidding at the polls.

Public opinion. —The wisest man or the most wealthy has but one vote. But his vote is not the only way in which he helps to govern. What he thinks, what he says, what he does, influences others. As one student in a school may persuade a dozen others to·act as he acts, so a man of positive opinion may be a leader for hundreds of voters. As one persuades another or sets another to thinking, and so moves men's minds, who again, like ivory balls, move others in the same way, public opinion is made. One, or a few, wise, thoughtful, or public-spirited men may start public opinion; but once started, a multitude by and by take it up. Public opinion is behind votes, for votes only express it. But it is often stronger and quicker than votes.

It is not in human nature to wish to resist or oppose public opinion. It requires a brave man to stand against it, even when it is wrong or mistaken. Public opinion is therefore a check against abuses of the government. A committee of Congress, however negligent of the public interest, will not venture far to do what the people really disapprove. When public opinion is aroused to require honest public service, no corrupt ring can stand. Even a little stream of sound public opinion, directed by a few brave citizens, and expressed by voice and helped on by the press, when aimed towards a reform or against an abuse, makes itself speedily felt, so that the politicians themselves hasten to heed it; as a hunger or a pain in the body, telegraphed through the appropriate nerves, urges the will of a man to satisfy its need. Thus, if at any time, through faults in the government or the practices of negligent officers, harm is done, a remedy is at hand when public opinion is sufficiently stirred.

CHAPTER XXII.

THE CITIZEN'S DUTIES TO HIS GOVERNMENT.

WE have seen how numerous and important the services are which the government renders to its citizens. It extends its protection over their lives and property; it provides courts of justice, schools, and education; it maintains roads and carries the mails; it brings water and extinguishes fires; it guards the public health and cleanses the streets; it supports public hospitals. All these things, and more, are done by the government for its citizens. It would plainly be unfair that citizens should enjoy these benefits without making any return. There are several simple duties, therefore, which the citizens owe to the government.

Obeying the laws. — In every civilized state there are definite laws. Some of them are very old, and no one knows when they were first made; others have been decreed by the government of the city, the state, or the nation, by the legislature, the Congress, the Parliament, or the king. They treat of all sorts of subjects, — of property, of commerce, of behavior. Some of the laws, and generally the oldest of all, are such as appeal to every one's conscience, such as we learn in our childhood; as, for example, not to steal or to injure another. We should obey these moral laws, if no courts threatened to enforce them. There are many other rules, ordinances, and laws, however, which have been found by experience to be necessary, or which serve the common convenience. Thus, the laws may require children to attend school, because no state can afford to let its youth grow up in ignorance.

Sometimes a law may seem to the individual citizen unnecessary or trivial, or may prove inconvenient. Nevertheless, no one has any right to put his personal preference or convenience before the laws which serve the public good. For example, in cities it is necessary to forbid the use of firearms, although a discreet or skilful person might carry a gun or pistol without injury. Employers are also liable to a fine for hiring boys or girls who ought to be in school, although sometimes their parents seem to need the money which the children might earn. If any business, however profitable, like making gunpowder or selling drugs, proves to be harmful or dangerous, the law may forbid or restrict it, to the inconvenience or even the loss of its owner. In all such cases the individual must submit to the laws. For it would be unjust to wish to indulge oneself, or to make money by any practice or business which either hurt or imperilled the public good; precisely as it would be unfair for a boy to throw stones upon the ball-ground where his fellows were playing.

The care of public property. — If we belonged to a base-ball or cricket club, every member of the club would try to take good care of the balls, bats, and wickets. For whatever waste or loss there were would have to come out of our spending-money. So in any home, no intelligent child would wish to break the furniture or waste the provisions, since the whole family would be poorer for every dollar thrown away. The same rule holds with the public property. All that belongs to the government really belongs to us all, like the furniture or the provisions of a great family. In the public buildings, the schoolhouses and the school-books, the fire-engines, and the machinery of all the different departments of public work, the highways, the lamps and lamp-posts, as well as the forts and navy yards, and iron ships, and lighthouses, — in all these things which have cost hundreds of millions of dollars, we each have a share. It is as if every child was born heir to a fortune. No one is so poor as not to be better off for this grand public property. To waste or injure or deface or destroy anything that belongs to the government, therefore, is to injure ourselves. To break the glass in a public building would be the same kind of foolishness as to break glass in our own house.

We do not merely owe the government, that is, our-- selves, the duty to do no injury to our own public property. We owe a positive duty to watch against harm or waste. If the treasurer of a club wasted the money, or the keeper of the bats and wickets left them in the rain, we should turn him out of office. So likewise, if we saw any officer wasteful of the public money, or careless in performing his work. Especially if we were ever hired by the government, we should be ashamed not to do as honest service as we should do for ourselves, since our work in such a case is really for the common good.

The duty to vote. — We have already seen that it is a right or privilege to vote, so that any one would feel defrauded if his vote were taken away from him, or if it failed to be counted. But it is also a duty to vote. In other words, we are not asked to vote for our own sake, to protect our rights or our property, but for the good of the public and because the ballot is the weapon to protect the rights of all. As in a club we must vote at the election of officers in order to secure good management, so every citizen is responsible through his vote for the kind of government that he lives under. There is an old rule that "Silence gives consent." If, then, a set of bad or worthless men should plot to get the offices, all the citizens who took no trouble to vote against them would help the bad party into power and would also be to blame for the harm they did.

Suppose, again, that the people were asked to vote Yes or No upon some proposed change in the constitution of the State, for example, a prohibitory amendment, forbidding the sale of intoxicating drinks; and suppose that many thousands did not vote at all. Whichever way the vote of the State went, those who did not vote would be to ·blame if harm came. For they did nothing to prevent it.

The duty to pay the taxes. — We have seen that the taxes under just government ought not to make people poorer. They are like money taken out of the pocket of the individual to put into the common purse, and by and by to expend for the common good; as when a party of boys contribute together to purchase a foot-ball or a boat which no one of them alone could have afforded. So all the people of a city contribute to build good roads and to buy fire-engines, or to provide waterworks. It is every one's duty, then, to pay his share. For it would be extremely shabby to be willing to enjoy the advantages that the government gave without paying one's share towards the cost.

The government may expend money for something that a citizen does not care for; as for a school when the citizen has no children of his own, or sends his children to a private school. Nevertheless, since the schools are for the public good, and the country is more prosperous and the government safer by reason of them, whoever shares in the prosperity and safety that the schools help to bring, ought not to shirk paying the cost with the others.

It may happen that some citizen does not see the value of the public schools, or does not believe in building forts and war-ships; ought he to be obliged to help pay for what he does not believe in? It would be fair, indeed, for him to vote, when he has a chance, against the forts and war-ships, but if the majority is against him and the taxes are levied, it would be disgraceful to try to make others pay more than their share, in order to escape himself; as he in turn would think it unjust in the others to refuse to pay their taxes towards the objects, like roads and parks, which he believes in; precisely as in a society, as long as one belongs to it, one must pay the assessments as the majority vote.

It has often happened that men have avoided their taxes and even lied about their property, on the ground that "others do the same." This is a good reason why honest citizens should have the tax laws made simple, and require them to be fairly administered. If any method of raising the taxes tempts men of weak conscience to cheat, it is probably a bad method. But since "two wrongs do not make a right," there can be no excuse for any one to shirk, much less to deceive, and therefore to throw a heavier burden on honest persons, because some one else is unfair. Indeed, it is a good rule everywhere to do yourself as you would wish all to do.

The truth is that, if one part of the citizens are expected to pay their share of the taxes towards objects which are good for another portion, — if the Western farmers must pay for the lighthouses for the sailors, these in turn must pay cheerfully their share towards other objects, like the levees on the Mississippi River. If, meanwhile, some citizens seem to themselves to pay more than their share, yet every one is better off than if there were no government and no taxes to pay.

The duty of public service. —It is an ancient requirement that every able-bodied citizen must bear arms in case of war. This duty extends so far as to demand the citizen's life if it is needful to help save the state. For it is better that a part of the citizens should die, than that the state should be destroyed or enslaved. As a good father or a good son therefore would risk his life for the sake of the family, so a loyal citizen holds his life at the call of the government.

It may happen that the government makes a mistake and exposes the citizen's life without cause. Should he disobey, shirk his duty, or run away in order to save his life? It is evident that, in case of public danger, a riot or a war, there must be very prompt obedience to the summons of the sheriff, the marshal, or the governor. If no citizen would risk his life for his country until he was first made perfectly sure that the government was quite 'wise, there would be no reliance on any one. The rule is, then, that the citizen must share the risks of his country or his government, even though at times some one has blundered. For it is nobler to lose one's life, like the soldiers at Balaklava, in trying to save the honor of the country, than to be too prudent in trying to save one's own life.

The duty sometimes to take office. — The public service is not only for times of war or danger. The state also claims of the citizen many forms of peaceful service. There are many offices which suffer, unless filled by able and patriotic men. Moreover, the office frequently carries no pay, as with the school committee and many town and city offices. Or, as in the case of jurors, the pay is small and the trouble is great. Or, as with the State legislatures, the duties of the office are tedious to many citizens. The faithful officer is also liable to partisan abuse, and in some cases to the loss of his place at the hands of those who want it for themselves. There are therefore many citizens who, for various reasons, do not desire office, or cannot, they think, afford to give up lucrative business of their own even to go to Congress, or to be made a judge or mayor, or a governor, much less to serve without pay on some public commission. But the state needs most the very men who desire office least, and who have no selfish ends to seek by taking it. Since the state can command even the citizen's life, it seems to follow that he ought equally to give up his time when called to take office for the public good.

Public spirit. — In almost every community there are certain men and women who are known as *public spirited*. Others may be selfish or narrow-minded, and vote or act as their own private interests seem to require. But the public-spirited citizens take broad and generous views, and even prefer the good of the state or the nation to their own profit. Thus in the Civil War, while a narrow-minded man feared about his business, or waited until bounties were paid before he enlisted, public-spirited men cheerfully risked their persons and property for the support of the government. The public-spirited are equally willing to be taxed for libraries and parks to benefit the people. In other words, they not only perform their duties to the state with honesty, but they take pleasure in serving the public, and are liberal beyond the requirement of the law.

Exceptions. — It is possible that a government might require of a citizen what his conscience forbade. Thus the laws of the United States once commanded the return of fugitive slaves to their masters. This is like the case where a wrong or foolish parent commands a child to act against his conscience. But though one must certainly obey his conscience, yet if he breaks a bad or foolish law, he must be prepared to take the legal consequences of disobedience, perhaps to go to jail, or to pay a fine; or, even to lose his life, as in the story of Socrates or of Sir Thomas More. Moreover, the individual who ventures to break a law on his own judgment may prove to have been wrong, and his conscience to have been unenlightened. We can imagine a fanatical Mormon, for example, who prefers to obey the command of his church, and to resist the United States government in Utah.

Although it is the general duty of the citizen to vote, there may be cases in which one cannot conscientiously vote. The voter might have to choose between two measures, both of which seem wrong, or between two candidates, both of whom are unfit for the place. It cannot be duty to do a wrong, or to tell a lie, by one's vote, or to seem to approve what one does not honestly wish for. Thus if two political parties appear for the time to further wrong policies, or to put up bad men, one may have to withdraw from voting with either of them until one or the other party changes its character, or until he can join others in forming a new party. But it would not be right to abstain from voting longer than is absolutely necessary. As before, one must do what he wishes every one else to do; but while he would wish every one to abstain from voting for a bad or unfit man, he would not wish others to be content till the government was set right and in good hands.

At the time of the War of Independence our forefathers complained that it was unjust to pay taxes to England without being represented in the British Parliament, which made the taxes. Their refusal to pay the stamp tax led to the war. In this case, however, the colonists had no peaceful means of opposing the odious tax except to petition the Parliament. In our government, if an unjust tax were imposed, we have the courts to redress wrong. We can also vote for representatives who would take measures to change a wrongful tax.

It has sometimes happened that a public officer has been required to perform duties against his conscience. Thus a marshal of the United States would once have had to arrest a fugitive slave. There would therefore be no obligation to take public office, if the laws require wrongful conduct. So if an army officer, who must obey orders as long as he holds command, believed any war to be unjust, he could resign, as Granville Sharp, the friend of America, gave up his place in the Ordnance Office of England because he could not conscientiously handle war material to be used against the American colonies.

CHAPTER XXIII.

THE ABUSES AND PERILS OF GOVERNMENT.

Abuses that the civilized world has outgrown. — As long as men tolerated the rule of the strong, and suffered bad men to hold power, government was often made the engine of cruel injustice. Kings came to imagine that the people existed to serve them or to fight for them. In Turkey and Egypt the peasants still have to pay for the luxury of the great court of the Sultan and the Khedive, and for the support of a crowd of idle officers. Even in England, till quite lately, a Roman Catholic or a Unitarian was forbidden to hold office on account of his opinions. A little further back, bigoted men thought it right to use the arm of the law to enforce their opinions or religion on others, or to prosecute those who differed from them. There were terrible punishments imposed by the colonial laws, and very cruel treatment of the poor and the insane was permitted. The power of government was used to hang men and women at Salem for the supposed crime of witchcraft.

Meddling with business. — Governments have been in the habit, too, of interfering with trade, with the prices of goods, or with the values of money. A dishonest king would issue coin of diminished weight or purity. It is said that between the years 1300 and 1600 the English pound of silver, which at first made twenty shillings, was at last divided into sixty-six shillings. The early Parliaments were often very ignorant. They thought it necessary to make laws to keep the money in their own country. They made it hard to sell goods out of their country, or to get foreign goods in return; they did not see that trade made nations richer. They imagined that they could fix prices for wheat or bread, or for a day's wages, by law; they did not understand that though the law can fix a low price for a thing, the law cannot compel any one to sell it for that price.

Governments are like the people who govern. — The truth is that the government always reflects the character of the men who rule. If they are stupid or ignorant, they will be sure to make foolish and injurious laws. If they are wasteful, they will contrive to squander the public money. If they are narrow and prejudiced, they will not mind hurting those who differ from themselves. If some of them are bad and dishonest, they will be sure to cheat in managing the government. If they are greedy, or think that the government is for every one to get as much as he can for himself, instead of being for the public good, they will make it selfish and oppressive. Thus the abuses and perils of government proceed from the faults of the rulers even more than from the faults of the system or method. This is equally true if the government is by the people. For while it rests with the few, it is good or bad like the few that hold it, but when it rests with all the people, it cannot easily be much better than the average character of the people. If many of the people of a republic, then, are ignorant, as kings used to be, if others are prejudiced, and some are bad and dishonest, it will be very hard not to have officers and representatives like the people who choose them.

It is as though a party of boys from one of the school

ships were cast on a desolate island and undertook to manage and govern themselves. If they were ignorant and selfish, they would be in great danger of destruction; but in case the majority of them were generous and intelligent, they might contrive to establish a little state, till they could build a boat or be taken off the island.

The best government. — The faults of the rulers will show themselves, and make trouble in any kind of government; but some modes of government make men's faults more perilous. We may suppose that the boys on the island allow the greediest fellow among them to keep the supplies. This would tempt him to help himself to more than his share. Or they might let the loudest talkers among them make all their plans, as men often do in government. They might, on the other hand, contrive to pick out the most trustworthy and intelligent of their number to take charge of the supplies and to make plans of escape, so as to secure a management even better than their own average; as though the body were to choose the brains and the conscience to determine what the muscles and bones should do. So we can perhaps contrive methods of government that, instead of tempting the weak, dishonest, and selfish to become worse, shall make use of the wisdom and integrity of the best and most capable citizens. We need now to see where the chief dangers lie in our American government.

Faults of American government; partisanship. — Men, in a mistaken sense of loyalty, will often follow their party to vote wrong, or to choose unworthy men against the plain interests of the public. It is particularly harmful in Congress, or in the legislature, when members who are paid to consult the public good think themselves bound instead to serve their party. For designing men, by gaining a majority in a party caucus, or a party committee, finally oblige the whole party to carry their bad measure through.

Provincialism. — This word, which comes from the simple word *province*, means local patriotism as opposed to the love of the whole country. Thus a man cares more for his village than for the good of the State, or more for his State than he cares for the nation. Provincialism is a form of selfishness. It was this which brought on the great Civil War. For men were once trained to be more loyal to the flag of their State than to the flag of the Union. It is the same spirit that wishes the prosperity of a section, as the North or the West or the South, instead of the welfare of all sections. It is the same, in a smaller way, when one votes against a man from another part of the State, and insists upon voting for a neighbor, or for some one of the same church, when the stranger is the better man.

Jobbery and patronage. — It is evident that if public work is to be done, as in the case of erecting a new schoolhouse, an equal chance ought to be given to architects and builders to offer plans and make bids for the work, so that the city shall secure the best and cheapest building. Suppose now, that, instead of trying to choose the best builder, the committee in charge should award their contract to the builder who would make them a present, or do them personal favors, or promise to buy his materials of them. This would be *jobbery*. The committee would be turning the public service into means of private gain.

It is evident also that if the government wants a number of laborers or clerks for the navy yard, all capable citizens ought to have a free and equal chance to offer themselves, and that the selection should be made of the most competent. But suppose the officer in charge filled the places with his personal friends, or with those who voted for him, or, as he was bidden by some congressman, with persons of his party alone. This is the misuse of *patronage*. It is unfair to the public, because it often puts unfit persons into office and keeps them there; and it is undemocratic, because it does not give equal chance to all who are deserving. It is to guard against the evils of jobbery and patronage that we require a pure civil service.

The government and trade.—It often happens that a business threatens harm to the public, as when the factories employ children too young to work. The railroads may seem to charge excessive rates of fare. The interest of money may appear to be extortionate. Manufacturers or miners wish laws passed to help their business, or to prevent foreigners from selling goods cheaper than the American goods. Workmen may wish foreigners to be prevented from coming here, or they desire by law to fix wages, or the number of hours of the working-day. The taxes may be laid so unfairly as to encourage one kind of business and oppress another. Sometimes the taxes are contrived so as to enrich a particular set of men, like the salt manufacturers, at the expense of every one who uses salt.

These are among the ways in which the laws may interfere with business. Sometimes the law is needful, as, for example, to protect women and children. But it has been found by long experience that it is very hazardous to make laws that meddle with business. The rule is to leave trade as free as possible of restrictions. If we thwart or harass any kind of business, it becomes more costly. If we favor it above others, besides being unfair, we take away from those who carry it on the natural spur to improve and cheapen their methods. If we fix prices or wages, or the hours of labor, we always tempt men to get around the law in some other way, and make it harder for those who are honest and obedient. For those who buy and sell of each other are more likely in the long run to secure fair play than the public who look on from the outside. In all these subjects, however, there is room for much difference of opinion, as there is need for wise judgment. In fact, legislators and congressmen are not generally wise enough to meddle with other people's business, and always do this at great risk.

Public debts and borrowing. — It is a good rule in housekeeping to live within one's income. But our modern cities have grown very fast; they have needed immense sums of money for buildings and waterworks and parks. Sometimes they have suffered from devastating fires. They have been tempted, therefore, to borrow money. The national government, especially in the Civil War, felt obliged to incur a gigantic debt. Many States also rolled up debts. Nearly everywhere a considerable part of the taxes now goes to paying the interest upon borrowed money.

The harm that debt does. — A habit of debt inflicts the same kind of harm upon a people that it works in a family. It makes men careless; it leads to further borrowing; it provokes extravagance, waste, and corruption; it sets a bad example to individuals; it is also very expensive. Though it is urged that posterity ought to help pay for the public roads, buildings, and sewers, the fact is that the present generation has to pay more than their cost in interest money, and then leaves the encumbrance of debt like a mortgage upon every one's property for one's children to pay. On the contrary, a small increase in the annual taxes would enable every city or State to pay its way without debt. In this case citizens would be more careful to watch the use of the public money which is taken from their own pockets.

The ignorant vote.—Our country has welcomed men of every nation, and has given to all free citizenship on easy terms. Many of the newcomers had never enjoyed our advantages of public schools; they had often been despised and oppressed. They came here, therefore, in great ignorance and with strong prejudices, sometimes against all authority. They had never before been trusted to help govern or to vote.

The freeing of the slaves in the South left a vast negro population, who became voters before they had generally learned to read and write. A large number of whites in the old slave States, being degraded by the touch of slavery, were poor and very illiterate.

These ignorant voters help govern; but they are easily excited and are apt to be led by bad or foolish men. In many localities they are numerous enough to turn the elections.

Popular crazes.—Ideas are often catching like wildfire. The new idea, if many people are thinking and feeling alike, will seize all their minds almost at once. Sometimes it is a good idea which seizes them, as after the firing on Fort Sumter, when the idea of saving the Union swept over the land. But the popular idea may be hasty and mistaken. Thus in the case of "the Greenback delusion," when multitudes imagined that the poor might be helped to be rich, if the government would print sufficient quantities of paper dollars. It is a craze when the farmers or others think that it is part of the duty of government to lend money, and so tempt every one to run into debt. It was also a popular craze that hurried the

Southern States into the War of Secession against the better judgment of their more careful citizens. Riots, revolutions, and even wars have likewise been kindled by such sudden movements of excited feeling. There is need, therefore, of trained and careful citizens who will hold fast like a rock against the waves of sudden passion or error; as in the school an older or more independent scholar may dissuade the rest from cowardly or foolish conduct.

The tyranny of majorities. — We have already seen that it is not only a king or a despot who may exercise tyranny. Sometimes the majority may abuse their power to the injury of the minority. It is possible for a party who hold the majority in a State to manage so that the other party shall hardly be represented in the government. It is possible for the majority to levy taxes that shall bear unfairly upon the minority. It needs, therefore, to be seen that gaining the vote of a majority for any action does not make the action right, any more than the command of a king makes a thing right.

The lobby. — There are many members of a legislature or Congress who are ignorant or uninformed upon the subjects on which they must vote. Thus the legislature may be asked to pass laws relating to railroads or gas companies. It has become the custom to employ agents both on the part of those who want the new laws and of those who oppose them, to wait on the members of the legislature, and use influence to secure their votes. These agents are often paid large salaries. They are sometimes in attendance at the capitol as long as the legislature is in session, to look out for the interests of their clients. They are even authorized on occasion to spend money to further their cause. If legislators are weak, and the agents are unprincipled, there will be bribery and fraud. These agents constitute what is called the *lobby*, a word which literally means the space just outside the legislative hall.

The saloon power. — The great abuses of the alcoholic drinks have required many laws to check or resist the traffic. These laws have led the persons engaged in the liquor traffic to stand on the defensive, and to combine to maintain their business. There are many millions of money and hundreds of thousands of people concerned in the various branches of this business. There is thus created a formidable power which is ready to purchase or threaten or bargain with either political party in order to get its own ends. In cities this liquor or saloon power too often controls elections, or nominates men to office, and even interferes with the management of the police.

It will be seen how many political perils and diseases are in the air. They demand intelligence, courage, activity, and patriotism on the part of the citizen. Good citizens are like the vital germs in the blood which fight off malaria. If these healthy vital germs are numerous, the body politic is safe and strong; but if they are few and meagre, the commonwealth suffers decay.

Rebellion and revolution. — The evils of a government through tyranny, through persecution, through corruption and iniquitous laws, may become intolerable. When citizens refuse to obey their government, or take up arms against its officers, it is called rebellion. If the rebellion succeeds and the government is changed, — as for example when our forefathers established the republic, — the change is called revolution. Rebellion is right on three conditions; namely, if a government seriously oppresses its citizens with abuses; if all peaceable measures of reform have been tried in vain; and if there is a reasonable probability of replacing the bad government with a better. Otherwise rebellion is a terrible injustice. In a republic, rebellion can hardly be conceived of as justifiable. For the constitution provides peaceable means to cure evils by persuading and enlightening public opinion. Rebellion, therefore, usually implies a condition of barbarism, where men are not yet good or intelligent enough to settle their differences like rational beings.

CHAPTER XXIV.

FACTS WHICH EVERY ONE SHOULD KNOW.—
OPEN QUESTIONS.

BESIDES the permanent facts about the system of our government, there are certain important practical facts, which every intelligent citizen should know, as regards the officials who for the time carry on the government.

The chief officers of the national government.— Every one is supposed to know who is the President of the United States and the Vice-President. One should also know who are the members of the Cabinet, or the heads of the great departments of the government; and especially the Secretary of State, who in the event of the death of the President and Vice-President would succeed to the Presidency. One should know who is the Speaker or presiding officer of the House of Representatives, who appoints the most important committees of Congress. One should also know who are the most distinguished members of Congress in both parties; and in particular the two senators from one's own State, and at least the representative of one's congressional district. One should know who is the Chief Justice of the Supreme Court, if not all the associate judges. One should also know who the ministers are who represent our country at the capitals of the great nations, as England, France, and Germany.

The State officers.— Besides the governor and lieutenant-governor of one's own State, one should know who the State senator is in his district, and who represents the town or city in the legislature ; the president of the State Senate and the speaker of the House. One should know who are some of the judges of the Supreme Court, the judge of the local district court, and some justice of the peace.

The town, city, and county officers. — One should know who the chief officer or officers of one's town are, as the mayor or selectmen ; the clerk, who keeps the public records ; the treasurer, who has the public money ; and the superintendent or committee, who manage the schools. If it is a city, one should know who are at the head of the important departments, with the alderman and the members of the common council from one's district.

It is well also to know what towns and cities make up the county, and where the county seat is ; who is the sheriff ; the county or district attorney, or lawyer who prosecutes offences ; the registrar of deeds, who has the records of property ; the probate judge, who has charge over wills ; the clerk of the court ; and the county commissioners.

Open questions. — There are certain questions upon which opinion is divided, or upon which citizens have not yet thought sufficiently to make up their minds to act. We have already hinted at the difficulties that arise from some of these questions. One of them is about the tariff.

The tariff, or free trade and protection. — Whenever trade follows its natural course, nations exchange their products with each other, somewhat as men do in the same country. As the farmer sells his hay, buys wheat, hires carpenters or buys lumber wherever he can trade to advantage, so India sends its cotton or wheat to England and buys of the English various manufactured goods. As long as the farmer can sell plenty of hay and wheat, he can better afford to hire carpenters than to do the carpenter's work himself. So when England will pay well for the cotton, India can better afford to supply it than to build factories to make her own cloths.

If there were no custom houses in the world, so that people of every nation could freely buy wherever they could get the best bargains, the various goods needed in trade would be produced wherever it was found to be profitable to produce them. If the climate and soil of Cuba were exactly suited to raising sugar, the countries which could not raise sugar so well would be glad to get it from the Cubans, and pay for it in articles which they could make better. This would be free trade.

But governments have to raise great sums of money. One easy way to collect a revenue is to take a toll or duty upon foreign goods as they cross the frontier. This tax is the tariff. In ancient times every little state and every city collected this kind of toll, as the city of Paris still does. As we know, the merchant first pays it, and then collects it in turn from his customers by adding to the price of his goods. This toll or duty may be for one of two distinct purposes, or for both of them together. One purpose is to raise a revenue for the state. Thus England raises millions of dollars upon articles of luxury, as coffee, tea, tobacco, and wines. Some say that this is all that the tariff rightly is for; namely, to produce an income for the government. Otherwise, they say, trade ought to be as free as possible.

The second purpose for which a tariff is used is to hamper or prevent foreign trade. If the foreigner and his goods can be kept away by the barrier of a high tax, the sugar, or the nails, or the cotton goods, will have to be made at home. This is called protection to native industry. Thus if the Frenchman can afford to sell silks at two dollars a yard, but the tax at the custom house is two dollars more, it might pay some one to start silk works here, and even to bring over French workmen. Every one who brought silk from abroad in this case would have to pay more in order that the American silk factory might be run at a profit. It is claimed by the advocates of protection that it is desirable for a country to produce, so far as possible, all that it needs; and also that after the silk factory or other industry has been protected long enough, it will be able to produce goods as cheaply as the foreigners.

It is one of the great open questions how far this nation ought to protect the home manufacturer; in other words, to adjust taxes so as to enable him to make money. One party claim that this policy increases the volume of work done by the nation, and thus adds to its wealth; that it is, therefore, American. The other party claim that protection is narrow and exclusive; that it is a survival in modern times of the barbarous jealousy which one nation felt towards its rivals as outsiders; that it adds to the gains of a few at the expense of all; and finally, that the educated and skilled American workman does not need protection.

Prohibition and license. — Another open question is the treatment of the liquor traffic. There are certain kinds of business which are especially dangerous, and which ought therefore to be under the control of discreet men only. The sale of gunpowder and the druggists' business come under this head, and require some kind of public license. The sale of alcoholic drinks is particularly dangerous, since there are great numbers who are excited or made crazy by these drinks. Besides waste and expense, injury to life and property very frequently attends their use. It is an open question how the public can best control this kind of business. For some hold that on the whole it does so much harm to the public, and so little good, that it ought to be, like gambling and lotteries, under the ban of the law. But others vote to tax and restrict it, and to grant licenses for carrying it on only to those who can give bonds for their carefulness by the payment of a large fee. As we have already seen in Chapter XVI., this is partly for the sake of raising the public money. But another reason is to control and lessen a dangerous business. This question will deserve further treatment under the head of social duties.

National education. — The intention of our government has been to leave the subject of education to each State to manage for itself. If any State neglects to educate its children to be intelligent citizens, that State will be first to suffer the consequences of its neglect. It is, therefore, for the interest of every State to provide public education.

The vast number of blacks emancipated from slavery and admitted to citizenship has put a new face on the problem of education. The cost of public education bears hardest upon some of the poorest States. The ignorance of the voters allows unscrupulous men to cheat at the elections. The voters in any state for the State officers are also voters in United States elections. It might happen thus that the election of the President would hang upon the correct counting of the ballots of a few hundred men who could not read.

There are some, therefore, who advocate the granting of aid from the national treasury to help public education, on the ground that this is a measure of national protection. On the other hand, it is urged by equally strong friends of public education, that the best way to secure good schools is to leave the responsibility upon the State which will benefit by having them, and which will suffer if they are neglected; and that there is no State which is not able to provide its own schools.

The question of woman's suffrage has been referred to in Chapter XIX. Other questions relate to the banks and the money; the treatment of the Indians; whether the old custom of having two legislative houses is better than to have a single house; whether it is desirable for the government to own and manage the railways and the telegraph lines, and in cities the gas, electric and water works, as well as the street railways; the various methods of taxation, and especially whether a tax might not wisely be laid upon the succession of great estates; the treatment of bankrupt debtors (bankrupt laws); the best method of securing justice to authors, or an international copyright law. On all these subjects persons of wide knowledge hold different opinions. It is well, therefore, not to make up one's mind without careful study.

CHAPTER XXV.

IMPROVEMENTS IN GOVERNMENT. — RADICALS AND CONSERVATIVES.

A SYSTEM of government is never completed. New conditions arise ; new laws have to be made ; old machinery wears out and needs repairing ; new machinery has to be invented. This is especially true in a new and growing country. There are, therefore, suggestions to be made of possible improvements in our system of government.

The presidential electors. — The framers of our Constitution believed that nothing demanded such wisdom and care as the selection of the President and Vice-President. They accordingly arranged that the people of each State should choose as many picked men as the number of its senators and representatives together. These leading citizens from all the States should form the electoral college, who should be quite free to select, from the whole nation, the fittest candidates for the two great offices at the head of the government.[1]

This beautiful plan has entirely failed. The presidential electors, so far from being free to choose the best men they can find, are really pledged beforehand to cast their votes for particular candidates. A great convention of each party fixes the candidates. A child could do all that is required of a presidential elector.

The method of choice for the electors, moreover, is thought not to work fairly. The voters of each State cast

[1] Consult Article XII. of the Amendments to the Constitution of the United States.

their ballots, not directly for the President and Vice-President, but for the list of their party electors. A plurality of votes for a list elects the whole list. That is, if there are three tickets or lists before the voters, and one of them has forty thousand votes, the next has thirty-five thousand, and the third has twenty-five thousand, the list which has more than either of the others wins the vote of the whole State. The votes of the other parties are thus thrown away, while a list may be elected which did not have nearly a majority of the vote of the State.

Moreover, in this way a minority of the people of the United States may elect President and Vice-President, while an actual majority of the voters prefer the opposite candidates. For the weaker party, which had, for example, only seven million votes in the nation out of fifteen millions, might, notwithstanding, by winning the whole electoral vote of the great States of New York, Pennsylvania, and Ohio, with some smaller States, finally get a majority by one or two votes in the electoral college, although the opposite party actually cast eight million votes.

This fact is a temptation to spend a great deal of money in carrying the election in States where the parties are nearly balanced. Whereas in other States, where a party has a very large majority, men often do not take the trouble to vote.

It would seem to be fairer, since the electoral college has failed of its purpose, to abolish it, and to permit every citizen to vote directly for the President and Vice-President, and to declare the candidates elected who have actually the most votes in the whole country. There would then be no temptation to spend money in carrying an election in one part of the country more than in another, and every citizen would be made to feel his responsibility to vote.

The time of the meeting of Congress. — The members of a new Congress are elected every other year in November. But the Congress thus elected does not meet till the December of the year following. Meanwhile the old Congress continues to serve, though the country may have voted to turn out many of its members, and to change its majority to the opposite party. A new President may also have been inaugurated in March. The long interval between the election and the meeting of Congress was perhaps well enough in the early days of the republic, when it required many weeks to travel from the more distant States. But it is quite absurd, now that a week will bring the most distant representative to his seat in Washington.

The responsibility of the executive. — Our fathers were afraid that governors and presidents might usurp too much power; but they did not foresee that committees of Congress and the legislature, and even the committees of parties, might also usurp the power and meddle with the government. It is as though the stockholders of a great railroad feared to trust their superintendent, or to give him the power to appoint his officers or to manage the road; but tried instead to keep the business in their own hands. If accidents then happened, or losses befell the road, no one in particular could be blamed.

The larger and more complicated the government becomes, the more directly do we need to make the chief executive responsible for its good conduct. The President must choose the best Postmaster-General, and he in turn must have command of the business of his office. If anything is at fault, it will be because the head is at fault, and will reflect so much discredit upon the President who made the appointment. So in the other departments of the administration. If there is waste of money in useless public works, we ought to know at once what head of a department is to blame. But if the public business is wisely administered, we shall like to re-elect the President who gives us good and honest service.

In the same way in the States, and especially in the cities. We need to make the mayor more directly responsible, like the railroad superintendent, and to give him power enough to carry out his work. He shall choose men as the heads of the various departments of the city, as the railroad superintendent or president chooses his assistants. The various committees, for example, upon the streets, will then be responsible not for the conduct of the work, but only to make report upon it, and to offer suggestions for its improvement.

The Cabinet and Congress. — It is customary for the President to communicate with Congress by letters or messages; it is also the custom for the heads of the various departments of government to make reports to Congress, and to recommend plans for the public service. It has not been the custom for the President or members of his Cabinet to appear on the floor of Congress and to explain the policy of the government, or to answer questions about it. It is as though the president and cashier of a bank were never to meet the directors or to be given an opportunity, except in writing, of stating what plans seem desirable for the prosperity of the bank.

It happens, therefore, that the executive and the legislative branches of the government sometimes work out of gear. Congress often fails to do anything to meet the recommendations of the heads of the great departments. The executive and Congress would be brought closer if the members of the Cabinet could at any time bring forward the business of their departments before Congress;

or again, could be invited to present their plans in person. The administration would thus be made more directly responsible for public measures. The country would know where a plan was started, whereas now many ill-considered plans proceed from committees, where no one can easily trace the blame. Moreover, a Congressman represents his district or State; but we need some one to speak for the nation.

So also in the government of the State, where the governor and the heads of the departments should have a hearing in the legislature, and be able to bring forward plans for the public service. The mayor and his chiefs should likewise directly present their plans for the public service before the city council.

Fewer elective officers. — The ordinary citizen cannot easily know the fitness for office of many candidates. He must choose by rumor and report, and sometimes unfairly. It is not desirable, therefore, to multiply the offices to be filled by general elections. There are many important offices now filled at haphazard by the vote of a multitude, which might more fitly be filled by the appointment of the executive, who would then be responsible for good appointments. All judges, sheriffs, and attorneys for the government ought specially to be chosen in this more careful way rather than by popular election.

Longer terms of office. — It would injure any industry or business to change the management every year. So it hurts the interest of the state or city to make frequent changes (rotation in office) in the heads of the government. As a rule, a good officer ought to be kept as long as he will serve. If another might do as well, the experience of the first constantly adds to his value. It must be remembered that the offices are not in order to give men places, but to serve the people as well as possible. There has been a bad law by which the term of numerous postmasters and other officers, appointed directly by the President, expires at the end of four years. This law ought to be repealed.

The two-thirds vote. — There are many cases where it seems fair or necessary that a bare majority should decide a question; or, when there are several plans or candidates, it may be quite fair to agree upon the one that has a plurality, or more than any other. But there are also cases when it does not seem wise or fair to compel a large minority by a majority vote. It is often agreed, for instance, that there must be a vote of two-thirds to change the constitution of a State. It is believed that for taking so important a step, a bare majority ought to wait till they have persuaded others to agree with them. Action that is thus delayed is likely to remain, whereas action which a bare majority hasten through may be soon reversed. It would be well if this courtesy towards a minority were oftener required by our laws. It is an application of the excellent rule, " to do as we would be done by," to respect the reasonable protest of a large minority.

The reform of the caucus. — It has been shown that many elections are practically decided by the caucus, or meeting, of the stronger party. Whatever the caucus decides upon is likely to be done. If a little ring or committee manage the caucus and arrange its business, it may accordingly happen that the citizen becomes merely a voting-machine to do what has been arranged beforehand. The party committee of the caucus also frequently collect and expend a good deal of money.

The caucus, therefore, should be so contrived as to give every citizen fair and independent opportunity to express his mind and make his own choice. The Australian ballot system, for example, if used at the caucus, would permit voters freely to use their influence in favor of the best candidates. A published account of all election expenses would also be a check upon the abuse of money at elections; for all evil practices shrink from publicity.

Radicals and conservatives. — There are some persons in every community who naturally favor new plans and changes. They hold that it is desirable to improve the government, and that no government is so good but that it may be better. These are the progressives or radicals. Men are sometimes progressives because they are wise, far-sighted, and courageous, but others, because they are fickle, and love change.

There are also certain persons who dread change, who are aware of the expense and risk that attend it, and who hold that it is wise as a rule to "let well enough alone," or at least to delay change till it becomes quite necessary. These are the conservatives. Men may be conservative because they are experienced and cautious; or, again, because they are timid and lazy.

Between the progressives and the conservatives are many citizens who are sometimes on one side and again on the other, or who favor one so-called reform but oppose the next. The discussion and opposition of these two tendencies help to bring to view the advantages and difficulties of every new plan proposed.

The great political parties, as the Tories and Radicals in England, sometimes shift places with each other, and the party which has once opposed change or reform will be found foremost in advocating some radical measure in order to get into power. The great mass of men are very liable, like a party of boys, to go with a rush where their leaders direct.

The fair presumption. — We rarely approach any question that needs to be decided without some bias in favor of one side or the other. Often we have a right to this bias. Thus we presume that any man accused of a crime is innocent until he is proved to be guilty. The presumption, as we say, is always in favor of holding a man to be good rather than bad. So in political questions. There is always a fair presumption in favor of the old or accustomed way and against change. It is for those who advocate change to show that the old way is wrong or unwise, or to prove that change is likely to be a real improvement, and so to increase the public good.

There is always a presumption, however, in favor of a principle, as justice or liberty. If a custom, however venerable, like slavery, can be shown to be contrary to the principle of human freedom, the presumption is at once turned against it. So if any change, like Civil Service reform, is demanded by justice.

The ideal citizen. — The ideal or best possible citizen is conservative and progressive at once. For he prefers the old and familiar methods of government as long as they continue to do good service; but he is perfectly willing to listen to any plan which promises better service. He is cautious in trying political experiments, but fearless as soon as he sees that the change is right. Thus the men who founded our republic were at the same time wise and brave and candid. The best citizen also is hopeful about the future of the nation, for he believes, whatever abuses there are, that Right will triumph in the end. He is quite willing, therefore, to act with a minority for a while, in order to further a just principle.

PART THIRD.

ECONOMIC DUTIES, OR THE RIGHTS AND DUTIES OF BUSINESS AND MONEY.

PART THIRD.

ECONOMIC DUTIES, OR THE RIGHTS AND DUTIES OF BUSINESS AND MONEY.

CHAPTER XXVI.

WHAT WEALTH IS.

THERE are two meanings of wealth. The larger meaning comprises everything which makes men "well off." In this sense a man's health, his home, his children, the salubrious climate, the air and the rain, the beautiful scenery of his country, are a part of his wealth. In this broad sense the man who enjoyed life most amply, whether he had much or little property, would be best off or most wealthy. In this sense, indeed, his best wealth, which made him most happy, might not have any money or market value.

In the narrower sense wealth is everything which has a market value; that is, which can be bought and sold. Houses, ships, lands, wheat, cattle, furniture, books and pictures, gold, silver, iron,—all such things constitute visible wealth, which we can see and touch. If such things, wherever they could be found, were added together, they would make up the wealth of the nation.

Natural wealth. — There is much that is often called wealth which has no present market value. The fish on our shores, the wild lands in the West, the timber in

Alaska, the ores in the mines,—all these things of unknown value may some time be wealth, but they are not yet wealth, till they can be bought and sold.

In the strict sense of the word, man always creates wealth; sometimes by his labor, as when he produces wheat or builds a house; sometimes by bringing a thing, like wild fruit, to market, and offering it for sale; and again merely by claiming it as his own, as when a man fences off a piece of land, or discovers a mine.

Wealth in public works. — That is not always wealth which costs money. Thus a city may spend millions of dollars in building sewers or constructing streets. But the sewers and streets are not strictly wealth, since when they are constructed no one would pay anything for them. There may be public works also, like jails and almshouses, in which wealth is sunk. The need of such things is a public misfortune, and stands for the presence of poverty and crime. In other words, a nation that had outgrown the necessity for jails and almshouses would be richer than a nation that had many costly buildings of this sort. As a well man, who has no medicines in his house, is better off than a lame or sick man who has a large supply of crutches and drugs.

Wealth is likewise sunk in fortifications and war-ships. The nation would be richer if it had no need of these things, as a man is better off who does not have to keep pistols to defend himself from burglars.

Wealth in men. — There is wealth in horses or mules, because they can work, and can therefore be bought and sold, or hired. There was also wealth in men, for the same reason, under the system of slavery. A large part of all the property of a slave State was in men. This kind of wealth did not disappear because the slaves were made free, as free men own themselves instead of being owned by masters. They can hire or sell their labor, their skill, or their knowledge. A man without owning any visible wealth may possess qualities in himself, such as experience and integrity, which will bring thousands of dollars a year. A young State which has many such men will soon have abundant visible wealth. But although wealth in men, that is, their labor and skill, can be bought and sold, so that a man with no money and a good trade is richer than an ignorant man with a thousand dollars, yet this kind of wealth is not generally counted. It is not shown in the census reports; in fact, it is not easy to measure it in money.

Wealth in paper. — A man may have large wealth and never see it. Some of it may have been lent to farmers or to help build warehouses in a distant city. Some of it may have helped a company of men to build a mill, or a line of steamers, or a railroad, in a new State. Some of it may have been put into a bank, and then loaned with other money all over the country. But while the rich man may not see anything which he owns, he has papers which show the amount of his wealth. Some of these papers are notes, signed by men who promise to pay so many dollars; or mortgages on the farmer's house and land; or railroad bonds, which are notes of the railroad company; or certificates of so many shares in the mill or the bank; or bonds of the government, which are really a sort of mortgage upon all the property of the people; or paper bills, which promise so many dollars in gold or silver.

This paper wealth, these bonds and notes and certificates, may be bought and sold in the market, but they have no value in themselves; the country would not be poorer if they were burned. Yet they are often counted as so much wealth. A State like New York is said to have so many millions of dollars in visible wealth, and so many millions more in paper wealth. It is evident that in this way the same wealth is often counted twice. For example: the railroad is counted once for its visible value in land, rails, stations, and cars; and then it is counted again for the paper bonds and shares, which merely show who its owners are.

So with the mortgage on the farmer's land. It shows that for the present some one else owns part of the farm. Perhaps a savings-bank has the mortgage, in which case all the depositors in the bank have a share together in the farm.

As we have already seen, the government often attempts to tax the same property, first as visible and again as paper wealth.[1] Thus the farmer will pay the full tax on his farm; the bank or company which loaned money to the farmer may pay another tax; and the individual who has a share in the bank may pay again.

The wealth in paper may sometimes mean an addition to the real wealth of a state. Thus the people of Great Britain own hundreds of millions of value all over the world in lands and mines, etc. The bonds and paper certificates show that other countries are so much in the debt of Great Britain. So the people of Philadelphia may hold paper bonds and shares in stores and mills in a number of cities in the West, and the people of other cities may likewise own in Philadelphia in the same way.

False wealth. — There may be wealth, or things which can be bought and sold in the market, which harm the persons who use them. Thus, if ardent spirits hurt and degrade a community, the distilleries and saloons used

---

[1] See Chapter XVI. p. 95.

by the liquor business must lessen the wealth of the people. Although, therefore, the census reports may add so many millions for the distilleries and saloons, or for buildings used by gamblers, a true estimate would be to subtract this value, since that cannot really be wealth which in some way does not make men better off. It is as if a farmer kept a vicious bull which destroyed every year several times its value.

How wealth varies.— That which is wealth in one place may not be in another. Land which is worth several dollars a foot in New York may be worth nothing in Greenland, nor a picture in Patagonia. This is because wealth depends on a market, or the desire of men to buy and sell. Even the same market may change from one year to another. Thus London is called the great market of the world, because all sorts of things are bought and sold there. But, in case of rumors of war, men's desire to buy and sell might be suddenly checked. In that case the value of many kinds of wealth would fall, although the things themselves would still remain.

Robinson Crusoe's lands and goats, though real wealth, would not strictly be wealth till other men appeared to purchase them, that is, to make a market. Even gold would not be wealth on the lonely island, for one man would have no use for it.

All wealth is constantly being destroyed, or used up, or worn out. Some kinds, like food, are only good for immediate consumption. Clothing lasts a little longer, but soon has to be renewed. Houses and buildings at last go to decay. The gold and iron wear out. Perhaps one-eighth of all the wealth in a country is used up in a single year. Among a poor or barbarous people probably the proportion is much larger. The land is the one thing which remains the same; but its fertility is often exhausted while the demand for it is constantly changing.

The increase of wealth. — Although wealth is constantly destroyed or worn out, it is also re-created. The harvests of each year renew it; the labor and skill of millions of persons change the raw products into new and higher values, as in the case of a steel watch-spring, worth many fold the cost of the crude iron ore. Even the land may grow in value by being tilled, or the growth of a city may give each square foot of land a greater value than an acre possessed before the city was built. A large part of the wealth of people in towns and cities consists merely in the land upon which stores and houses are crowded together. The greater the city, the more the value of this land.

The wealth of a people is thus like the body of a man. It is in a state of constant change or flux. It is always being renewed or made over. On the average, it is all made over once in a few years, but some parts of it are more durable than the rest.

CHAPTER XXVII.

THE CONDITIONS OF WEALTH.

IF a household of children were rude and destructive, or had not learned how to use toys or articles of furniture, it would be impossible for them to keep anything of value: they would have no wealth. So with a savage people. As long as men were barbarous, the duties of business and property were extremely simple. The land belonged to the whole family or tribe. There was little furniture in the rude tents or huts where the people lived together in alternate plenty and want. There was little or no barter or exchange of goods, and no shops or merchants, and not for a long time any coined money. The chiefs lived much like the common people, as is still the case among the American Indians. As men came to live in cities, life grew less simple; all sorts of luxuries were demanded; various trades arose; and there became everywhere a wealthy class, living differently from their neighbors. The growth of cities brought travel, and therefore the more trade, as the people of one place learned to desire the things which another place produced. There came to be great trading cities, like Tyre and Carthage, which sent their ships beyond the Mediterranean Sea.

Unfavorable conditions. — There were serious obstacles, however, in early times in the way of industry and commerce and the amassing of wealth.

War. — There was almost constant war. A rich city was always liable to be pillaged and burned. The caravans of merchants were likely to be attacked by robbers. Men had to defend themselves, or to obey ambitious kings, and had not the leisure to work and earn money.

Piracy. — The seas, too, were infested with pirates, who thought it right to seize merchant-ships, and sell their crews for slaves.

Slavery. — Slavery also obstructed industry and business. The slaves did less work than free men could do, and the latter were less willing to work. Thus there came to be everywhere a great class of idle people.

Caste. — In some countries also, as in India to-day, there were castes, that is, classes of people, the members of which could not change their occupation. The son of a tanner had to be a tanner too. Thus bright men in the lower castes were kept from rising. Ambition and invention were checked, and warriors were thought better than workers.

Prejudice against foreigners. — There was a prejudice everywhere against foreigners, who were not given an equal chance with native citizens, and whose goods were often heavily taxed, and sometimes confiscated.

Thus war, piracy, slavery, caste, contempt of work, jealousy of foreigners — in fact, all unjust customs — hindered business, and prevented the increase of wealth.

The physical conditions of wealth; the climate. — There are certain countries in which, so far as we know, there has never been any wealth. In the arctic regions, for example, where the energies of man are nearly exhausted in the fight with winter, there could never be a rich civilization. In the heart of Africa or under the equator civilization has never flourished. On the contrary, the richest nations dwell in temperate regions. The climate of a country, then, is one of the conditions that help or hinder the wealth of a people.

Natural resources. — Certain countries are poor by nature. The soil may be sterile, fuel may be scarce, the supplies of valuable minerals may be scanty. Other countries enjoy rich lands, ample forests and coal fields, vast water power, good harbors, and inexhaustible mines. The United States are thus magnificently endowed with the materials of wealth.

The spur of necessity. — In the Garden of Eden, as in one of the beautiful islands of the Southern Pacific Ocean, there would be little wealth. The people would be too comfortable to need to labor. The abundance of fruit would content them; the mild climate would not require much clothing or the building of permanent houses. There never would be art or books unless men learned to work, and few would learn to work unless there was some necessity.

As soon, however, as the conditions of living become harder; when fruits do not grow of themselves, but have to be cultivated; when cold and wet demand clothes for men's bodies; when men require shelter and permanent houses, wealth begins through the spur of necessity. Necessity teaches men to work; all work requires more work to perfect and secure it; the field once tilled has to be fenced or protected from wild creatures; the house has to be enlarged and improved; inventions come to save labor, and the inventions themselves demand new kinds of labor and new appliances, that is, more wealth. The introduction of the telephone into a town requires an increased force of men and women to manage the business, and the increasing numbers require more houses and more telephones.

The necessity at first seems to be a misfortune. Thus in the north the long and cold winter requires fuel and hay, and more labor to supply these necessaries. It comes to pass that a considerable portion of the wealth of the nation consists in wood, coal, and hay, which the rigor of the climate demands.

Everything that men esteem precious thus arises from some kind of necessity, either real or imaginary. The need of bread or shoes or tools stirs them to work to overcome the need, and thus to grow rich.

Intellectual conditions; enterprise or energy. — There are some races, and certain persons in every race, who are more easily contented or more indolent than others. They do not feel so keenly the spur of necessity. One condition of wealth, therefore, is energy or enterprise. The enterprising farmer will work more hours in a day; take better care of his cattle; provide warmer buildings; fertilize his land; and grow rich by his labor.

Intelligence. — An ignorant people have few wants, and therefore little wealth. An ignorant people could not have invented the steam-engine, neither would they have felt the need for the articles which the steam-engine helps to produce. It is when the average intelligence of people has risen to demand a vast supply of many things, that the spur of necessity urges inventors to harness the forces of nature to help them in shops, mills, and railroads. The single invention of the steam-engine, called forth by intelligence, has within a few years increased many times the wealth of the world.

Taste. — A certain portion of all wealth is for enjoyment or decoration. Pictures, statues, beautiful buildings, instruments of music, the products of the various arts, constitute this kind of wealth. It arises from higher kinds of need, as men come to want satisfaction for their sense of beauty. As soon as a people have learned how to provide plenty of the great necessaries of food and clothing, they can afford to set a larger number of their workmen free to produce and to cheapen the articles of taste. Many can now have pictures and books, and pianos, which once the few only could enjoy. The more taste the people have, the larger will be the production of this form of wealth. The call for works of art, taste, comfort, and luxury requires more shops and houses; that is, greater wealth of other kinds. So the taste for natural scenery adds a new value to rocky hills and wild shores, for which persons without taste would see no use.

Moral conditions: Honesty. — There are certain moral conditions of wealth. There would be little wealth, if thieves and robbers were abroad. For it would be hopeless to labor and gather abundance, only to be snatched away. So, too, if the government were dishonest and took men's savings ruthlessly from them, like the government of the Turks.

Good faith or trust. — Wealth is daily changing hands. A vast portion of business consists in trade. Wool, cotton, wheat, must be brought from distant States and manufactured articles returned. But trade would be impossible unless men could trust each other. Trade is carried on in the faith that men will do as they promise, that they will pay for what they buy, that they will furnish articles as good as they agree. Even a few men who break their word injure business, cause distrust, and require higher prices in order to induce merchants to take the risk of being cheated. The honest have thus to suffer for the faithless. On the contrary, if all men would keep their word, more business could be done, at cheaper rates, and every one could have more wealth.

A state of peace. — When our forefathers were at war

with the French and Indians, they were liable to see their corn-fields and towns burned, and their ships captured. They could not make wealth in time of war. But as soon as peace returned, the French and the Indians helped them to get more wealth. The Indians brought them furs, and took cloth and iron in return. Their ships sailed to France, and both the French and the Americans profited by trading together. The Americans sold their furs and salt fish, of which they had more than they needed, and bought from France silk and other articles, such as they could not make so well as the Frenchmen. Trade made more wealth in both countries, but trade depended on the nations being at peace.

Courage. — It sometimes happens that vast amounts of wealth are suddenly swept away, as by a fire or a flood. Such occasions demand courage, not only at the time, but afterwards, to go to work again, to repair the damage or to rebuild from the ruins, like the men of Chicago after the great fire of 1871. In various industries also, in the management of steam and electricity, on railroads and on ships, there is daily demand for the same kind of daring to take necessary risks and even to brave death, as used to be called for in a military age for the hazards of battle.

In general, when men are friendly with each other, when their ships can sail freely into all seas and foreign nations welcome each other to their ports; when many travellers from one country can go to another and see what others can do better than they, such friendly travel and interchange help to make more wealth. Men who see superior work abroad, feel the spur of new needs and go to work to meet them. Men desire foreign fruits and products, — tea and coffee, rice and bananas, — and bring them to our markets. New ships and steamers must be built to carry the trade of the world; new warehouses must be erected to accommodate the growing trade; more fields must be tilled and more mills built to make things with which to pay the people over the sea for what they send us. Wealth not only rests upon good faith and friendliness, but the getting of wealth brings distant peoples together, and teaches them to trust each other rather than to fight.

CHAPTER XXVIII.

TO WHOM WEALTH BELONGS, AND HOW IT IS DIVIDED.

It has been seen that labor alone does not make wealth, as some think. Wealth is partly natural, as the land, the fisheries, and the ores in the mines. Intelligence, skill, and taste are necessary in creating a large part of all wealth. Good morals make wealth by setting higher standards of living, and making men honest, industrious, and faithful. If religion enhances the worth of human life, or furnishes stronger motives for noble conduct, it also shares so far in creating wealth. Thus property is worth more in the United States, with its schools, benevolent institutions, and churches, than in Morocco or Siberia.

The useful. — If a colony of persons were to settle for the first time in a new country like New Zealand, and take up land and build towns, it is easy to see that their wealth would rightfully belong to all who had been in any way useful to the colony. None of it would strictly belong to the idle, to the wasteful, to the injurious, if such were among the colonists. There are various divisions of the useful in every community, who ought, therefore, to share in the wealth, according to the part which they play in making it.

Discovery or invention. — In our new colony there would be certain persons to go out as pioneers and scouts to discover the natural wealth of the country, the fertile lands, the fruits, the minerals, the springs and waterfalls.

If they did nothing but discover, and tell others where to go, they would deserve their fair share in the wealth which would come in their track.

The inventors are like the discoverers. Whoever shows a new use to which iron or copper can be put is as useful as if he discovered a new mine. Whoever invents a process or a machine to save labor, that is, to set workmen free to do something else, may be as useful as a thousand men.

Production. — The largest part of the working-force of the community must be employed in producing food and all kinds of supplies. There must be farmers, black-smiths, carpenters, operatives in shops and mills, to make boots and shoes, clothing, tools, etc. Whoever produces something useful for the community ought to have a share in the wealth. Artists and painters belong under this head, if they make things which add to the happiness of the community. A great deal of domestic work, done by women, comes under the same head. The woman who cooks the man's food, or repairs his clothing, is useful in the same way as the farmer who reaps the wheat.

The work of distribution. — It used often to happen in old times that there would be plenty in one place, while men were starving a hundred miles away. The farmer did not know how to get his produce to market. In a civilized country, on the contrary, thousands of persons do nothing else but help distribute supplies where they are needed. The grocers do this on a small scale in every village. The great merchants do it by wholesale in the cities. Their agents travel up and down through the country, buying and selling.

Transportation. — The distribution of supplies requires a host of teamsters and draymen. The railroads and steam-ships are built largely to carry freight, and so to assist in distributing the product of the nation. The farmer need not now stop working in order to go to market with his wheat. Multitudes of passengers must also be carried, mostly to their work and business, and also for their pleasure. An army of men must be detailed for conductors and brakemen, who also deserve to share in the wealth of the country. Horses and stables must be kept for the same purpose.

Protection. — The duty of protecting against violence and fire cannot be altogether committed to the government. There must be private watchmen besides in stores and mills. There must be patrols on the railroads to prevent accident. Whoever prevents injury ought to share with those who produce the wealth. The physician or nurse, too, who defends against disease, claims a rightful share.

Administration and accounts. — The vast business of the community needs a certain class of skilled men to manage and direct. The wise management of a good engineer, architect, or superintendent may save the labor of hundreds of men, while poor and shiftless management may cause enormous loss or waste. The administration of business needs also a large force of accountants and book-keepers in offices, factories, banks, warehouses. There must be many trained heads which can superintend accounts, and make a multitude of figures tell the truth, or else, through error or fraud, injustice will somewhere be done, or supplies will not be distributed where they are needed.

Economy; savings. — Economy is the care of values. There are numberless holes or leaks through which wealth is wasted by ignorance or carelessness. Whoever saves wealth, therefore, whoever stops the leak, whoever keeps what another would lose, deserves something of the community. A housekeeper, for instance, may save enough food, which another would throw away, to feed one or two mouths. This is the same as producing the food. The larger one's responsibility is, the greater the chance of wise economy.

Instruction. — Since intelligence is a condition of wealth, there must be a certain number of persons detailed to the service of education. Whoever teaches, or waits on the teacher, or learns the facts of nature or history, or makes books, must have a share in the wealth. There must also be libraries and museums with their attendants. So, too, whoever teaches good morals, or the laws of faithful conduct, so that men learn to be more just and friendly, becomes a worker and a sharer along with the direct producers of wealth.

Comfort. — Men work more efficiently when they are made comfortable. Thus a man who has a comfortable house or lodgings will do more work than if he is badly housed. There are, therefore, in a civilized country numerous appliances requiring much labor, purely for comfort. A very large part of woman's work is to promote and increase comfort. In general, whoever can help make men more comfortable at their work, or in their homes, whoever can lessen drudgery and render labor more pleasant deserves a share in the wealth.

Recreation. — Every one needs, not merely rest, but sometimes amusement or play. Men who work hard, like children who study, need vacation; they will do more if they have it. This requires another body of workers. Others must carry on the work while the first set have their change. Moreover, there must be those who can entertain and amuse. More cars and steamboats must be run; there must be musicians and singers; there must be hotels and restaurants. The producers must cheerfully share with those who enable them to enjoy recreation.

Personal and domestic service. — There are a large number of persons who need help and service. Sometimes they are sick or aged persons who cannot help themselves. Others may be overworked, and therefore require assistance. In many households such assistance is needed in the care of young children. There are also those whose time is very valuable. A great engineer like De Lesseps, a great scholar like Agassiz, a wonderful painter or singer, the President of the United States, ought not to use up his time or strength in manual work which some one else could do for him. We are, therefore, willing to allow certain persons extra service, provided they need it, by reason either of their infirmities or the superior value of their work.

We grudge this kind of help, however, where it is not needed or deserved. We grudge it to a young person who had better wait on himself than be waited on by another. We grudge it to the indolent, who are harmed by it. In the new colony which we have imagined, in which we should need every skilful hand, we cannot see why a lazy person should be entitled to the assistance of another to wait on him, or why either of them should rightly share in our wealth.

Luxuries. — There are certain articles of which there are not enough to go around, or at least not for common use. They are like the sweetmeats or jellies which are brought on at a feast. Because they are comparatively scarce they are more costly than the necessaries or comforts, of which there may be enough for all. Many of the luxuries depend upon the cultivation of taste, and are not luxuries at all to those whose taste is not cultivated. A gem or a work of art, for example, might not be a luxury to a savage. There are certain luxuries which seem suitable for a feast, when we entertain friends, which would not be wholesome for ordinary use. There are other luxuries which we should set apart for the sick or the aged, the use of which would be enervating for the young or the healthy.

We have already spoken of personal service, in order to save valuable time or life. There are other such luxuries, like travel abroad, or more ample houses, or horses and carriages, or more costly dress, which we should cheerfully allow to men and women whose lives are specially useful, or whose service might be prolonged by extra care. In other words, there may be lives which the community would do well to serve specially, as we give a nicer care to rare, valuable, or delicate tools. The work of furnishing luxuries ought never, however, to be suffered to lessen the supply of the necessaries of life, upon which all depend. Thus, the empire of Rome was on the way to ruin, when the rich rioted in luxury, while the poor starved.

The family. — A considerable part of woman's work must always be directly for the family, and particularly in the nurture of children. The health, the morals, and the working power of a people are high or low in proportion to the character, the care, and the wisdom of its mothers. Whatever improves this care sooner or later enriches the country. Whoever gives such care to make the children stronger or better deserves a share of the wealth.

The division of labor. — In a poor or uncivilized country the same person carries on various kinds of work. The farmer is his own carpenter and blacksmith; spinning and weaving go on in the same house. But this causes great waste. As men learn better to help each other, they divide their work into trades and professions, so that each shall do what he can do best; as when boys wish to play a good game of ball, they choose the one who can catch best to be catcher. By this plan each worker, who is useful at all, is entitled to his share of the wealth produced by the whole people, while the total product becomes greater.

The division of wealth. — We have seen that the wealth ought strictly to belong to all who are in any way useful to the community. It is not quite easy to see how to apportion it exactly. Some are very much more useful than others. Some are useful for a time and less useful afterwards. Some have far greater needs than others. An artist, a student, an architect, has needs different from a farmer. We cannot tell precisely how useful one is as compared with another. A distiller of strong drink may not really be useful at all. A skilful teacher may be more useful than any one knows. Fortune may increase or lessen the usefulness of the farmer or the fisherman. No tribunal of men is wise enough, therefore, to divide the income or the wealth of a people. It would not seem fair to divide equally, for all do not work equally hard, or need the same amount. Even at the same table one eats more than another. It would not be just to let each take what he wishes; for many, like young children, are greedy and wasteful. If it were fair for the people of one city or country to divide their wealth equally, it would be difficult to treat the people equally who might flock there from poorer and more barbarous places, in order to share in the wealth of the richer place.

The law of supply and demand. — The way in which wealth is really apportioned is according to the supply and the demand. If, for example, anything like coal is scarce, and the demand for coal is great, the natural rule is that fewer can have it, or in other words, that a man must work more hours in order to earn his share of the coal. If flour is abundant, so that there is plenty to go around, less labor will provide enough for the family, and there will be so much more time to provide other things. If little labor of a certain kind — of carpenters, for instance — is needed, their pay will be less; that is, they can have less flour or coal, or whatever else they need. If, on the other hand, there are few carpenters, and there is much work for them to do, so that they become very useful, they will have so much more for their work.

This is the law of supply and demand. The law of supply and demand works on the playground as well as in the market. If there are not boys enough to play, even poor players are welcome; but if there are plenty of boys, the poorer players have to stand aside, or do something else less agreeable.

The law of supply and demand declares that some articles are more useful or valuable than others, as also certain men and women are more useful than others. It brings the less valuable things more nearly within reach of every one, but makes the scarcer things, like luxuries, expensive. It gives to the many persons whose work is less in demand, or less useful, or whose places could be readily filled, less of the wealth, but more to those whose places are hard to fill.

The law of supply and demand is a law of *things*, not of men. Like the fire or the steam, it makes no allowance for men's feelings and needs. As gravitation does not protect a falling body from hurt, so the law of supply and demand would not save men from starving. It works out only a rude kind of justice. It requires to be controlled and supplemented by friendliness.

As on the ball ground the better and stronger players will try to make room for the poorer and younger, and to teach them to play better, so the abler and stronger men ought to find out how to make room for the less capable and intelligent. We shall have occasion to speak further of supply and demand in another chapter.

CHAPTER XXIX.

THE INSTITUTION OF PROPERTY.

WE can imagine a people holding their wealth in common, as a club of schoolboys own their bats and balls together. Among a savage people like the North American Indians, a considerable part of the wealth is common to all. The tribe hold the corn-fields. When game is taken, all the village share; a number of families will often live in the same house. As long as any one has food, his neighbors, or even strangers, will come and eat.

Difficulties in holding wealth in common. — There is never much wealth in a savage tribe. There is little encouragement to the more enterprising members of the tribe to work hard and to lay up stores of provisions, where the lazy and improvident may come in to devour and waste. Few would be likely to build new and better houses, or to take the trouble to have a garden, or to plant trees, unless they could hope to enjoy the reward of their work. Men who hold things in common are like children playing together with blocks. It is hard for one to make anything with the blocks unless the others agree, or unless the blocks are divided.

The beginnings of property. — Property is that which is one's own, which no other person has a right to take away. Property begins even among savages, as it begins among children. Thus one's clothes are one's own. It would obviously be inconvenient for more than one person to claim the same clothes. So of one's implements and weapons, the axe or the bow and arrows, especially such as one makes himself. So of the ornaments and decorations, the shells or gems, or bits of metal that any one finds. "These are mine," says the child, with a sense of injustice, if any one else claims them. So of the Arab's horses which he has reared and tended, or of the flocks which he pastures.

Differences of men in tastes and capacity. — Property also begins with men, as among children, from their differences of taste and capacity. One is fonder than another of shells or bright colors, and therefore takes more trouble to collect them. One cares more than another for horses or cattle, and has therefore better success in raising them. One is fond of ornaments, and carves a beautiful handle to his axe or knife, while another does not think the carving worth his trouble. The ornamented axe is the rightful property of the man who had the taste and skill to make it. So one man loves books and pictures, and is willing to work in order to obtain them. They ought to be his, then, rather than the property of another who does not care for them.

Property by earning. — Suppose now that one man works for another. The man who has a herd of cattle hires another to help him take care of them, and pays him in cattle or in skins, or money. Here is property in what a man earns by his labor or skill. This rightly belongs to the man who has worked for it, and not to others who have not worked, or who perhaps did not care to work. Indeed, it would promote laziness in the men who did not work, if the cattle or the money which another had worked for were to be shared in common with them.

Property by exchange. — It might be that the man

with the herd of cattle could raise wheat. Suppose he exchanges some of his young cattle, or some of the bright gems that he has found among the hills, for a supply of wheat. This, too, is his property. It could not rightly belong to others who had sat still and not helped to raise the wheat. Moreover, it would hurt their character to claim a share in what they had not helped to produce.

Property by gift or inheritance. — It would be fair for the man who had the wheat or the horses to make a gift to his friend or his son. The gift would then be the property of the friend, and not of any one else. A great deal of the wealth in existence is handed down from parents to children, and belongs to the children by inheritance.

Property by natural genius. — Suppose a man has the genius to invent a useful machine, or to write a valuable book, or one has a beautiful voice, or can play the violin. That which any one can make or do that others cannot do is his property; that is, it rightly belongs to him, in the same way as his eyes or his hands are his own. It would not be right for the family or the nation to claim this man's genius as theirs, or to compel him to write books, or to sing for them whenever they pleased. So the rewards or the pay which he received in return for his genius would be fairly his. Other men would have no claim to compel him to divide or to share with them. Neither would it be honorable in them to think that they had such a claim. On the other hand, it would be shameful in him to withhold the gifts of his genius, or to extort unreasonable pay for it.

Property by accident or good fortune. — If a fisherman has a lucky catch, we say that it his. The unlucky fishermen, or those who do not go fishing at all, have no claim to force him to share his good fortune. They will take their turn at fortune another time. Men enjoy their fishing better so: they are also more watchful and daring than they would be if their prizes were taken away from them.

So if a man finds a nugget of gold or a mine on his land. We say it is his. If we could rightly compel him to share it, we should not know how to divide it, for it would no more belong to all the persons in the town than to all in the state or the nation, or even to all in the world.

So also if a man has property, such as wheat or a house, which rises suddenly in value. We call this increase his property, although he may have done nothing to earn it. For as before, if we demanded that he should share it, we should not know how fairly to divide it. If we claimed that it ought to belong to our city, the nation might claim it equally, or even other nations. Moreover, as the man has to bear his losses when his wheat or his house falls in value, it seems right that he should enjoy the exceptional advantage when the value rises.

Property by possession. — Suppose one found some of Captain Kidd's treasure, it would be impossible to restore it to its rightful owners. It would, therefore, be the property of its discoverer. So also in case one had inherited property from an ancestor, who had long ago made his money by fraud, or by the African slave trade. It would still be the man's property, since no others could rightly claim it.

Property in land. — We have mostly considered so far such kinds of property as may be moved, or carried upon the person. Movable property, such as clothes, furniture, ornaments, cattle, produce, money, etc., is called personal property. This also includes paper and certificates of property, such as bonds and bank shares. There is another kind of property in land. The land and the buildings upon it constitute "real estate." What gives any one a private right to own the land?

When Robinson Crusoe came to his lonely island, although savages sometimes roamed over it, they were not using it, and did not therefore rightly own it. Crusoe, accordingly, took what he needed of it, partly for pasture and partly for tillage and garden. Suppose now that another ship had been wrecked on the island, and its crew had come ashore. It would neither be fair for him to claim to own the whole island, and to make them pay him for the wild land; nor, on the other hand, for them to take from him any of the land that he was really using.

Suppose, finally, after the best land had all been taken up, another company of men should come ashore. It would certainly seem hard that they should not have as good lands as the earlier comers; but it would not be right for them to demand the fields that had already been occupied, cleared, and improved. As, when strangers come to the table at the hotel, it is well, if those who are already seated are willing, to move closer and accommodate the later ones, but otherwise they must wait for the second and perhaps poorer table.

As long as there is plenty of land, as in most of the United States, there is no difficulty about the private ownership of it. So, also, if every one used all his land, and if every one had got it fairly in the first place, there would be less question about the rightful ownership of it. But often the land was acquired in war or by violence; or by injustice, as when the Highland lords in Scotland dispossessed the clansmen of land which rightfully belonged to all the tribe; or by a fiction, as when the king of England granted or sold vast lands in America which did not belong to him.

The laws also and custom have allowed men to take up much more land than they could use, and to keep it unemployed even when others needed it.

When wrongs have been done, it is hard to right them at once without doing more wrong. For the present owners of the lands that were once wrongly acquired may have honestly paid for them, and may really use them. Even if it were fair to take away that which one had purchased in good faith, it would be impossible to say to whom it should now be given.

In general, property in land is right and fair, in case the community have found on the whole that the custom of permitting such property is a public advantage. If, for example, there proves to be more enterprise and better care of the land when each man is free to acquire and use it as he pleases, than when a whole village, as in barbarous times, owned it together, it is a sufficient reason for the custom that it works to the advantage of the community. If, however, it could be clearly shown that some other custom of using the land would be better for all, and would at the same time be freer of objections and injustice, every one ought to be willing to adopt it.

The right of eminent domain limits the right of individuals in land. — Property in land is always held subject to the needs of the State or community. Thus if the government required a piece of land for public buildings, or if a new street or a railroad needed to be laid out through a man's farm, the individual has no right to insist upon keeping his land in the face of a public necessity. But he is entitled to fair compensation, as for any other property.

Common property. — There is much wealth which is owned by persons in common. Thus several farmers may own a threshing-machine or a creamery. A great number of persons unite in establishing a savings bank. We have already seen that all the people of a town or city own the public buildings and schools, the parks and the streets. Every newcomer who is enrolled as a citizen, and every child born in the city, becomes a sharer in this property on equal terms with the rest. So with the property of the State, which every citizen is a sharer in. So with the vast property of the nation, including great tracts of lands in the Territories. Our government claims such lands as belonging to the American people, and not to people in Asia or Africa, because the land is within our boundaries; precisely as a farmer claims the land for which he holds a title.

All, too, become sharers in the knowledge, the inventions, the discoveries, by which each generation inherits the labor and thought of all previous time. The value of this common knowledge is immeasurable.

Property and the public interest.—We respect private property for two reasons. One reason is our regard for the individual. We respect his claims to his various belongings as we would wish our own claims to be considered by him. A second reason is the public good. There will be more work, industry, energy, and thrift, if we allow individuals the freedom to own and use and give away their own property, than if we forbid them to have anything of their own. This is the general experience of mankind. It is the same in a nation as in a family. The whole family will have more if each member of it can have his own things, than if no one can call anything his own. So the community will create and possess more wealth, and all will therefore be likely to be better off, if each is reasonably free to acquire and own property, than if all the property were held in common.

If, however, it is discovered that there is any kind of property, like turnpikes, bridges, or waterworks, which it is better for the interest of all for individuals not to hold privately, it is fair for the individuals, in such case, to consent to let the public acquire such property in common, only in such way as to be just to the former private owners.

Responsibility for property. — We have seen in government that every official does his work best when he is directly responsible for his conduct. We respect property, likewise, because we thus make every one directly responsible for what is his own. If the boy has his own clothes and hat, he and no one else will be bound to take care of them. If he has his own allowance, he will be bound to keep account of it, and not to waste or lose it. So if a man has his own property, he learns to use and save it. If he has his own land, he is responsible for the care he takes of it; he will take pleasure in tending and beautifying it; he will be likely to put permanent improvement upon it, in clearing and draining it; he can afford to build a substantial house, where an Arab would only set up a tent. To respect a man's property is thus to make him responsible for it. And responsibility develops his character and makes more of a man. Whereas if he is too slovenly to take care of his own, he would be unlikely, like the savage, to take good care of the common property.

CHAPTER XXX.

HONEST MONEY.

MEN do not trade together long before they invent something to measure the value of wealth. Money is that by which they make such measurement, as they measure distance by the length of a pole, or by a yard-stick. They begin with a very rude kind of money, such as wampum or beads or cattle. Thus an American Indian would sell a valuable package of furs for so many strings of wampum. The precious metals, and especially silver and gold, have been the chosen forms of money among most civilized nations for thousands of years. In early times the money was weighed. Afterwards it was coined; that is, a bit or piece of a certain weight was stamped by the sovereign or the government.

Changes in the value of money. — It would have been very convenient if there had been some one kind of metal which was always of uniform value. But there is no such metal. The supply of gold or silver, like the supply of other things, varies from one time to another. The opening of new mines or fresh discoveries of the precious metals, tend to lower their value, as a large harvest lowers the price of wheat. On the other hand, increasing trade causes a demand for more money, and tends to absorb the supply. Ignorant people, as in the East, often hoard or hide their money, as though it were buried again in the mine. There is a changing demand, also, for the gold and silver for other purposes besides money, as for articles of ornament or luxury. The same amount or weight of gold or silver will not therefore buy as much at one period as at another.

The double or single standard of value. — It has been common to use both gold and silver money, though gold is worth much more than silver; unfortunately the two metals vary with respect to each other like all other values. Thus gold is estimated to have been worth eleven times as much as silver in the fifteenth century, fifteen times as much at the close of the eighteenth century, and more than eighteen times as much in 1879. There have been further changes since. Thus, one common silver dollar, if melted down, would not now buy nearly one hundred cents' worth of labor or produce.

A moral question. — When government stamps a coin, and makes it "legal tender," that is, good money to pay debts, the stamp is a sort of guarantee or pledge that the coin has as much value in it as it says on its face. Thus the gold eagle says, "I am honestly worth a fixed sum in the markets of the world." But if the government should make eagles with one-fifth less gold in them than before, or one-fifth less than the English or the Germans put into their coins, and still mark "ten dollars" on the coin, it would not tell the truth. So, too, if the government coins silver dollars, and puts less value into this coin than it puts into its gold dollar. The silver dollar would not tell the truth, unless it has in it as much value as the gold dollar contains.

The money of commerce. — Governments coin money, but the commerce of the world fixes its value. For commerce, in her great markets, like London, where the business of the world meets and is settled, asks of all commodities, and the coins of every nation also, What is their real worth? A government may put a false mark on a coin or mix alloy with the metal, but commerce weighs and tests the coin, and will not give more for it than it really is worth.

For the present, the standard of commerce seems to be gold. This is because the great commercial nations use this metal in settling their accounts. Even when they use silver coinage along with the gold, as a matter of fact, they refer their values to the gold basis. Thus the United States practically counts values, not in silver dollars, worth perhaps eighty cents, but in gold dollars that correspond to the gold sovereign of London. When money has to be sent back and forth between nations, the gold is also more convenient, being far less bulky.

Paper money. — Although a dollar means a certain weight of precious metal, most of the money in use consists of paper bills. There is, in fact, risk and inconvenience in carrying coin, and especially in doing a large business with it. If, for example, all the wheat and cotton of the West and South had to be paid for in metallic money, there would be great cost and often loss, merely in sending the vast weight of coin thousands of miles. Civilized men have therefore invented paper money of various kinds as a substitute for coin.

Bank bills. — A bank, for instance, which has coin in its vaults may issue bills, which are really written promises or orders, for so much coin. The use of these bills or orders depends upon the trust or confidence which men have in the integrity and honor of the bankers. As long as men believe that the bankers will keep their promises and pay the coin when requested, they do not care for the coin, but find the bills more convenient. In order that the people may be protected from loss, it is the custom for the government to superintend the banks which issue bills. They are not allowed to issue too many bills; that is, to make more promises than they are able to keep.

Checks and drafts. — Besides bank bills there are millions of money in private paper orders which are sent by mail, or pass from hand to hand. Thus, a merchant in New York, instead of sending a great roll of bills to pay for lumber or iron, deposits the money in a bank, and writes a check or order upon the bank for the amount of his debt. If the merchant is honest, the check is the same as money, and another bank in Michigan or Tennessee will accept it from the lumber or iron dealer. Or, a merchant in New York wishing to pay for his goods in Bordeaux, will get a draft or order for so much money from a banker in his own city upon a banker in London. This draft upon a well-known and honorable bank will be as good as money anywhere in the world where ships go. Thus orders for money become themselves a kind of money. The orders may even be sent by telegraph over the continent or under the ocean. Thus a bank in Chicago, which is known in London or Paris, may telegraph an order to pay some American student a sum of money which the American's father had deposited in his bank at home.

Government and paper money. — The government of the United States was obliged to borrow on an enormous scale to pay the expenses of the Civil War. Besides other methods of borrowing, hundreds of millions of dollars in bills were issued. These bills were the promises or pledges of the government to pay as many dollars in coin as was printed on the face of the bill. The bills were used as money to pay for supplies and the wages of soldiers. The government, however, was not able to keep its promises and to pay specie, that is, the real coined money of commerce, to merchants and others who wanted it. On the contrary, the quantity of paper notes was so great that some feared lest, as in the case of the continental currency, or the paper money of the Revolutionary War, the bills would never be paid. It therefore happened, finally, that almost three paper dollars were required to get the value of one gold dollar. A yard of cloth worth one dollar cost almost three paper dollars. The value of the paper dollar varied with every victory or defeat of the national arms. The gold and silver were hoarded away or sent abroad to pay the merchants' debts. This was because the paper dollar no longer told the truth.

Specie payments.— After the war, as soon as confidence was restored that the government could keep its promises, the paper money rose in value. The yard of cloth that had sold for nearly three dollars could now be had for, perhaps, a dollar and a quarter. At last government resolved to make the paper dollar tell the truth again. It was announced that any one who wished might have gold coin at the Treasury in exchange for the paper bills. But very few persons now desired to draw the bulky gold, since the paper dollar at once became as good as the gold to buy the yard of cloth.

Gold and silver certificates.— Besides the notes of the government or its promises to pay, other bills or certificates have been issued which entitle the holder to so many gold dollars, and again another class which entitle the holder to so many silver dollars, deposited in the Treasury vaults. These certificates are also as good as money, and much more convenient.

A national danger.— It will be seen that our government has gold dollars which correspond to the money of commerce, containing the precise value marked on the face of them; secondly, silver dollars, stamped by the government, but at present containing less than their true value; thirdly, silver and nickel currency, used merely for convenience, but not containing nearly the worth stamped upon it; and, fourthly, paper notes and certificates, worth nothing in themselves, but guaranteed by the wealth and honor of the nation. These different kinds of money all circulate together as long as the government honestly keeps in its vaults sufficient gold coin — the money of commerce — to enable every one who has silver or paper dollars to come and get an equal number of gold dollars, if he needs them, to pay for goods abroad. If, however, at any time, the government should refuse to give the merchant the real value in gold in exchange for the silver or the paper, the same thing would happen as in the Civil War: the silver dollar and the paper would cease to tell the truth; the yard of cloth would rise in price; all values would change.

It would be precisely as though the government, like the despots of old times, had clipped the coin or mixed alloy with it, so as to make a new kind of dollar of less worth. The true dollars, such as the commerce of the world buys and sells with, part company with the false or debased dollars, and disappear from the hands of the people whose government does not keep its faith or make its money tell the truth.

CHAPTER XXXI.

CAPITAL, CREDIT, AND INTEREST.

WE may suppose a number of men to go on a fishing-voyage. It is not enough that they possess skill and strength: they also need boats, fishing-tackle, and a stock of various supplies to live upon while they are gone. The wealth which is required to begin any enterprise, or to carry work through, is called *capital*.

Thus if a man proposes to be a farmer, he cannot succeed without some capital. If his land were given to him for nothing, he would still need farming-tools, cattle, and provisions enough to support him till he got his first harvest.

In the case of a great enterprise, like a factory or a railroad, an enormous capital must often be laid out to purchase materials and hire the labor of a large force of men before any return is made to those who expend their capital.

A barbarous people can make little progress, because there is not wealth or capital enough among them to draw upon in order to feed and clothe workmen. As long as every one is poor, men have to supply their own daily necessities. There must at least be laid by an accumulation of food before any great work can be undertaken.

The accumulation of capital. — Whoever produces more than he consumes accumulates capital; for example, a farmer may produce food enough for a dozen families, or a shoemaker can make shoes enough for a neighborhood. Wherever men labor, their industry accumulates capital, or produces and lays up a supply of produce or material to be drawn upon for further work. In the most simple society, the harvest of each year is the capital to provide against the needs of another year.

The use of machinery, and especially of steam, water, and electric power, enables a few workmen to do the work of armies of men, and so to accumulate capital on a grand scale.

Credit. — A man does not always need to have accumulated capital himself. If he can work, and is honest, he may find some one willing to make him a certain advance of money or provisions on the expectation that he will do work or business enough to repay. The amount of this advance is called his credit, and depends on his ability and character. Thus if he is a skilful fisherman, he may find some one who will lend him a boat. If he has at the same time a piece of property, as a lot of land, his credit will be greater; and some one will trust him with a vessel, without his needing to sell his property.

Thus a farmer owning his land and buildings may not only work his farm, but through his credit obtain additional capital to make improvements, and increase his products.

Or the owner of a mill may go to the bank and get money to buy raw material or to expend in wages to his men till his returns come back from the sale of his goods.

All this is made possible by credit, or the trust which men repose in one another's good faith in keeping their promises.

Corporations. — Many individuals, each with small earnings or savings, often combine together, and trust their capital to directors or trustees who manage for all as they would for themselves. Thus large masses of capital may be employed to use machinery, and pay many workmen, and both to produce and to save to better advantage than could be done with a small capital. Railroads, gas companies, cotton mills, savings banks, and many other corporations are formed by this kind of union among many individuals. These corporations for massing and using capital are made possible only where there is a considerable number of able and honorable men, who can be trusted to hold and manage the money of others.

Profits. — In most kinds of industry — in farming, for example — labor produces something more than its bare equivalent. There is a natural increase besides the cost of production. We call this surplus the *profit*. It is the encouragement which nature gives when man begins to work. Thus a farmer ought to be better off at the end of the year than he was at the beginning. There will be an increase of cattle and sheep and fowls. The amount of this increase will depend, not only upon his skill and intelligence, but also upon the capital which he has at his disposal. If he has money enough, he can employ extra labor to drain his boggy land; he can fertilize his fields; he can buy machinery, and harvest larger crops. For nature, by showers and sunshine and the richness in the soil, will always add something to encourage his enterprise; as, on the other hand, if he is lazy and dull, nature will prod him with various discomforts to urge him to labor and to learn.

So in other kinds of industry. Besides barely enough to support life, the patient fisherman will bear home a profit which he can dispose of to enable him to add to his capital. If he has already capital enough to buy the best sails and fishing-tackle, and intelligence to direct a number of men, he can increase the profits of his whole crew.

The merchant, likewise, who contrives to bring supplies of goods to the points where men need them most — from the farms where the owners are burning the corn for fuel to the towns where, without the corn, people would starve — will get more than the bare cost of his business and his living.

In short, the whole community, if intelligent and industrious, will do better than merely to live; it will be enriched by the natural increase or profit which nature gives for labor wisely expended.

This profit will be larger in proportion to the skill, education, patience, industry, and integrity of the people. It will tend to come to those who show these qualities, but will be reduced if many of the people lack them. It will not generally fall into the hands of those who are dull, incapable, shiftless, dishonest, or unwilling to work; it will certainly not stay long with such people.

Rent and interest. — We may suppose that a skilful young fisherman borrows a boat and tackle of a widow whose husband has been drowned, and goes fishing. When he returns, he shares his catch of fish with the men who went to help him, and with the woman who owns the boat. This is her *interest* in the fishing, on account of her boat. This would be the simplest form of interest. It would be the same in fact, however, if the fisherman, instead of paying a share of his catch in fish, engages to pay her a fixed sum for the use of the boat.

It would still be the same in case the fisherman, instead of hiring the boat, borrows from the widow the value of the boat in money. The young fisherman can then buy a boat for himself, and pay the widow the same sum for the use of her money, which he might have paid for the boat.

Likewise, if the widow had a farm which her husband had cleared and drained, or which he had paid for out of his earnings, some one might like to borrow the farm, and pay her a share of his harvest. He might thus do better for himself than if he took up wild lands. Or one might borrow of the widow in another way; for she might have sold the farm outright for money. He could then borrow the money that her farm brought, and buy a new farm for himself, and pay her so much every year for the use of the money, instead of paying for the use of the land.

By the use of the widow's capital, the fisherman or the farmer increases his product; without it he could not have made so much. He therefore, in fairness, shares with the owner of the capital. If he borrows a thing, a piece of property, or land, the share that he gives is usually called the *rent*. But if he borrows money, the return upon it is called *interest*. As we have before seen, money is practically an order to pay things or property, so that the borrower of money really borrows the things, whether boats, supplies, provisions, or materials, that he purchases with the money.

Thus the farmer who borrows money to improve his barn or buy stock really borrows fertilizers or cattle. The money is merely a convenience in making the exchanges. When at the end of the year he realizes larger harvests on account of these improvements, he owes a share as interest to the person whose labor or whose saving had enabled him to have the use of the money.

So with the mill that has borrowed money to buy cotton to make into cloth. Part of the returns must go to the savings bank; that is, to the persons who had gone without the use of the money themselves to lend to the mill. They deserve their share as well as the workmen who furnished the labor, or the superintendent who managed with his brains to make the mill a success.

The rate of interest. — It might be agreed that the interest or rent should depend upon the amount of the product, whether more or less, of the fishing-boat or the farm. The lender should have a certain share, and the workman another share, and the manager who borrowed the capital still another. This is done in some cases. All, then, would share in the risks and in the profits.

But suppose the widow who lends the boat or the money prefers to take a smaller fixed rent or interest rather than to share in the risks of the business, and sometimes, perhaps, fail to get anything. This is usually the case. The bank, for instance, lends its money at so much per cent; for instance, six dollars a year for every hundred. The borrower gives security, as a mortgage upon his farm, and takes all the risks himself. The bank then gets a regular return for its money to divide among the persons who have trusted their savings to its care. The borrower has all the profits, after paying his interest and his men.

How interest is fixed. — The amount of interest upon money, or the rent of capital, varies like all other prices. It depends upon the amount of money to be lent, whether it is plenty or scarce; upon the times, whether they are peaceful or stormy; upon the demand for money, whether few or many want to borrow; upon the security that can be given, whether there is much or little risk of being repaid; upon the prosperity of the community where the money is used, whether the profits of business there are large or small. Thus the same money which will only bring three per cent when loaned to the government in

London might bring five or six per cent if loaned to a private person; or, sent to a new growing country like Australia, might get ten per cent or more. If the lender shares at all in the risk, he also shares in the larger profits. If he wishes perfect security, and the borrower takes all the chances, he must be content with a small regular share.

Usury. — Interest now means the price paid for the use of capital; but it once had a bad name, — *usury*. For in old times, before the science of money was understood, many supposed that it might be wrong to exact interest upon money, although no one saw any harm in taking interest, that is, rent for property or land or boats. Money was scarce; and many lenders also were extortionate, and took cruel advantage of their debtors. Laws were therefore often passed, forbidding more than a certain rate of interest. To take higher interest than the law allowed was then called usury. But these laws never did any more good than the laws which governments used to pass to fix the prices of other things. In many of our States such laws still remain, although they are constantly disregarded.

The fact is, that all prices of money, land, labor, or products depend upon " the law of supply and demand." Ten per cent may therefore be as fair interest on the Pacific coast, where the demand is great, as five per cent is in New York. In New York, too, money may be better worth six or seven per cent in a good year of business than five per cent in a very dull year. Neither can any legislature compel a man to lend his money or his land unless a fair return is offered him.

The widow, for instance, will not risk her property with the fisherman if she can do better with it herself. Neither would it be fair to require her to lend it at six per cent if he were able to make twelve per cent with it.

In general, the rate of interest upon good security tends to diminish. This is because civilization produces such large capital and vast credit that all reasonable enterprises can get what they need.

If interest is low, other things are also likely to be low; and no one has to pay so much for hiring his house or for the cost of living. But if the interest is high, every one who has a dollar in the savings bank or a single share in a corporation shares in the increase. This is because the whole community is linked together, so that whatever affects the whole affects each one.

Should the government lend money to its citizens?— It is sometimes thought that the government ought to use its credit and borrow money to loan to needy citizens, for instance, to poor farmers, at a low rate of interest. There are two serious objections to this. One is that the government, that is, all the people would often be in danger of losing both principal and interest. The second objection is that, when merchants and others must pay five and six per cent, it is not fair to help any class of the people to borrow money for two or three per cent. This would be the same as giving presents to one part of the people at the expense of all.

CHAPTER XXXII.

LABOR AND COMPETITION.

The law of life. — The general rule is, that men must work for their living. The amount of work required may vary with men's wants, or with the climate in which they live. A native of Samoa may get all the breadfruit and cocoanuts that he needs with very little effort. But the higher the standard of civilization, the more things men want; and the more labor therefore becomes necessary.

The use of machinery, with the forces of steam and electricity, does not serve to change the general law. For the more men learn to save by the use of machines, the more their needs increase, so that the demand for labor still continues. Thus when cloth could only be woven slowly by hand, men could have very little. But now that water power or steam can be made to weave cloth, every one wants much more, so that men and women still have to work for their clothing.

The law that men must work for their living, though at first it may seem severe, proves to be a kindly law; as on the playground, those who join in the play, not only are stronger, but enjoy more than those who only look on and watch the others. Even persons confined in prison must have a certain amount of work in order to keep well.

Labor and wages. — If any large number of people should stop working, the whole supply of the nation would be cut down. Those who did work, as well as those who did not, could not have as much. Wages and salaries, therefore, would fall. On the contrary, it is evident that the larger the number of the workers is, and the more they accomplish, — the fewer the drones in the hive, — the greater is the product, and the more on the whole every one will have. All wages, therefore, will tend to rise. It is the same with a nation as it is with the household of a farmer. If all his children work, they will have produce to sell, and will grow prosperous. The reason is seen here why wages are higher in the United States than in Europe. It is because our whole product is greater.

Labor and wealth. — Moreover, besides the increase of men's needs and wants, there is a constant increase in their numbers, requiring new lands to be opened, new houses to be built, and new mills to saw lumber or weave cloth. If all the wealth of the richest nation were divided equally, it would therefore last but a short time before men would have to go to work to make more wealth. The richest nation is thus only in the condition of a farmer who has on hand a rather better supply of tools, stock, and farm buildings. But because he has this better supply, even more care is required to keep them in order, and more constant labor in using them. Thus, though the richer farmer lives better than his slovenly neighbor, he must still work equally hard or even harder, like the winning crew in a race.

A common fallacy. — It is sometimes imagined that it would be better for those who work if their numbers could be restricted. They fancy that they could then have better pay. Or it is thought that the workmen would be better off if they worked fewer hours a day. There are exceptional cases where this may seem true for a little while.

But it is obvious that the fewer laborers there are, the less will be the product of the nation. If only half as many men make shoes, there will be fewer shoes for all. If ten million men work, and five million are idle, the latter will have to be fed by the others, with less food to go around. In short, the more intelligent labor is used, the greater must be the product which all will at last share.

The reduction of the hours of labor. — On the other hand, there is a limit beyond which men do not work efficiently. They will not work to advantage if wearied, oppressed, or discontented. Free men will do more work in eight hours, putting good-will or interest into their work, than in ten or twelve hours of slave labor.

The general duty of labor. — It follows that every one ought to contribute his share towards the sum of the product of the nation. For if any one only eats and drinks and enjoys, but does not labor, he makes the nation poorer. To work is indeed a necessity if one is poor, but it is an honorable obligation equally upon the rich. That a man is rich, gives him no right to consume or lessen the wealth of the nation. On the contrary, his wealth, like the richer farmer's tools and stock, is an added reason why he should do a larger share for the good of the whole.

Different kinds of laborers. — The word *laborer* properly covers all kinds of service in behalf of the household or the community. In the larger sense not only the miner, the stevedore, the farmer, or the blacksmith, but also the clerk, the book-keeper, the teacher, the superintendent of the mill, the president of the bank, the trustees of property, are laborers or workmen. Socrates the philosopher, and Tennyson the poet, Macaulay the historian, and Darwin the naturalist, all have added each in his way to the resources of mankind.

Disturbances in industry. — It is difficult to divide the labor of the nation equally, so that each shall do his fair share. For some are more willing or more capable than others. Some are quicker in finding their proper places. If any part of the body fails to take its share of the burden, strain comes upon all the rest. Moreover, if the body is exposed to sudden change, the circulation is checked and one suffers a chill. So in a great industrial society, any sudden change of conditions is likely to cause disturbance. Thus there are frequent changes in the demands for labor. There will be a need of wheat, or of boots and shoes, and many will start wheat-farms, or go into the shoe-shops, till presently there is more wheat or more boots and shoes than are called for. Every new invention or improvement, however beneficial in the long run, is apt to cause disturbance and inconvenience for a time. Thus if the farmer buys a reaping-machine, he will not need to hire so many men, who may not at first find a new employment. The use of steam has multiplied the power of the world, but it has also caused a great deal of disturbance to the old-fashioned kinds of industry that worked by hand.

So again, there may often be too many men trying to get a living in the cities, where expenses are greater than in the country. Or there may be more lawyers or architects than the nation needs till it grows larger, and the extra lawyers need to find something else to do. This irregularity causes inconvenience and trouble and often serious suffering.

Business crises. — It is said that "there are tides in the affairs of men." So business and work have their high and low tides. This is partly because men have not yet learned to see far enough ahead to provide exactly the amount of wheat, iron, and other materials that they need. There are not likely to be too many people to work, but there may easily be too many workers in certain industries. The law of supply and demand acts in such cases to cut down profits and wages, and to turn men from employments where they are less needed to those where they are more needed. Meanwhile, during the process of change, work stops, thousands of men are thrown out of employment, less wealth is therefore created, business becomes dull, merchants fail, the mills which are not well managed go into bankruptcy, and new enterprises are checked. Thus whenever men work too fast or unwisely, in any direction, a period of reaction is likely to set in till the right proportions can be adjusted; as when one uses the muscles of his arm to exhaustion, and rest must be enforced till they recover their tone.

The free system. — Whenever men are quite free to get a living or to pursue wealth as each chooses, this is commonly called *competition*. This really means *free industry*. Thus any one may choose his own trade or profession, or if he does not like it, he may change. He is free to work hard or not; he may make his own bargains and set his price upon the value of his labor or his products. He is free to acquire property to any extent, or to part with it. He is free to invest his money wherever he thinks that it will bring him the largest return, in the land or on the sea, or to hoard it, if he can afford to be so foolish. If any one by working harder, or by his skill, or by intelligence, can make better wages than his neighbor, he is free to live better; as his neighbor is free to follow his example and to learn to excel him in turn. If any one has a genius like Rothschild, for handling and managing money, he is free to exercise his genius, as another is free to handle his tools.

The law of free industry. — Any one is free to work when he chooses and at such terms as he can make for himself, provided he does not interfere with the rights of other men. He is not free to snatch what belongs to them, or, being stronger, to push them aside, or trip them up, or hinder their freedom. As he may not interfere with them by force, so he ought not to hinder or oppress them by fraud, or by getting laws passed to the disadvantage of others; as on the playground, the rule is that all boys shall be free to play as they like, only so as not to interfere with each other's games.

The good side of freedom. — The freer men are to choose their work and to use and enjoy its results. the more work they are willing to do. Their energy and enterprise are called out, their wits are sharpened, their hopes are stirred. If any one wins unusual success, others are encouraged to try better methods. If any one enjoys his money, his neighbors are urged to work the harder, that they and their children may have the same enjoyment. Thus every one accomplishes more work in a condition of freedom, and the whole nation is richer, than if customs, like slavery and caste, or a system of laws, fettered and restricted men and compelled them to work according to rule. This is on the same principle that children enjoy their sports better, when left to themselves, than if a parent or teacher were to meddle and make rules for them.

As a matter of fact, wherever men are thus free to work, to earn, and to save or use their earnings as they please, the capable, the industrious, the temperate, and the intelligent everywhere tend to rise to prosperity. A considerable and increasing class become "capitalists" by the value of their houses or shops, or the amount of money in the bank. The skilful are always in demand, and at good wages. In fact, a day's labor never purchased so much in supplies as it does in the United States, where we use the free or competitive system of work.

The moral side. — Besides, when men labor, earn, and save or spend with perfect freedom, they develop many moral qualities, such as patience, self-reliance, self-sacrifice, venturesomeness, integrity, respect for others' rights, generosity. The slaves of the kindest master could not develop these qualities so well. If a committee or government of the wisest men could manage and make rules for the rest, and provide for every one's necessities, men would not learn to exhibit these sterling qualities of manhood so well as by being thrown upon their own resources. We know this also from the fact that the strongest characters have been worked out in brave and patient conflict, often with difficult circumstances; whereas the men who have never been thrown upon their own resources rarely amount to anything.

Certain evils. — If some are free to work hard and earn more, others must be free to work less and earn little; as, if boys race, some will come in behind. It may be that those who get less will be jealous and suspicious of the success of the others. Instead of trying again and doing better, they may fall into the ranks of the discontented, like sulky children. This happens in some cases with men of small natures, however fair, honorable, and merited the success of the others may be.

The men at the bottom. — It is a wonder that we have learned to feed and clothe the population of great towns or of vast armies. But such a task is always attended with difficulty and the risk of occasional suffering through mistakes and accidents. Our free system does not work perfectly, or as well as it ought.

In a crowded city like London or New York there are generally more workmen than there is work to be done. This is partly because new people, frequently foreigners, are constantly coming into the city. They cannot find employment as fast as they come. In such cases competition brings much suffering. Men and women, who must live, will accept work for a meagre pittance; then the wages of others are cut down. This is because men are free to seek a living where they please. If they were not free, fewer could be allowed to press into the city. If men, therefore, choose to be free, they must sometimes suffer the consequences of their freedom.

It seems very hard that evil consequences should so often fall upon the poor and ignorant. This fact is a constant incentive to better education, since faithful and skilled men and women more readily find occupation. It also prevents the more prosperous from selfish contentment; for there can be no assured health in the great body politic while any considerable number of individuals are allowed to suffer.

Two kinds of competition. — There are two kinds of competition in vogue. One is like that of brutes who struggle with each other. It is as if there were a table with just so much food spread upon it, and men tried to get as much as they can for themselves, by pushing and crowding the others. There are thus always some men in a community who seek to make their living at the expense, or by the loss, or out of the labor, of others, like the robber barons who once infested the valley of the Rhine. Not only the laws now restrain violence, oppression, and fraud, but public opinion is growing to condemn men who seek to live by getting away the property of others. Public opinion is even more effective than laws;

for men, like boys, are ashamed to do what their fellows regard as mean and despicable. So far, however, as public opinion praises men who manage to snatch more than their share, and calls them "smart," men, like boys, will do as their fellows permit.

The competition of men; emulation. — The competition of brutes is to get away what the others possess. The competition of men is to do more and better work; it is to economize material and power; it is to add to the sum of human wealth and enjoyment. In the competition of men every one in the end becomes better off; besides those who excel, the level of all is raised and the opportunities of all are enlarged. The object of intelligent men is not, therefore, to snatch the food from the limited supply on the table, but to heap the table with larger and more varied supplies. Thus the world says to each individual, " You are free to gather all that you can from the land, the sea, the mines, and beds of ore. You can use and enjoy as your own whatever you gather, for we know that the more each one has and uses and enjoys, the more all will have."

CHAPTER XXXIII.

THE GRIEVANCES OF THE POOR.

The two extremes. — The condition of mankind in barbarous times was that of constant peril from disease and famine. Men frequently could not have known where their bread would come from. Our present civilization has not yet succeeded in raising all above this chronic condition of danger in which our forefathers once generally lived. We have seen that there are many, especially in the cities, whose meagre wages barely keep them off the verge of want. They cannot always get work. Frequently their wages are cut down, or they are thrown suddenly out of employment.

There are thus two extremes in society, — one made up of those who live in luxury, and have even more than they need or deserve, and the other of those whose toil seems to be hopeless. Justice and humanity alike raise the question, how this very unequal distribution of wealth can be kept from working cruelty.

The socialists. — In some countries there are many who are bitterly discontented about these things. They are sometimes called socialists: some of them are called communists. They all believe that something must be wrong in a community which allows some to grow so rich while many remain in abject want.

There are various divisions among the socialists. A few who have suffered from bad government, like the Russian nihilists, favor revolution. Some, the anarchists, do not believe at all in governments, with armies and police to enforce laws, but think that men would behave better, if they were quite free of the control of the state. Some go to the opposite extreme, and believe that the state should own all the capital, and furnish every one with work and supplies. Others think it is a great abuse that individuals can own the land and make others pay rent for it. They would have all the land owned by the community, and no one could have any land which he did not use. Every one should then pay a fair rent to the government, that is, to all the people, to be expended in place of the taxes, for the benefit of all.

Others claim that the government should own the rail-roads, the telegraph, the gas and water-works, and perhaps also the mines and factories, and other property, now worked by great companies. The government could then furnish employment to laborers with fair wages and shorter hours of work.

In general, whoever wishes to add to the kinds of wealth which all the people own together, is so far a socialist. In a free and civilized country most men are partly socialists, inasmuch as all favor common schools, parks, public buildings, sewage, water-works, and the post-office, and in fact, a common government.

The men and the system. — It is well, before a man pulls down or alters his house, to find what part of the inconvenience from which he suffers is owing to the fault of the house, and how much comes from his own negligence. It is also necessary to have some clear plan of what he will build in place of the old building, and how he will make the change. It is evident that one cause of men's poverty and distress lies in the fact that the individual men and women who make up society are as yet very imperfect. The whole body cannot be sound and well unless the parts are also sound.

The inefficient. — There is everywhere a class of ne'er-do-well people, feeble in body or mind, lacking in energy or skill. Their most serious misfortune is not in being poor, but in their want of life. If there are many of the inefficient, as there are in certain tribes of savages, the whole community is poor.

The ignorant. — So, too, if a large proportion of people are ignorant. For the ignorant not only cannot earn or produce as much as the intelligent, but they also waste food, fuel, money, and life itself, in a thousand ways. If, then, a people, or a single household, had the best arrangements possible, they could not succeed in acquiring wealth, as long as they were ignorant.

The idle. — There is a certain proportion of idle or lazy persons who do not care to study or read, or sometimes even to play, but prefer to watch others; least of all, do they care to work. The more of these there are, the harder must others work. However excellent our social arrangements were, the idle would tend to keep us poor. If their own needs no longer urged them to work, it is to be feared that the arm of the law would be needful to compel them, as in the army, where uncomfortable discipline has to be enforced.

The unfortunate. — There are many who, without being imbecile or inefficient, are, through sickness, accidents, losses, and the death of friends, from time to time rendered helpless. Among these are widows and orphans who are perhaps permanently unable to earn their living. All these necessarily lower the average of the prosperity of the community. Others must cheerfully work the harder in order to make good their misfortunes. But no mere change in the arrangement of property will remove this class.

The vicious. — Besides the cost of prisons and police, the labor of the community has to bear the constant burden of all the vices which waste property, destroy health, and ruin character. Drunkenness alone is the cause of a large proportion of the poverty.

On the other hand, vice, and especially drunkenness and idleness, are apt to prevail whenever many are discontented or suffer injustice or oppression; as boys do not behave as well unless they believe in the fairness of their teacher. So it is necessary that men should have confidence that the arrangements of society are on the whole just.

A problem. — The individuals who make human society are more or less imperfect, only partly educated, partially successful or happy. No plan will therefore give us perfect results till the individuals are better; as a crew cannot row successfully in the best boat unless the rowers are all strong and skilful. Can we now contrive any new plan or improvement by which all can have and enjoy more? Before we answer this question we need to see the main objects to be secured by human society.

The objects of society. — One object is material, that is, an abundant supply of all sorts of products. If, then, our present arrangement barely gives an average of forty cents a day to each person, we should still require as large or larger supplies. We want, therefore, to be quite certain that men would do as much work under another system as they do now.

No perfect justice with imperfect men. — Another object to be secured is justice and the contentment felt when every one receives it. We fail of justice as long as some have more and others less than they deserve. But we should not secure justice or contentment by sharing alike, however much or little each did. Neither is any one nor any number of men wise and good enough to award perfect justice and remove all discontent.

Freedom and manhood. — The greatest of all objects to be gained by human society is manhood or character. We want capable, faithful, patriotic, and disinterested men and women, since a state made up of such citizens will be stronger, richer, and happier. We have seen that a large freedom stimulates character, as fresh air stimulates physical life. If any new system could even increase our supplies, it would still need to be shown that it would also make our people more energetic, capable, generous, and high-minded.

It is with men as with children. If they abuse or waste their playthings, or cheat with their marbles, the remedy is not in taking the playthings away from them, or in compelling them to change their game for a new one. What we want is not to prevent them by force from cheating or abusing their sports, but to train them to play with skill and fairness.

Faith or trust in men. — Human society is bound together by justice and confidence. We trust, on the whole, that our fellow-men will do right; that if we show them evident wrongs, they will be fair enough to correct them; that if help is needed for the unfortunate, they will cheerfully render it. If men cannot be trusted in the long run to do right of their own will, no laws or rules or systems can be trusted. For men must make and enforce the rules. But if men can be trusted voluntarily to do justice, the fewer rules we make to bind and compel them, the better they will behave; like students trusted by the college, who respond better to trust than to rules or force.

Our laws, then, are for the exceptional cases of those who cannot be trusted; but society, as a whole, ought to be like the model school, where rules are least needed. This is the idea of our free society. This could not well be under any plan which gave to the government the control of the work and the wealth, as well as the power to command the idle or unwilling.

Summary. — However much we desire to cure injustice, or to bring relief to the poor, we must still seek to preserve the greatest possible freedom, since we cannot make men just by compulsion. We cannot cure one kind of injustice by doing another kind. If we knew that some one had more wealth than he deserved, this would not make it right for his neighbors to appropriate his wealth by a majority vote.

It is probable that the permanent common wealth will largely increase, at least in the form of schoolhouses, hospitals, museums, public grounds, and buildings. No one can foresee sufficiently to be sure that various offices, now performed by great corporations of individuals, may not sometime be advantageously performed by the whole body of the people.

The fact seems to be that, when all are faithful and honest enough to be trusted to act freely as individuals, all can then be trusted to act justly together. Neither can all work together, without doing each other any injustice, unless the individuals have first learned to be just; as the boys of a club cannot play well together till all its members are willing to do their share of the work.

CHAPTER XXXIV.

THE ABUSES AND THE DUTIES OF WEALTH.

The significance of property.—Property gives its possessor a lien on the produce of the world. Besides the share which his work or skill buys, he is also entitled to an extra share representing his property. He may even do nothing, and yet draw from the world an income equal to the value of the labor of scores or hundreds of men. It is as if the world carried a mortgage upon its shoulders. If one thinks of all the products of the world as put into a vast pile, a certain part of the pile must be given to the owners of property. On the other hand, the pile is larger on account of the property which has been used as capital. The owners of property have furnished necessary tools, machinery, and materials. The property-owners have often made the tools by their skill, or invented the machinery, or gathered the material by their frugality. So far as this has been the case, no one grudges them their larger share in the products. Neither is any one poorer because they have more.

The rich.—A few rich men in every community often possess a disproportionate share of all the property. This is true on a small scale in a fishing-village or among farmers. It is partly on account of good fortune, by which one man out of a hundred finds the school of fish or the nugget of gold. It is partly the result of training and character, since only the few know how to manage and keep their property. It is partly also because property, like a snowball, after it has rolled up to a certain size, tends to grow very fast.

Besides those who are rich through the ownership of property, such as houses and lands, there is a considerable class who are practically rich through the large incomes which genius, special ability, or skill enables them to draw. The voice of a great singer, the acumen of a great lawyer, the insight of a physician, or the rare administrative ability of a railroad superintendent, naturally brings the same sort of exceptional income as the possession of visible property, and raises its possessor into the class of the rich. Rare skill or genius, in fact, like good fortune, is a natural inequality, making one man to differ from others.

The rich who have done no service. — The custom of mankind has not only allowed men themselves to enjoy the advantage of wealth or exceptional ability, but also to give property to others, and especially to their children. Many are therefore rich who have done no more service themselves for the enrichment of mankind than if they had not been born. In some cases the law of inheritance has doubtless made children rich by fortunes, like those of pirates or gamblers, which their fathers had acquired by fraud. The truth is, that if it is deemed best to permit the good and deserving to grow rich, and to transmit their wealth to their children, the dishonest will sometimes do the same.

The different uses of wealth. —There is no danger to a family, in case one of the children takes better care of his toys than the others, or is ingenious and makes playthings for himself, and so possesses more than the rest. For the whole household has more resources than if he had less. It would be quite different if the ingenious boy undertook to get away the toys and playthings that belonged to the others. There are two kinds of uses, likewise, which may be made of their wealth by the rich.

One use is to make the great pile of the products of the world larger, in which case every one will be better off. Thus if a millionnaire were to lay out his income in building houses, although he might grow still richer by the rent from the houses, the city would be richer, and every one might have better and cheaper shelter. So if he built a mill, gave work to a thousand men, and made flour or cloth.

But suppose the rich man used the power of his wealth to get away what others possessed; suppose that he bought up all the houses in order to charge a higher rent; or suppose he and others with him owned a railroad and refused to take corn to market unless the farmer paid a ruinous charge; or suppose that rich men bought all the salt-springs, so as to tax every one in the country for their own selfish benefit. This would be to create a *monopoly*.

Monopolies, good and bad. — It is a monopoly when one or a few hold and control the use of any valuable thing. A monopoly is not always bad or unfair. Jenny Lind's voice was thus a sort of natural monopoly. It gave her the opportunity to become very rich. The laws also confer a monopoly upon an inventor or author. No one can use the invention or publish the book without paying the man who holds the patent or copyright. The laws even give the inventor the right to charge more than is fair if he chooses. There are many monopolies, however, which are plainly oppressive. If Robinson Crusoe had secured the only spring of water upon his island, and refused to let new colonists have water without working for him, this would be a cruel monopoly. So whenever men buy up some great article of universal necessity, like rice, coffee, or quinine, in order to get their own price out of other's pockets; or, again, when they get laws passed compelling every one to use the product of their mines or their mills.

The limit of monopolies. — The great moral laws which govern the world limit monopolies. If the monopoly is abused, it checks or kills itself. The great singer may ask too large a price; the author or the inventor may charge so much as to stop his sales. The railroad will not make so much money by high rates as by carrying more goods at fair rates; or if its rates are exorbitant, another road may be built. The salt or the sugar must not cost too much, or people will send abroad to get their supplies. This is in case the monopoly is not protected by force or by law. But if the laws make the monopoly, giving advantages to one or to the few, or to a class of nobles or rich men, the only remedy is in making the laws equal for all.

Land monopoly. — It sometimes happens in a city that one man or a few, owning land needed for building, hold it so as either to keep it out of the market and arrest the growth of the city, or else to require unreasonable prices. This makes a monopoly. The owners may finally lease their land, so as to draw a large income from the business of the city.

So when men get control of great tracts of fertile land, or of timber, or of mines. The time may come when these men have a monopoly, and can therefore demand their own price for the land. This price has to come out of other men's pockets. For the men who hold the land monopoly do not add to the wealth of the world, or confer any benefit by holding their property out of the market.

The cure of land monopolies. — The laws may be made either to encourage monopolists of land or to discourage them. It rests largely with the assessors of taxes to see that the men who hold more land than they really use, hoping to make money by keeping it, shall pay as much into the treasury as would be paid if the land were sold to those who would put buildings upon it or cultivate it.

The rivalry of the rich. — As kings used foolishly to fight with each other to extend their domain, so the rich may employ their wealth to ruin each other's property, or in the hope of winning more at others' loss. Thus fortunes sometimes change hands on Wall Street as at a gambling-table. Or men contrive to injure the trade or the business of their rivals, and even to drive them into bankruptcy, or to make it unprofitable for them to run their mills. This sort of struggle plainly does not make the pile of the product of the world larger, but lessens the general wealth and often produces great hardship, as in any kind of war.

Waste by the rich. — A great fortune may be like a great reservoir in which the water is stored for further use to irrigate the fields. But suppose the man uses his great income for his own indulgence, for his whims and fancies, like the famous mad king of Bavaria. Suppose he spends it in costly banquets, or locks it up in private pleasure-grounds. Even so he cannot spend without giving his money back, through the goods he pays for and the men whom he hires. Nevertheless, his waste and extravagance become a public loss. For while the investments of his income in new buildings or railroads cheapen prices and rents, his expense for extra service and luxuries makes prices dearer for others.

We can imagine the evils of gigantic wealth to be such that the community would be forced to erect some limit or safeguard against the abuse of money — as we do in the case of the insane, or to guard against a public enemy; nevertheless, the peculiar evils of riches in the hands of a few depend mainly upon the character of the rich men, and disappear when they are wise, just, and public spirited; as power in the mayor or president is only dangerous in case of his incapacity or injustice.

Capitalists. — The poor man begins to be rich as soon as he has acquired any kind of property, as tools, or land, or a house. He then becomes a capitalist. He may be an owner of shares in the great railroad for which he works. The bank or railroad company in which he is an owner may possess more property than any man in the state. Like the rich man's fortune, so the company composed of many little capitalists is a reservoir for accumulating and using money. It has also some of the same dangers of wasting its resources, or of using its power to fight with others, or of making monopolies, or even controlling legislation. It is not, therefore, the rich who are to be feared so much as wasteful, reckless, or unscrupulous men, whether they have much or little.

The duties of wealth. — The possession of wealth is not merely a right which certain ones enjoy, or a luxury of which a few accidentally may have more than their share. Wealth imposes certain obvious duties upon its possessor.

Trusteeship. — There are in the United States hundreds of millionnaires, holding the title to a large proportion of the land, banks, railroads, mines, and factories. Their actual or personal services to the community cannot generally have been worth as much money as they possess. They may, therefore, justly be considered as so many trustees, having for the time the care and management of the accumulation of the wealth of the whole community. This great fund, as we have seen, is partly the product of human labor and thought, and partly the bounty of nature. It is morally sacred for purposes of good. The fact that this obligation is not legal, but moral, makes it more honorable. The idea of trusteeship does not apply merely to millionnaires. Every person is responsible for all that he uses or spends.

So far as rich men acknowledge and act under this obligation of trusteeship, there is no hardship in their acquiring and holding as much wealth as they please. Moreover, if any one is a foolish or incapable trustee, the general rule is that his wealth goes out of his hands, as power disappears from one who does not know how to use it.

Service. — We have seen that the possession of property gives no one a right to lead a useless or idle life. On the contrary, however much one inherits or accumulates, one is bound to the universal duty of some kind of service in making the world better, richer, or happier. The more wealth one possesses, the meaner he therefore is, like the stronger or older brother in the household, if he does no good with his money, or if he makes of himself only a bigger drone in the hive.

Sharing. — The trusteeship of property makes it shameful for any intelligent person to lavish expense upon himself. So with unnecessary exclusiveness, especially with regard to grounds, paintings, and works of art. That a man should attempt by his wealth to fence out the public from a great forest, or appropriate for himself alone a tract of seashore, betrays the selfishness of a small mind. The rarer products of wealth ought to be held with a generous consideration towards the community upon whose labor wealth is based. We appeal here to the same principles of honor and kindliness which hold in every home and schoolroom. If it is better to let the child own his knife or ball for which he is responsible, it is still his duty to share its use with the others, as it is wrong to lock it up for his own pleasure.

Public munificence. — It was the custom of the Athenians to expect of their richer men to undertake certain special kinds of public expense, as the fitting out of a trireme, or the cost of a festival. So in our times there is a just expectation that no rich man will live and die without some worthy public benefactions. A generous public spirit should spare the rich the envy of their poorer neighbors.

It is not merely generosity to give; it is the return of an obligation, or the discharge of a trust. For much of the accumulated wealth of the world has arisen from the toil and effort of the men of the past, from whom we all inherit. A portion is always due, therefore, not only for present needs, but also to keep good what we have inherited, in special provision for the future, — for public works and buildings; for schools and colleges; for works of philanthropy or religion. The more property one has, the larger his honorable responsibility for these purposes.

How property ought to be distributed. — That community would not be most prosperous and happy in which all had precisely the same income, for this is not just; nor where the state held everything, and the individual's freedom to follow his natural bent was taken away. But the truest prosperity would come about, where the laws gave free scope to the skill and energy of the people in earning wealth; where, among rich and poor alike, least money was wasted and squandered; and where the accumulated wealth came to be distributed, according to each man's wisdom, integrity, and capacity for using it well. In such conditions, if the wiser and more able were also friendly and considerate, no one could fall into grievous poverty, and no rich man who held himself as a trustee of his wealth could use it for oppression. Thus the free system of acquiring and holding wealth promises to work out justice and happiness, as fast as individuals learn to be fair, and to do by others as they wish others to do by them. Whereas, unless there are plenty of such fair-minded individuals, there can be no happiness or prosperity enforced by rules, whether made by a sovereign like the Emperor of Germany, or by the majority of a republic.

CHAPTER XXXV.

BUYERS AND SELLERS; OR, THE MUTUAL BENEFIT.

THERE are two theories of the conduct of business. One theory is, that each party in trade aims to get an advantage over his neighbor: one should try to get as much and give as little as possible. If goods are defective, the seller should conceal the fact. The only rights which this theory of business recognizes are legal rights. One must not overreach far enough to come within the penalties of the law. Otherwise, so far as the law does not prescribe, the other party to a bargain must look out for himself.

The notion underlying this theory of business is that whatever one makes, the other loses. As in gambling it is thought to be for the interest of the winner that all the others should lose, so in business it is sometimes supposed that the successful merchant grows rich at the expense of his neighbors. Business is thus a game in which every one is trying to win. The laws are merely the rules of the game.

The idea of business. — The fact is, that buyers and sellers perform mutual services to each other. Mercantile business is not a game, but an industry, like farming or manufacturing. The merchant increases the value of goods by bringing them to market. He therefore deserves wages or salary for the services which he renders in collecting and distributing his goods. He receives his wages in the form of the surplus of his sales over their cost. The larger

his sales and the greater his skill, — that is, the more valuable his services, — the greater his income deserves to be.
The law of supply and demand regulates this.   The income
of merchants is not, however, uniform. Sometimes it is
less than the equivalent of the work and cost which they
have spent, and sometimes much more. In the long run,
it is nearly the same as equal labor, skill, and experience
would produce in any other industry.

It follows that what the merchant honestly makes is not
at any one's expense or loss. The wheat gathered in the
warehouses is actually worth more than in the farmers'
granaries. Neither the farmer, therefore, nor any one else
has lost by the merchant's profit in the purchase and sale
of the wheat. So with all other products.

The rights of buyers and sellers. — The earliest kind
of trade was barter. In barter each party was both buyer
and seller. In fair barter each shared the mutual advantage of the exchange ; as, for example, a pack of skins for
a sack of wheat. So in modern trade, which is only a
more complicated kind of barter. In a fair sale the buyer
and seller divide the value of a mutual advantage between
them : each, therefore, ought to be better off than before.
If any dealer, as a rule, got for himself the whole advantage of his bargains, it would be the same as getting what
did not belong to him.

It follows that all overreaching, even though the laws
do not specify it, is an attempt to get what belongs to
another. The sale of goods which are defective or below
the standard — the adulteration of food or the watering
of milk — is not trade, but an attempt to get what belongs to others. So, too, of purchasers who seek to beat
prices down to less than the cost of goods : they not only
try to get what belongs to others, but they tempt men to
cheat them.

The interests of buyers and sellers. — It is not only just that buyers and sellers should share in the mutual advantage of their bargains, it is also for their interest. This is the meaning of the proverb, that honesty is the best policy. Thus business is best when every class gets fair pay for its services. If the farmers do not get their share of the proceeds of their labor, the merchants will feel the loss in the end in the diminution of business. This is also true in individual cases, because, as a rule, men appreciate just treatment, and tend to do as they are done by. In a community where men aim to share equitably, there is a general increase of values, and there is, therefore, more wealth to share.

Legitimate and illegitimate business. — It follows that only those kinds of business are righteous which result in benefit to the public. A business which does no good on the whole, or which even results in harm or loss to the community, no just man ought to engage in. It makes no difference with this principle, that custom and the laws sometimes allow harmful business. Thus when no laws forbade the sale of powder, firearms, and liquor to savages, the business was no less bad in its effects. So if the owner of a building rents it for an injurious purpose, as, for example, a low drinking-saloon.

The law of supply and demand, or competition in buying and selling. — One can imagine all the cattle of the country to be in the hands of a few families, who have cattle and nothing else. They must therefore have wheat and other supplies from the farmers. They begin by exchanging with the nearest farmer at his own price, which happens to give him a large profit. A second farmer presently appears and offers his wheat for less; and the first farmer, rather than not sell, reduces his price.

Thus, after a time, by competition, the farmers fix a price as low as they can afford. Henceforward the exchange of cattle and wheat regulates itself according to the plenty or scarcity of the one product and the other. If the cattle men have a good year, they can afford to furnish cattle at a lower price; if wheat is scarce, it must be dearer.

It is in some such way as this that the prices of all sorts of things are fixed. The more valuable or the rarer a thing is,—in other words, the more work it costs to obtain it,—the higher the price which is fixed upon it. If the demand is so great that many set to work to supply it, and it presently becomes plentiful, or if the demand falls, the price is lowered accordingly. Thus, once iron was scarce and costly, till men learned to produce it on a great scale; the more iron mines were worked, the cheaper became all sorts of iron ware. So there was once great profit in trading on foreign shores, as in China; but as more ships were built and plenty of tea was brought home, the profits finally fell so that it scarcely paid better to build ships than to build houses.

Selling in the dearest market.—We may suppose that a farmer raises fruit and vegetables, which few of his neighbors in the country care to buy. But a few miles away, in the town, there are many people who need his products. Their demand, being active, will allow the farmer a good price. This is because he brings his fruits where they are most wanted. If now he can send to the great city, and if he can furnish fruit of superior quality for persons who demand the best articles, he will reap still better prices. The "dearest market," then, is wherever the demand or need is greatest. Whoever will take the pains to meet such a demand will be well paid. The dearest market, also, is usually, though not always, where people can best afford to pay a higher price. Thus the dearest market for the farmer and fisherman is in the city, where most money is. It is therefore an advantage to both buyer and seller for goods to be brought to the dearest markets.

Buying in the cheapest market. — The cheapest market is where there is a most plentiful supply. The cheapest market for the fish is on the shore when the fishing-boats come in. Here, then, is the place to buy to best advantage. The best place, likewise, to buy clothing is in the great shop where clothing is piled on the shelves. Whoever will buy where goods are plentiful, that is, cheapest, accommodates the seller also, who wants money instead of his goods. Thus it is to the advantage of every one when purchasers buy in the cheapest market. If, however, many purchasers crowd into the cheap market so that the goods become scarce, it is fair to all to raise the prices. In this case those buy the goods who need them or care most for them; but those who can get along without them do not buy, or purchase something else, or they seek a cheaper, that is, more plentiful, market. Meanwhile, as soon as prices rise, men set to work to provide a cheaper market again; in other words, to furnish a fresh and larger supply.

The attempt of men to sell in the dearest market and to buy in the cheapest, constantly works to bring goods of all kinds precisely where they are most wanted, and also to distribute money where it is needed. It is a part of the great natural process through which the result of the work of the world is divided.[1] It is like the circulation of the blood in the body, which is always seeking to flow where there is a hunger for it or a loss to be replaced.

[1] See Chapter XXVIII., pages 188 and 189.

Freedom in trade. — In barbarous times it was so perilous and costly to travel, and transportation of goods involved such risks, that men might perish within a few miles of a cheap market. For many centuries, also, there were so many tolls collected of merchants and so many custom-houses on the border of every little state, that men could not afford to bring their supplies, where they were wanted, to the dearest market. There was, therefore, great poverty and suffering, as when tight cords restrict the flow of the blood to the limbs.

Civilization cuts the cord and gives the body freedom to act. It makes the turnpikes and bridges free for all; it unites the little states into great nations; it builds great lines of railway. In the United States there is perfect freedom of trade among all the States and Territories. When, therefore, the crops fail in one section, supplies flow freely in from other quarters to meet the demand. Famine, the scourge of ancient times, is rendered almost impossible. The farmer in Dakota, with his great wheat-fields, is brought close to the hungering markets of New England. This is because every one in the nation is free to buy in the cheapest market and to sell in the dearest.

International freedom of trade. — The world is not yet so civilized that every one is free to seek the cheapest market abroad as well as at home. The German is still forbidden by his government to enjoy the cheaper American markets in buying his meat. The American does not yet see his advantage in giving himself freedom to buy goods wherever he can find cheaper markets in England, France, or Cuba. Meanwhile as long as we refuse to permit our neighbors in other countries freedom to use our markets, we must expect to be denied the freedom to sell our goods to them. Thus if we lay a duty or tax to restrict merchants from buying wool in South America, we shall naturally suffer retaliation from the South American Republics, who will levy taxes on the products which we send to them. Full civilization, on the contrary, makes no restrictions on freedom of trade, and inflicts no retaliation.

On the other hand, those who believe in restrictive duties maintain, that as long as the world is not yet civilized, our nation cannot afford quite freely to carry on intercourse with foreign peoples, who have different laws, customs, and rates of wages, and often lower standards of living.

Freedom in trade; what harm it may do. — While freedom in trade works out good on the whole, it sometimes does harm; as the laws which work well for the many, may do injustice to individuals. Thus it is good for the nation that we can buy corn in the cheapest market, which is in the West; but this is hard for the farmer in Vermont, who cannot raise corn so cheaply. It is good, on the whole, that the Vermont farmer can sell his eggs and chickens in the dearest market, which is Boston or New York, but this makes eggs and chickens dearer for the people in Vermont; as when there is demand in the brain for nourishing blood, which is drawn away for the time from the extremities.

The two sides. — Competition in trade may be very selfish and cruel, as when one neighbor outbids another or undersells him, on purpose to get rid of him and to control the whole business; or when a great firm seeks to crush its lesser rivals. So in case of a great snow-blockade, cutting off a city from its supplies, if the milkmen wring extortionate prices from the needs of suffering children.

But competition or freedom of trade need not be selfish. As a class of boys may aim each to get the most perfect mark of excellence; so every man who sells, if he be honorable and high-minded, may aim at furnishing the best quality of articles on the most favorable terms which he can afford; so purchasers may, and often do, scorn to exact unreasonable advantage from the necessities of the seller. In short, there is no need, because one carries on business, to forget that one deals with men like oneself. If the laws, then, allow meanness and extortion, enlightened public opinion, not to speak of religion, calls for humanity and friendliness, and brands with shame any species of competition which forgets the *man* in the bargain.

Paying one's debts. — Men are debtors and creditors in turn, according as they owe money to others or others owe them. If, now, a man's debtors put off payment or do not pay at all, there will be difficulty in his paying his creditors as he has promised, and again in their paying to others. As the failure of any link in the chain weakens the whole, so wherever a promise is broken there will be suffering and loss. If many do not pay, money will be hard to obtain, and business in general will suffer; whereas prompt payment by one gives the means of payment along a whole line of men. The money which before failed to circulate, moves on freely and makes more business, as well as the means of happiness, every time it is promptly paid.

Bankruptcy. — It often happens that merchants and others fail to pay their obligations. No one then will trust them longer, and they have to stop their business. This is not a hardship to them merely, but to many others who depend upon them, as clerks and employees, as well as those who have lost by giving them credit. Often the greatest suffering falls on those who are thus turned out of employment.

Bankruptcy sometimes happens through the failure of others ; but it occurs often by the extravagance, the folly, the unskilfulness, and even the fraud of those who fail in business.

Bankruptcy laws. — When men fail to pay their debts, there are often many creditors, all of whom ought fairly to share in the assets or property of the debtor. It may be that the debtor also, if the creditors will agree to give him time to settle his affairs, will contrive to pay them more than if they seized and divided his property at once. It may be fair, too, if the debtor honestly gives up all that he has, for his creditors to release him from further payment and leave him free to go on in business. Bankruptcy laws, therefore, provide through the proper courts for the protection of the interests of both debtors and creditors. Whereas once a debtor could be cruelly imprisoned by a hard-hearted creditor, the debtor is now given a fair opportunity to retrieve his fortune.

Sometimes creditors live in different States. · A national bankruptcy law is therefore needed, in order that the creditors who live in the State where the failure took place may not have unjust advantage over the others.

As with other laws, dishonorable merchants may sometimes use the bankruptcy laws to wrong their creditors and to secure a release for themselves without giving up their property. On the other hand, men of honor can and sometimes do more than the law requires, and after being released from their creditors, insist, as soon as they are able, upon paying the full amount of their debts.

CHAPTER XXXVI.

EMPLOYERS AND THE EMPLOYED: THEIR INTERESTS IN EACH OTHER.

ALL men are either employers of labor or employees. Most men are at the same time both employers and laborers.

The rights of employers; fidelity. — The meaning of fidelity is to do another's work as well as possible, or as well as if it were one's own. The truth is, that the workman sells something — namely, his work, whether of his hands or his brain; and, like everything else sold, it ought to be of standard quality. The right to faithful service is not lessened if the employer pays insufficient wages or salary, neither is the service merely for the employer: it is for the whole community, which is poorer for every wasted hour or blundering piece of work. The man, also, who performs unfaithful service becomes degraded and demoralized. Fidelity includes honesty, sobriety, and punctuality. Courtesy is also due to the employer, and tends to make permanent and friendly relations with him.

The rights of employees; wages or salary. — Whoever sells his work or skill, is entitled to its fair price as truly as if it were corn or cloth. Fair pay is not only a righteous amount, but also punctuality in payment. Fair pay has reference to the hours of work and to the amount of vacation or holiday time given.

Respect. — The employer has not discharged his duty in paying a laborer; he owes him also courtesy and friendly respect as a man.

Honest management. — The employee is not only entitled to fair wages, but a wrong is done him by dishonest and speculative management of business, which results in failure and bankruptcy. He is in a certain sense a partner with his employer, and his interests ought not to be risked.

The labor market. — In one view, labor, like everything valuable, is subject to the law of supply and demand. The men who have their labor to sell will bring it to the dearest market; that is, wherever labor is most needed. It will there get the best pay. On the other hand, those who wish to hire labor will go to the cheapest market; that is, wherever labor is plentiful. Thus if a company wish to build a factory, they will consider where they can get workmen to the best advantage. They could not build their factory in Oregon so well as in Massachusetts, because the latter State is a more abundant market for labor. Meanwhile, wherever they build their factory, workmen will flock there. It is thus of advantage to both employers and the employed to buy labor in the cheapest market and to sell it in the dearest. On the whole, work is thus distributed where it is most needed and where the best pay can be given it. If any considerable number of workmen are getting small wages, a free opportunity is afforded to get better wages wherever a larger demand is made for their help.

A difficulty; the human element. — Labor is not simply valuable as a commodity. It is human also. When corn is plenty, or inferior in quality, it is no great hardship if it brings a low price, or does not sell at all. But the workman must live; he may have a family dependent upon him; even if he is an inferior workman, he must still be housed and fed as a man. Neither can the laborer be easily transported, like corn or commodities, wherever the demand and the pay are greater. Many circumstances may render it costly or even impossible for him to move to a place where his labor will be in more demand.

Low wages; the limit of decency. — While at times the number of workmen may be far greater than the demand, there is a limit below which it is not the custom to let wages fall. This limit is fixed by men's considerations of humanity. The more high-minded employers are, and the stronger is public opinion, the higher is this limit of wages to which a man's work is entitled, on the ground that he is a man.

Employees who cannot help themselves. — In years of good harvests and prosperity there is more money to spend, and there will be employment in all industries for men able and willing to work. But bad years also come when there is less to divide and to spend, and therefore less work is called for. The inferior or unskilled workmen are the first to suffer for want of employment. Moreover, the conditions of civilized life require costly tools and machinery: no man can easily work alone, as the savage can, but the civilized man needs the co-operation of others. One cannot even till the soil without assistance or capital. Although the law of supply and demand works after a while to correct disorders of industry, and to set men again to work where they will be needed, this law has often to be supplemented by sympathy and humanity to prevent the innocent from suffering. For the whole body of the community is bound up with the welfare and prosperity, or the loss and misery of any portion. If individuals, then, cannot provide employment for their neighbors who wish to find work, it may sometimes be the duty of the state or the city to provide public works, such as the building of streets and other improvements. Better education will also train a larger proportion of the children to such skill and faithfulness as may find permanent employment.

Employers who cannot help themselves. — We have seen that the number of workmen may sometimes be greater than can be employed at all; or business may be dull and unremunerative; or certain factories may have greater expenses in rent and interest than others, and so cannot afford to pay sufficient wages to go on making their goods. In general, unless the employers are successful and can accumulate capital, they cannot weather the storms which will sometimes occur in the financial and industrial world. The poorly managed shops and factories are often, therefore, obliged to stop altogether. This is not because the employers are unwilling to help their workmen, but because they are themselves unfortunate.

Industrial warfare; strikes and lockouts. — It will happen sometimes that employers and employees disagree and quarrel. It may be by reason of misunderstanding, or for actual fault on one side or the other. In some cases the men agree to quit work until their demands are granted. This is called a *strike*. Like war, it means loss of time and money on both sides, and often great suffering to the workmen's families. Like war, it ought to be justified, if at all, only by urgent necessity. It might also, like war, almost always be prevented.

The employers may make war upon their workmen by shutting down their works and stopping wages till the men accede to their wishes. This is called a *lockout*. As in war, the evil is not merely at the time, but in the loss of good feeling afterwards.

Trades-unions. — The printers or the telegraph operators, by union among themselves, may make a monopoly of their skill, and for the time set their own terms for their labor; exactly as rich men who own a railroad, or who buy up cotton or wheat, make a monopoly. The union may also attempt to limit the number of workmen, to forbid the employment of non-union men, or to demand the same pay for unskilled as for skilled workmen; as the monopolists of coffee or salt try to interfere with the law of supply and demand.

The good of Trades-unions. — On the other hand, the trades-unions are often friendly and benefit societies, and may use their influence to raise the standard of skill and intelligence among their men. As with all societies, the membership is of a higher character when members are free to join it or to stay outside, than when they are brought in by any kind of compulsion; as an army composed of volunteers is more efficient than an army raised by conscription.

Arbitration. — It is impossible for individuals or majorities, whether in a trade or in the state, permanently to fix prices or wages. As a rule, it is unwise, as well as unjust, to try to prevent the free and natural relations of employers and employees. For the industrial machinery of the world is very complicated and delicate, so that meddling with it at one point may disarrange it somewhere else. It sometimes happens, however, that difficulties and questions arise between employers and their men, in which impartial advice may remedy misunderstanding or injustice on one side or the other. This is called *arbitration*. So far as employers are fair, and their employees are intelligent, arbitration may be expected to save the waste and ill-feeling of the more barbarous and violent methods of strikes and lockouts. For the quarrels of men, like the quarrels of boys in their games, would mostly be averted by yielding to the decision of a wise and friendly umpire.

The interests of employers and the employed together. — It is obvious that the interest of the employer is in the most faithful, intelligent, and willing workmanship. The best workmen, even when they must be paid high wages, are the most economical, as goods of standard quality are cheaper in the end than inferior goods. The employer, therefore, with skilled and willing men, may easily afford to pay the best wages and yet produce goods which will sell at a profit.

The success of the employer is equally for the interest of the workmen. His success means permanence in work, whereas the less successful shop will often have to be closed. His success means also the ability to pay better wages, and to continue to pay them through dull seasons. For the successful employer will have a large capital and credit, and will be able to keep his men employed even at times when he makes no profits himself.

Co-operation and profit-sharing. — Enterprises have often been undertaken in which all who have part in the work share in the profits; as, for instance, in the fisheries and in certain factories, — notably in the case of the *Maison Leclaire* in Paris. It is found that men, if made partners in a business, take a personal interest in it, work better, and accomplish more. This is especially the case in work requiring skill. The advantage is not merely in the fact that the workmen hope to receive better pay, but that by this method employers signify that they mean to deal fairly with their workmen.

All kinds of business, however, are really co-operative, whether called so or not. For the payment of regular salaries and wages (which are apt to rise in good times, and fall in poor times) is simply a method of sharing the profits of business with all those who are concerned in carrying it on. On the whole, a man's share depends upon how useful or necessary he is. Moreover, many great corporations, like the Pennsylvania Railroad, advance their wages according to the length of faithful service, or give pensions to aged workmen. It is also possible for employees to invest their savings in the shares of the company for which they work, unless they can do better by some other form of investment. On the other hand, it is fair for those who expect to share the profits of their work, to be willing also to meet the chances of loss.

Men who have been the employees of others, like the coopers of Minneapolis, sometimes combine, and establish a business or an industry of their own. The new enterprise, like any other corporation, is then subject to the usual conditions of success; namely, the energy, prudence, and honesty of its managers.

Women's work and wages. — We have seen that wages follow the law of supply and demand; although, when they become very low, humanity interposes, and forbids paying less. As a rule, this limit to which wages fall is lower for women than for men. This is partly because of the survival of barbarous ideas as to the worth of women. It is partly because there are fewer employments open to women's strength, while the number of women seeking work constantly increases. Many women who live at home are glad to earn a little money at very low wages, lower often than they could afford if they had to support themselves wholly. But the employers who can find willing hands at fifty cents a day cannot easily afford to pay more to other women, no more skilful, who need a dollar a day.

Moreover, the wages of women are allowed by common custom to be lower than in the case of men, even for the same work, because it is considered that a man must have enough to support a family, while a woman more often has only herself to support. This custom frequently works great hardship, but it holds largely for the sake of the wives and mothers whom the men ought to support. Men's work, as a rule, is also for life; whereas working women are apt to marry, in which case their work changes to meet the calls of domestic life.

The commonwealth of labor. — The best commonwealth which we can think of would be where every one started with a suitable education and a fair chance to rise to the place for which he was fitted, — where all had an opportunity to work according to the strength and skill of each; where every one had a living according to the worth of his services; and where no one could squander the fruits of other men's labors. It would be a commonwealth where men saw the interests of each in the interest of all; where all men worked side by side as joint partners; where each endeavored to add as much as possible to the sum of human advantage; and where friendliness as of men, not the suspicion or jealousy of brutes, was the prevailing spirit of their work. So far as individuals carry on work, as they would wish every one else to do, they help to bring about this commonwealth.

PART FOURTH.

*SOCIAL RIGHTS AND DUTIES; OR, THE DUTIES
OF MEN AS THEY LIVE TOGETHER
IN SOCIETY.*

PART FOURTH.

*SOCIAL RIGHTS AND DUTIES; OR, THE DUTIES
OF MEN AS THEY LIVE TOGETHER
IN SOCIETY.*

CHAPTER XXXVII.

THE RIGHTS AND DUTIES OF NEIGHBORS.

WE have already seen that even in making money and
bargains it does not work to treat men as machines or as
rivals; but as the famous Roman emperor said, "We
are made for co-operation, like feet, like hands, like eye-
lids." We have also seen with what good temper we
must work together as fellow-citizens in order to secure
an orderly and prosperous state. On many sides of our
lives we meet men in society simply as neighbors.

The growth of the neighborly feeling. — The old idea
used to be that members of the same tribe, caste, or class
were bound to help each other. Thus Romans should
help Romans, and Brahmins should help the poorer Brahmins, and noblemen should stand by each other; but
Romans need not help Greeks, nor nobles spend their
money in aiding peasants. Jesus taught that every one is
our neighbor; but this teaching has never been very much
believed till lately. It is now coming to be the creed of

the world that we ought to treat all men, of every race and condition, as neighbors.

The neighborly feeling has its rise in the family. We easily know how we ought to treat our elders, our guests, our brothers and sisters. We learn what our duties are towards the younger members of the family, towards the feeble, the sick, or the dependent. The village is a greater family; so is the state. In a large way all mankind make a family together. The same rules and the good temper that show us what to do in the home show us also how to live together whenever we meet men.

Our rights. — We have a right to respect and courtesy from others as befits men. We have a right to be considered for what we are really worth. This right holds good whatever dress we wear, or however humble a station we occupy. As the poet Burns says, "A man is a man for a' that." .

We have a right, unless we have thrown it away by misconduct, to be treated as honest, to be trusted and not suspected.

Privacy. — We have a right to our privacy. There are many personal matters which only concern ourselves or our most intimate friends. It is not well for us, neither is it desirable for others, that our private affairs should be made the subject of gossip or published in the newspapers. We have a right, therefore, to keep these things to ourselves, and not to be intruded upon by idle curiosity. As "every man's house is his castle," so every man's private life, his plans, thoughts, and feelings, his personal correspondence, and his conversation with his friends, ought to be sacred from publicity.

With most of these humane rights, however, we have no power to compel or enforce them, unless they are freely given to us. They are not like legal rights, such as the right to our liberty or to our property, for maintaining which we may need to ask the assistance of the government. Neither would they be of any use to us if we had to quarrel or go to law to obtain them; for respect unwillingly shown would not be sincere, and our private affairs would become public as soon as we carried them into court.

We have no right, on account of pride of family or of education, to claim peculiar respect, as though we were of finer clay than other men. We must expect others to take us, not at our own value, but at their estimate of us.

We have no right to any one's intimacy or to be taken into another's confidence, or to be asked to visit him. We have no right to insist upon being taken into the employ of another.

We have no right to demand assistance from our neighbors. If we have a right to live, we have no right to force others to help us to live.

Our neighborly rights are only such as others will freely allow us. For it destroys neighborly feeling to insist upon our rights.

Neighborly duties. — We have, in most respects, to trust others to give us our rights. Our main business is with our duties.

The duty of just judgment. — As we meet in business, elect men to office, or choose our friends, we have constantly to pass judgment for or against each other. The risk is that we shall judge carelessly, that we shall make up our minds hastily or on worthless evidence, and shall therefore do our neighbors injustice. We owe it, therefore, to every man, as we would wish to be treated ourselves, to take care to value him for what he is really worth. We ought to err on the side of overvaluing rather than undervaluing others.

Especially when we publish our judgments and opinions or tell them to others. We owe it to men not to report mere suspicions to injure their reputation or credit. If we must ever speak evil, we must know and not guess.

Respect as a humane duty. — We are bound as neighbors to give each other respect; by which we mean not only courteous behavior, but respectful feeling. This respect is based on the fact that every man has the same human qualities which we have. If, then, we slight or despise the common human nature, we both hurt others and cheapen ourselves. Moreover, men show their noble qualities — courage, fairness, generosity — to those who treat them well and expect their best. This is true of the horses and cattle, which do their best for the masters who treat them most kindly.

Sympathy. — Sympathy means that we are glad to see others happy, and sorry to see them in pain; that we are glad to hear good of them, and sorry to hear evil. Sympathy is easy inside our own family or our set of friends. The good of one is evidently the good of all; the hurt of one hurts all. This is true, although it is not so evident, outside our own set or family. The good of every American is the good of all; the loss or hurt of one is the loss or hurt of the whole people. As when any little wheel of the machinery of a great mill is injured, the mill cannot turn out so much work.

Forbearance. — Forbearance means that we do not condemn our neighbor till we know the circumstances against which he has to struggle. He may be ill, he may be misinformed, for no fault of his own he may be incapable. We are bound, therefore, to be patient with him, as we wish others at times to be patient with us. Even when another does us injury, we have no right, like

an ignorant savage, to wish him evil.   For that would be
to wish evil to the whole family, or to the community.

Assistance. — If our neighbor's wagon has broken
down, if his boat has capsized, if his house is on fire, we
owe him the same help which we should need if we were
in his place.   If one whom we have never seen needs help,
we owe the same common humanity.   Even a dog has
been known to jump into the water or plunge through
snowdrifts to save a stranger.

Different grades of neighborly duty. — Our neighborly duties are of different grades of importance.   Thus
we are naturally responsible for the care of our own family
and relatives.   We owe more to our friends than to strangers, to those who are near than to the distant, to our
workmen or employers than to others, to our townspeople
than to another town, to our countrymen than to foreigners.   The closer bonds make greater obligations.   We
also know better those who are near us, and can treat
them more intelligently.   Thus if a brother or a towns-
man was in trouble, we should choose to have the first
chance to assist him.   So when the great flood destroyed
Johnstown, every one was glad to help, but the first duty
was upon the people of Pennsylvania.

This rule, however, has its exceptions.   A guest or a
stranger or a foreigner might for a little while need more
attention or help than a friend or relative.   He might also
happen to deserve more on account of his character or
services, as when a distinguished man visits this country
from abroad.

What we do not owe to neighbors. — We owe kindly
feeling to every one, but we do not owe every one a place
among our intimate friends.   For no one can have many
intimate friends.

Neither do we owe help which would have to be given at the expense of another. Thus it would be robbery to give an employer's money to relieve distress, as truly as to use the money for our own pleasure.

The difficulty in treating men as neighbors. — If all men were equal in intelligence, power, and goodness, there would be no special difficulty in treating them as our neighbors. We have seen, however, that there are all sorts of inequalities. The actual difference between a savage and a great statesman, poet, or philosopher, is as great as used to be thought to exist between a slave and an emperor. The difference between men in moral character is equally great. We cannot, therefore, truthfully treat all men in exactly the same way, or give all equal respect or sympathy, since there is much more to love and honor in some men than in others. Indeed, it would be very unfair if we treated idle, ignorant, or vicious people with the same respect which we show to the industrious, intelligent, and virtuous.

The social aim. — We found that, so far as the duties of wealth are concerned, the aim of men was to produce more wealth, and that the great law which guided them was justice. The aim of men, as they live in society, is happiness, and the great rule is benevolence.

CHAPTER XXXVIII.

THE TREATMENT OF CRIME.

The dangerous class. — There are thousands of people in our country who are confined in jails and prisons on account of their crimes. There are many more at large who are regarded with suspicion as dangerous. Many children, also, either by inheritance or unfortunate circumstances, belong to this class. It is sometimes called the dangerous class. We learned in our study of the duties of citizenship that the government was bound to protect its citizens from this class.

Who are criminals. — Whoever is willing to injure his neighbors or the welfare of society is so far a criminal. There are many ways of injuring others. Besides those who rob and do violence, those may also as seriously injure society who get money by fraud, or by bad kinds of business, or who pursue a vicious or idle course; as the body is not only hurt by cruel blows, but sometimes even more by wasting and insidious disease. Some of the worst offenders may not, therefore, be touched by the laws. Thus a mayor or senator who bargained for men's votes might do more harm than a burglar who broke into a house. Or, if a rich man led an impure life, he might hurt the community — like a poison — as much as one who passed counterfeit money.

Our duties to criminals. — When people have been shut up in prison they do not cease to be our neighbors, and we still have duties towards them. It is for their good as well as our own that we confine them, as we would wish ourselves to be prevented from doing injury. Idleness ruins men; it is our duty, therefore, to furnish them employment in prison. Many criminals have no education or trade: it is our duty to teach them how to earn an honest living; it is our duty to give them a fair chance to recover, if they can, a respectable place in society. If they cannot or will not behave themselves out of confinement, it is equally our duty, for their sake as well as our own, *to keep them confined*, on exactly the same principle as we confine madmen. For no one who has shown himself dangerous to society has any right to be at large.

Punishment. — The ancient idea of punishment was revenge or retaliation. It was thought that the wrong-doer ought to suffer enough to offset the harm he had done. The law once was "an eye for an eye." The modern idea of punishment is to prevent more harm being done. It is partly for the sake of society, to remove dangerous persons, to warn the thoughtless against doing wrong, and specially, if possible, to deter evil doers through their fears; it is also designed to cure the criminal and persuade him to become useful. Thus no punishment is good for society which tends to make men worse. The purpose of punishment is exactly the same as in a well-ordered home.

Modes of punishment. — The modes of punishment used to be intended to cause pain, and were often terribly cruel, like the rack, the thumb-screw, and stoning to death. They were inflicted also for numerous small offences, such as ignorant or feeble-minded people might commit. These painful modes of punishment hurt and brutalized every one who witnessed them. They never made any one better; neither did they prevent crime.

These cruel modes of punishment have been largely given up in the United States. We punish criminals by fines or payments of money, by imprisonment for longer or shorter terms, and in some States, for the crime of murder, by the death penalty.

Fines. — If one has caused the State loss or cost, it is fair that he should be obliged to make the loss good by a payment of money. For many slight offences or for negligence, as when a citizen leaves ice upon his sidewalk, a fine is a good way to remind him not to offend again. But fines which are a slight burden to the rich are often a severe penalty to the poor, who are perhaps obliged to go to jail for want of the money to pay. They lose work, their families suffer, the cost of keeping them in jail has to be borne by the State, and no one is better in the end.

Imprisonment. — There are certain bad, worthless, or desperate men who doubtless ought to be shut altogether away from human society, as we separate a case of small-pox. There must be jails or prisons for such dangerous characters. There are also those who are so hot-tempered, and have so little self-control, that they need for a time to be deprived of their liberty, till they have shown that they can be trusted to be at large again.

It is a grave question, however, whether our laws do not work more harm than good through our use of jails and prisons. It is as if we sent cases of measles, scarlet fever, and small-pox all to the same hospital and treated them alike. So when young persons who have never offended before, or when poor men who have been sent to jail for want of money to pay a fine, are herded together with dangerous criminals. Many are sent to jail who do not need the stone cells and the thick walls, which are only good for guarding the few dangerous criminals. A bad and disgraceful name is also given, often very unjustly, to those who have been sent to a jail, as men fear the taint of a malignant fever. It is harder for men to get employment after they have been in jail, and they are likely to have made bad associates. It is a terrible thing, therefore, to expose any one to the penalty of imprisonment, unless it proves to be necessary. Moreover, it is very expensive to shut thousands of men and women in prison, and we ought to be sure that the imprisonment does good enough to warrant the cost.

The death penalty. — The savage law has always been "a life for a life." The death penalty is the survival of the old custom. In many States this penalty has been changed to imprisonment for life. The fact is that the death penalty has never prevented bad or hot-tempered men from committing murder, neither has it made careless men feel the sacredness of human life. Moreover, few persons would be willing to inflict the death penalty upon another. It is not well to require a sheriff or officer to do that which conscientious citizens would be unwilling themselves to do.

The rights of wrong-doers. — Every man has the right to be treated as innocent until his guilt is proved. If found guilty, he has a right not to be thought worse than he really is. If he has done wrong in one point, it does not follow that he is altogether bad. In fact, a criminal keeps all his rights, except such as he has distinctly forfeited by his offence. He still has the right to be treated as a man. But he may have thrown away the right to be believed, or to be trusted, or to his freedom, or to his franchise as a citizen. What right he has thrown away depends upon the nature of his offence. He may not deserve to be trusted or believed, but he may not have wholly sacrificed the right to his liberty. Another may be honest or truthful, but so violent or bad-tempered as to have lost his right to liberty. Another may be safe and decent while he is kept out of the way of intoxicating drink, but very dangerous where drink is accessible.

Even the right to life may be forfeited in case a bad life threatens the welfare of society. Thus if there were no prisons to confine dangerous persons, it might be necessary, as in the army, to sacrifice the life of murderous men, since society must somehow protect the weaker and innocent from the violence of bad men, precisely as it would defend them from ferocious animals. Indeed, one should much prefer to die than to be allowed to destroy society. If, then, we deem it best, on the whole, to give up the death penalty, it is not because desperate men, such as train-wreckers or incendiaries, have any longer a right to live.

What we ought to do. — We ought to give every offender a prompt and speedy trial. For this end we should improve the slow and cumbrous machinery of our laws, which frequently impose great delay and expense.

We ought to adapt punishments to the nature of the offence, so as to carry with us the offender's sense of justice. We should not lightly lock men up in jail, or throw them into the company of hardened offenders.

We ought to divide public offenders into different classes and treat them accordingly. Some would most fairly be required to work, as, for example, on the public streets. Some would need to be sent away to public farms or shops, where they could learn a trade and acquire habits of self-control. As soon as they could be trusted, they should be given a trial of their freedom again. Some could be entrusted, like the harmless insane, to the care of discreet and friendly persons in different parts of the State. Those only who needed restraint should be locked behind walls and bolts.

We should probably do wisely, when prisoners work, to credit them with a part of the product of their labor. This might go either to support their families or to provide them with means to secure an honest living when they come out of prison. We ought also, when they come back to society, to see that they are befriended and helped to find employment.

The indeterminate sentence. — The old and barbarous custom was to assign to every offence a particular penalty, — as of so many stripes, or so long an imprisonment for stealing a loaf of bread. It was as if a physician treated every case of pneumonia with the same dose of medicine. The new way is to treat each case with some regard to the circumstances. The "indeterminate sentence" means that the judge does not prescribe how long an offender must be confined. By good behavior he may soon prove that he can safely be trusted to return to his home. For all that the State desires is that he shall take his place in the ranks of the good citizens. But otherwise he ought never to be set free to do harm. Some States already use the indeterminate sentence. The laws ought to allow its more general use.

Prison reform. — In some States prisoners are largely kept in idleness, especially in the county jails. Nothing is done to help them to earn a decent living after they are discharged. There is a prejudice against prison work, lest the wages paid for it may lessen the wages of men out of prison; although it is evident that if prisoners do nothing for their support, they must be kept at the cost of the people.

In some States again, especially in the South, prisoners

are hired out to contractors, who pay the State for their labor. The contractors then try to make as much money as they can out of their bargain, as if they had hired so many cattle, but do not try to help the men to become good citizens.

A few States, notably New York, have adopted new methods in the care of prisons, in order to educate and reform the men and women committed to their keeping. In Elmira Prison, for example, the men are divided into classes according to their conduct. They may earn the right to be trusted. They are treated as fellow-men and taught trades. The indeterminate sentence is used, and "tickets-of-leave" are given on good behavior, entitling the men to release from prison, as long as they use their freedom honorably.

As we have seen, very much remains to be done, even in the most progressive States, in getting rid of old ideas of punishment, and learning to treat prisoners with a view both to their good and to the best interests of society.

The power of pardon. — In the early days the king could pardon an offender. Now that the people are sovereign, the governor, or in certain cases the President, has the power, as representing the people, to grant pardons; as it is his duty in capital punishment to sign the death warrant. But the power of pardon has been found liable to great abuse. It is, therefore, believed by many careful persons that the granting of pardons, as well as the care of prisons and the proper treatment of offenders, ought to be given to a board of the wisest men and women in the State, who shall be made, like judges, responsible for their action. In some States, as Massachusetts, there are already Prison Commissions, but their authority and usefulness are limited.

The prevention of crime. — With crime, as with every other evil, the chief hope of remedy is in prevention. This requires an understanding of the causes which lead to crime. These causes are partly the inheritance from weak or vicious parents. Other causes are the unfortunate circumstances in which many live; such as bad and crowded tenement houses, pressing poverty, and the abuse of alcoholic drinks. Very many of the criminals, also, are ignorant.

The prevention of crime consists largely in the removal of the prevalent causes which make criminals. The improvement of the houses of the poor, more wholesome sanitary arrangements, the spread of intelligence, a firm moral training, the forming of habits of temperance and self-control, — all surely tend to prevent crime. The children of vicious parents have also to be taken away from bad homes and placed under new and moral surroundings. Great good is done by the societies which thus aim to find homes for the children of the destitute.

The detection of crime. — It has become customary, besides using police and constables, to watch against and overtake wrong-doers, to employ a class of men called "detectives," to ferret out crime in its hiding-places. There are certain fair and honorable means to be used in tracking guilt, but there is always grave danger, if the State hires "a rogue to catch a rogue." The State thus pays some one for lying and deception — the very crimes which it wishes to prevent. It is very doubtful if it is ever important enough to bring any offender to justice, to warrant the use of tools which true men would be unwilling themselves to handle.

Lynch-law. — In wild and half-civilized communities it sometimes happens, for want of upright judges or righteous courts, that the people take justice into their own hands. They appoint their own judge and jury, and hurry the culprit to punishment, sometimes with terrible injustice. It is possible that lynch-law is better than no law: its promptness may at times be more just than the wearing delays of too many courts; but its terrible spirit of revenge and its risk of punishing the wrong person brand it as barbarous.

A final caution. — There is sometimes a harsh feeling towards criminals, as though they were a different race from other men, or as if detection and civil punishment made wrong-doing worse than if it had escaped detection. On the contrary, all improvement in the treatment and reform of crime has come from the efforts of those who, like John Howard, held the wrong-doer to be a man like themselves, and pitied him accordingly.

CHAPTER XXXIX.

HOW TO HELP THE POOR.

It was seen, in our study of economic conditions, what causes lead to poverty. One of the great questions which society has to answer is, how best to help the poor. It used to be answered very easily. Alms, it was said, ought to be given them.

Pauperism. — This plan of giving alms was tried for hundreds of years, till it was found that the more money was given to the poor, the poorer they became. In some countries, like Italy, there came to be a large class of professional beggars. In England vast numbers of the people became paupers; that is, they were dependent for more or less of their living upon the support of the government. At last it was seen that gifts of money and of food, instead of helping the poor, took away their manliness and independence, and made them less capable of earning their living.

Moreover, when the poor could get their living for nothing, honest and industrious workmen had to suffer in consequence. This was partly because the taxes, which always come out of the industrious people, were made higher by the support of the poor. Besides, when much money is given to paupers, the wages of the industrious class are likely to fall. For the poor who are partly supported by private or public charity can afford to work for lower wages than the industrious and independent class, who support themselves. The competition of pauper laborers, therefore, always tends to bring down wages to the lower level.

The effect is the same when any of the poor are given board or food at less than market values. Thus we will suppose that there are in New York ten thousand poor girls for whom kind people provide rooms free of cost. These girls can afford to work at perhaps fifty cents a week less than those who have to pay the rent of their rooms. Now employers prefer to hire the girls who can afford to serve for the smallest wages. These employers, again, can afford to sell their goods a little cheaper, and other employers, who compete with them, are forced to lower their price to the thousands of girls whose kind friends do not furnish free lodging. Thus unwise giving tends to hurt the people whom one meant to help.

Work not a curse. — Underneath the custom of giving alms to the poor there was a strange old notion that work was a curse. For it used to be thought that the most desirable condition was a life of ease and idleness. This is no longer believed. Work, if not excessive, is now known to be favorable to health and happiness. Even the struggle necessary to overcome difficulties often develops the most successful and the noblest men and women.

Charity ; the general law. — The wisest and kindest charity is *to help the poor to help themselves.* This is the working of nature, which rewards exertion, and has all sorts of penalties against imprudence and laziness. Thus it is charity to find a poor man work, or to show his wife how not to waste food, or to persuade the poor not to spend their money in drink. It is charity to teach co-operation among the poor, in order to provide for the expenses of sickness. It is charity to help the children of the poor to learn trades in which they can earn better wages. It may be charity to start a new industry in a poor neighborhood which shall distribute regular wages to a great many people. It is charity to build wholesome dwelling-houses at fair rates of rent. The greatest of charities would be investments of capital by the rich to enable men to become owners of their own homes.

Exceptional cases. — There are, however, certain poor people who, for various reasons, seem unable to help themselves; as the aged, the sick and feeble, and widows with little children. There are also times in which, for want of work or failure of the harvests, large numbers of people are thrown out of employment. In ancient times such people were often left to suffer terrible hardships, and to starve to death. It is now regarded as the duty of society to provide for these exceptional cases of poverty.

Why society relieves exceptional poverty. — The duty of helping the needy poor, society partly owes to itself; because it would lessen the happiness of all and narrow men's sympathies to witness suffering and do nothing to relieve it. In some cases — for instance, in a famine — it is necessary to assist the poor for the welfare and safety of society. Society also owes its help, in cases of extreme poverty, to the innocent and to children, of whom it is the natural guardian. So far also as the working of bad laws and customs has caused poverty, society ought to help pay the penalty of its own faults. Our common humanity specially requires us never to rest content while fellow-men are in distress.

On these grounds the state raises considerable sums of money by taxation to relieve distress and to support hospitals and asylums. The feeble-minded and insane are largely cared for by the state. Every city or town pro-

vides that no citizen or stranger, if possible, shall be left
to starve.

There are many, however, who only need to be tided
over a period of misfortune, and who do not wish the
assistance of public officers. Neither is it well for any to
form a habit of looking to the public treasury to save the
trouble of helping themselves.

The fact is, the spirit of kindness and gratitude grows
whenever friends or neighbors help each other; but kindness and gratitude hardly grow at all if a policeman or
official gives public aid, which comes out of the labor
of others. Moreover, friends and neighbors may render
wiser aid than officials, and know better when it may be
discontinued.

Who is responsible. — Near friends or relatives ought,
naturally, to help one another in misfortune. Near neighbors are more responsible for one another than distant
ones. Employers ought to have friendly care for their
employees. Owners of houses ought to bear some responsibility for their tenants. If relatives, neighbors, employers,
and landlords all bore their fair responsibility, there would
still be a considerable amount of distress to be otherwise
provided for.

The city poor and the country poor. — In the country
the people generally know their neighbors. If any one
is in trouble, the fact is easily discovered and the causes
and circumstances are known. If sickness or accident
cause suffering, every one sympathizes and wishes to help.
When bad habits make a family poor, friendly neighbors
can see what to do in behalf of the neglected wife or children, or may even have influence enough to change the bad
habits.

In the city, however, people often do not know their

nearest neighbors. The very poor are apt also to live crowded together, somewhat apart from the homes of the more prosperous. Employers may not be acquainted with their workmen; or great corporations hire thousands of men who are constantly changing. Often the owners of a tenement house, where poor people live, do not know who their tenants are, but merely collect their rent through an agent, like the absentee landlords of Ireland. When trouble comes, therefore, no one may at once know of it, or what caused it, or how best to help it. Those who have means to relieve suffering may never happen to learn of the need of a poorer neighbor a few blocks away from their own doors. These facts make it difficult to help the suffering in a city.

What kinds of help do no injury. — We have seen that it harms people to look to the public for support. This is because it is unfair for one set of people to expect the rest to work and to pay taxes, in order to give them bread, or free soup, or clothes; for every honorable person wishes to give as much as he gets. The kinds of help which do good are those which all share in enjoying and in paying for. Thus the whole city is better off when it cleanses and lights, or widens and improves a bad street, or requires a dangerous or unhealthy house to be renovated or torn down. The city cannot afford to let any of its people live in filth or exposed to disease.

So, too, it helps every one when a town provides education, libraries, and parks, free for all. Whatever tends to make the citizens more healthy, capable, and intelligent, will "help the poor to help themselves." The enlightened commonwealth especially wishes to give every child a fair start in life; as a parent believes that the better equipment his son has, the more honorable and useful he will become.

Friendly gifts and alms: the difference. — The person who gives alms to a beggar is like one who fires a gun without taking aim; for he does not know what the beggar really needs or whether his money will not do harm. He may give in order to get rid of the beggar. Even if the beggar needs money, too many strangers may waste their money upon him, to the neglect of some more needy person.

The gift of a friend, however, is directed with some intelligence. We may always hope to make some return to a friend. The friend can have an eye upon us to see if we make good use of his gifts, and will stop giving when the gift does no good. Friendly gifts, intelligently directed, not only stir our gratitude and generosity, but may leave us more capable or useful than we should be without them. Thus every one who receives such gifts ought to be willing to share them. A poor person may receive friendly gifts from a wealthier neighbor, and may himself help in turn a more needy person.

Not alms, but a friend. — In the old-fashioned almsgiving there was one noble thing; namely, sympathy, or humanity. True charity aims to foster this sympathy and to direct it to the most permanent good. It asks us to "put ourselves in the other's place," and to think what we should need if we were in distress. The motto of modern charity is, "*Not alms, but a friend.*"

What is being done. — If all the kind persons who wished to help the poor in a city were to work, each by himself, some needy families would receive more than their share, while others would be quite neglected. It is necessary, therefore, in order to secure efficient action, to organize people into societies. Sometimes, too, it is necessary to organize a number of societies together, like the various divisions of an army, so as not to interfere with each other. This is called *the Associated Charities.*

The Associated Charities endeavors by its agents to discover what are the real needs of the poor in a city; to find who are worthy and deserving, and who are false or bad; and to send its friendly volunteer besides to those who need friends. Sometimes employment is found for those out of work; or actual assistance must be obtained for a little while; or a suitable hospital or home must be provided, or perhaps a regular pension is needed for an aged person or an invalid. The leisure time of many persons, as well as the benevolent gifts of many more, are thus directed where the most good may be done. The aim of the Associated Charities is, as far as possible, to assist the poorest to self-respect and self-support.

Savings banks. — The trouble with multitudes of people is that they have nothing between themselves and want. If, then, illness befalls them, or they are thrown out of work, they have to run in debt or else suffer. The savings banks enable people to put by, " against a rainy day," very small sums to accumulate and draw interest, which would otherwise be spent or wasted. The habit of using the savings banks induces every one to become more industrious and wards off bad habits.

Many believe that our government, like Great Britain, ought to provide postal savings banks, so that the people could safely invest their earnings at every post-office in the country.

The co-operative banks are another kind of savings bank. They also help those who save their money to build or to own their home. The life insurance companies furnish another method to encourage industry and self-denial for the sake of one's family.

The housing of the poor. — In some of the great cities abroad, as Glasgow, where tenement houses have become terribly crowded, the law permits the public authorities to buy property and to build decent houses to be rented. This is because the old houses were a menace to the public safety. We have already seen that it is a grave question how far it is well for the public to attempt to carry on business, like building, owning, and renting houses. It seems better that people should themselves own their houses and be responsible for the care of them, as they so largely do by the aid of the co-operative banks in Philadelphia and other cities.

Cautions. — The duty of exceptional help for the unfortunate poor is still attended with serious dangers. No man must be encouraged, when ill or out of work, to depend upon public aid or benevolent societies instead of his own prudence and savings. It is unjust to the thrifty and industrious, if the improvident are helped so as to fare as well as themselves. The complaints and sufferings of all who ask help must, therefore, be carefully investigated before aid is rendered. The inveterate beggars must be found out, and punished, if necessary; the intemperate husband must not think that he can spend his wages in drink, and have his family supported by charity. The Associated Charities must keep careful records of the results of their investigations.

Rich beggars, paupers, and tramps. — It must be observed that all which we say of beggars and paupers holds of the well-to-do class as truly as of the very poor. It is quite as disgraceful to wish to live at the rate of five or ten thousand dollars a year out of the labor of others, and without doing any useful service, as to be willing to live on a pittance from a charitable society. It is as bad to beg for an office under government in order merely to draw the pay as to beg alms of a stranger on the street. And he who selfishly spends the money, which others have earned, in travelling over the world may be only a better dressed tramp.

CHAPTER XL.

THE GREAT SOCIAL SUBJECTS.

The growth of moral habits. — The world learns what is right and wrong slowly, as children learn. There were thus habits and conduct allowed in old times which civilized people agree to condemn and punish. We are told that the Spartans once taught their youth to be adroit thieves. All the ancient nations permitted human slavery. There were tribes who lived by raiding their neighbors; and cities, like Tripoli and Algiers, till recent times, whose chief business was piracy. Whereas we have now many laws and a long list of crimes, our forefathers long ago had but a few very simple laws. Neither were their consciences quick to protest against cruel deeds.

The great rule of morals. — Men once did wrong, like children, without fairly seeing what harm the wrong did. Or, they supposed that wrong did harm to others, but did not see how it also hurt the one who committed it. Thus when men knew that it would be bad for themselves to be slaves, they were slow in finding out that it was bad for themselves and their children to keep slaves. So with brigandage and piracy. Men discovered at last that it was not only bad to be robbed, but very bad also for a people to live by robbery.

As fast as men discovered that any practice or habit was *hurtful*, they began to call such conduct wrong, and to make laws to prevent it. Their consciences also made them uncomfortable at doing what they now saw was hurtful. Thus, as soon as any man saw what harm there was in slavery, to the masters, and to society, and to the state, as well as to the slave, his conscience troubled him for helping on this harm.

The rule of morals is, that whatever is found to hurt men or harm society is wrong. That which harms may seem at first to give some one pleasure or profit, like the brigand's booty, or the slave's service to his master; as a poisonous draught may give a moment's pleasure in the mouth, while destroying the health. It is possible, too, on occasion, that a few men may have to suffer some harm, as patriots who die for their country, in order to save all from greater harm by oppression. The simple rule, however, holds good, that any conduct or habit is bad, and therefore wrong, which on the whole hurts or weakens society, or leaves men poorer and worse.

Moral subjects that have been settled. — There are already many practices, such as slavery and piracy, the harm of which civilized men have clearly found out through very painful and costly experience. So in this country with fighting duels, although as late as 1804 the distinguished statesman, Alexander Hamilton, lost his life in a duel, and Germans and Frenchmen still practise the barbarous custom. The world has also learned the terrible harm and social disorder that comes by unfaithfulness in marriage, so that the laws and men's consciences make unfaithfulness a grave crime. When we say that such subjects as these are settled, we do not mean that every one does right with regard to them, but that men generally know the difference between right and wrong.

New questions. — There are other subjects on which men are only now fairly learning what is right; there are some important subjects upon which they are as yet disagreed. Thus, cruelty to animals is a new crime, which men have only lately agreed upon, and the harm of which many men need still to see. About gambling, about purity and the family, about the use of the alcoholic drinks, there are still grave questions of right and wrong, which are only slowly becoming settled.

Lotteries and gambling. — There was once a time when our forefathers appear to have seen no harm in gambling, and lotteries were even approved by the state, and permitted to aid colleges and charitable enterprises. But it became at last evident that gambling always did great harm to society. It led to idleness and waste. The losers not only had to suffer, but they dragged their friends to loss and want; the winners only gained by their neighbors' losses — a mean kind of gain! The whole of society was poorer and not richer by gambling, as though the body were to try to live by devouring itself. If gambling then hurts society, any one who for his own pleasure, or excitement, or gain engages in it, is as truly an enemy to society as the thief or the highwayman.

Gambling in prices, or stock speculation. — Men are not, however, yet fully agreed as to what constitutes gambling. Thus while the laws forbid lotteries and games of cards for money, the laws cannot easily prevent men from betting or gambling upon the rise and fall of the prices of goods or stocks and bonds. But all kinds of betting, where men hope to win by others' loss, hurt society precisely as the lotteries do. For after men have finished betting, nothing has been done to make society richer or happier; on the contrary, the waste of time of the losers and the gains of the winners must at last come out of the labor of the industrious, and leave every one poorer. Those, therefore, who wish to get their living by the chances of business, and out of other men's pockets, must be classed as gamblers, and enemies to society, since no honest man wishes to be made rich at others' expense.

The family. — Men had made various experiments in savage times about the family, before they came to see the true law of the marriage of one man to one woman. Every other relation of men and women to each other has proved to be fraught with mischief to society. Every other relation has done harm and wrought degradation both to men and to women, and has proved especially bad for children. Every other relation, then, since it hurts both the individual and society, becomes wrong. It becomes wrong none the less, even when in particular cases it might seem not to do immediate harm. As a thief is still the enemy to society, when he robs a rich man, even if he gives away the proceeds of his theft.

Thus the Mormons in Utah became enemies to society in reviving the barbarous habit of polygamy, and none the less, when they did it in the name of their religion; and society in self-protection justly required them to stop the hurtful practice.

The equal law of purity for men and women. — While society has long agreed that all offences against the law of the family are disastrous, and therefore wrong for women, unfortunately it has been slow in seeing that the same kind of offences against purity are equally wrong in men. In fact, nothing is meaner for a man than to do secretly a kind of wrong which, if every one did likewise, would ruin society.

Whoever, then, degrades womanhood, or encourages such degradation, puts himself in the place of the criminal. Even if he is never found out, his wrong, like that of a sneak-thief, remains the same. True men, therefore, gladly accept the same standard of purity for men and women.

The marriage laws. — That which makes real marriage is, of course, the love and devotion of husband and wife. Without love and devotion marriage cannot be real. But it is necessary to the order of society, and for preserving the rights of children, that certain simple marriage laws should be observed. The intentions of marriage should be registered beforehand, as in Massachusetts, at the office of the town or city clerk; the two persons should appear before some authorized person, a priest, or minister, or magistrate, and affirm their serious purpose to be joined in marriage; and a public record should be made of each marriage. The laws of the various states differ, and some of them are somewhat lax. The laws also require that the two persons shall be of suitable age. It is a pity that the laws cannot require the husband to prove himself capable of giving a wife proper support, or to guarantee the care and education of children. But, as we have seen, the laws alone cannot compel people to be thrifty, industrious, or honorable.

Divorce. — There are certain causes which prevent marriage from being happy, or even tolerable. Such are unfaithfulness, cruelty, and crime. It does not seem just to require the life of the innocent husband or wife to be blighted by the guilt of the other party. The state, therefore, which by the marriage law unites husband and wife, may also, by a special permit, sever the bond. This is called divorce. The authority to grant divorce is generally vested in the courts, in order that injustice may not be done to innocent parties and to children. The reasons, however, which are held sufficient for divorce vary in different States; and this difference of custom and law sometimes helps unscrupulous persons to obtain an easy divorce.

It is unfortunate that our present laws so easily permit the guilty, who have ruined the happiness of their marriage, to marry again and so to endanger other innocent lives. As we have already seen, however, it is difficult to protect by law those who are too foolish or unintelligent to protect themselves.

CHAPTER XLI.

THE PROBLEMS OF TEMPERANCE.

AMONG the moral questions which have come into view in modern times, like the questions of slavery and gambling, is the treatment of the alcoholic drinks. For in old times, although wise men saw dangers in the use of wine and strong drink, there were few who believed that their use was wrong. Moreover, the manufacture of the stronger drinks, such as brandy and wine, is comparatively modern.

The old world idea of temperance. — It used to be thought that the only harm in the alcoholic drinks was by their abuse. Temperance was to exercise self-control and not to become intoxicated. As this was the general opinion of the world for thousands of years, it is not strange that multitudes still hold it; most of the foreign people who come to our shores bring this idea with them. There are doubtless persons who have easy control of their appetites and are naturally temperate. There are probably certain races and nations who are more temperate than others.

Facts upon which all are agreed. — All thoughtful persons agree that the harm, the waste, misery, and poverty, the degradation and crime which come from the use of the alcoholic drinks are a terrible evil to the nation. The amount of money which goes every year in the United States to the purchase of these drinks rises towards one thousand millions of dollars. The public cost for courts, prisons, and police is largely increased by men's habits of drunkenness. The children of drinking parents are apt to have enfeebled bodies and minds. All these evils are perhaps worse in America, on account of our stimulating climate and the somewhat nervous character of our people, who are easily hurt by the whip of an artificial stimulant.

Moreover, the physicians, who once used wine and other alcoholic drinks quite freely in the treatment of disease, have discovered that they are likely to do harm rather than good, and that their use even as medicine is extremely narrow.

It is agreed that the alcoholic drinks, as a rule, are bad for women, whose finer nervous organization is easily damaged by the poison of the alcohol; so for men who lead a sedentary life, as clerks, students, and men in professional work; so especially for the young. Even the milder alcoholic drinks contain alcohol enough to injure the growing body.

It is also agreed that no one in health needs the alcoholic drinks, as was once supposed. Indeed, extremes of heat, cold, and exposure, such as soldiers, sailors, or explorers endure, it is now known, are better borne by those who do not habitually use these stimulants. The fact is, the intoxicating drink, the stronger it is with alcohol, acts so much the more like a poison. If, then, the body has already been subject to this effect, like a bow frequently bent, it becomes less elastic.

It is agreed that the alcoholic drinks are specially insidious. Their use easily grows into an enslaving habit and begets a craving for a larger and more frequent use, which at last becomes a disease, paralyzing the will of the patient. It is evident that those who have decided or, especially, hereditary taste for these liquors, expose themselves to peril in using them at all.

It is agreed that the alcoholic drinks are particularly subject to adulteration, often with poisonous substances, as well as to artificial strengthening with cheap and bad alcohol. The character of many of the persons connected with the liquor traffic is such as to make it difficult and costly to obtain pure liquors.

It is agreed that it would be well for the great class of working people and their families, who make up the strength of the nation, if they did not touch intoxicating drinks. The universal disuse of these drinks may be reckoned as equal to the average increase of their wages by one-tenth. Already, indeed, in a great many kinds of employment, drinking men cannot get work. Thus the Civil Service Commissioners will not recommend them as laborers or for the police. The managers of the best railroads do not want them for engineers or switchmen.

The modern or American idea. — Since the use of alcoholic beverages does terrible harm to multitudes of individuals, and to the nation, the question is, whether the rule does not hold good, as in the case of polygamy, slavery, and gambling; namely, that what is so harmful to society, is therefore wrong. This is what many say of the use of intoxicating drinks. Their use was excusable while men had not yet come to see the mischief which they caused. But as it does not make slavery right that there were some good masters, so, now that intoxicating drinks are on the whole proved to work vast moral evils to society, it does not make their use right, that certain individuals are able to get a little pleasure for themselves from them. If their use does harm rather than good to the nation, every friend to society should let them alone. Whoever persists in encouraging their use makes himself so far an enemy to society.

This new idea may be called American, because it has made its way faster in this country than anywhere else. But it has adherents everywhere, and especially in the English-speaking countries, in which new ideas always win hospitable attention.

A new moral rule. — When a new moral rule appears, there are two stages in accepting it. First, many individuals take it up and obey it themselves; then, when public opinion at last becomes strong enough, and men's consciences generally own the rule, laws are made to express the new public opinion, and to help enforce it. Thus many pure-hearted men gave up polygamy long before public opinion was strong enough in the world to make laws about it; and many individuals refused to gamble while the laws still permitted the harmful practice. So great numbers of people have become total abstainers from intoxicating drinks before their neighbors have recognized the new moral rule which they believe right.

The reformers. — There must always be those in society who are pioneers, to hew the way in advance. Sometimes these pioneers have to try dangerous experiments; often they have to brave the old established public opinion; they may even run the risk of being mistaken, or disappointed, like the navigators who expected to discover a northwest passage from Europe to Asia. When the pioneers endeavor to change men's habits, customs, or laws, and establish new and more beneficial customs, we call them reformers. Such have been the noblest men who have lived; for they have not sought anything for themselves, but only the good of society. Wilberforce in England, and Garrison in America, were such reformers in getting rid of slavery. There are men of the same spirit in every State, who are trying to get rid of the old bad habit of intemperance. The reformers have to give up their own time, or money, or pleasure for the good of the people.

What is being done. — All are agreed that intemperance will not cure itself. Public opinion, therefore, already demands certain laws to restrict the sale of intoxicating drinks. Liquors ought not to be sold to children or to drunkards; they ought not to be sold by reckless and un-principled persons; the places of sale ought to be closed within certain hours; there ought to be no adulteration of the liquors sold; dealers who break the laws should not only be punished, but also forbidden to sell again; drunk-enness perhaps should be punished.

License. — It is held by many citizens that the sale of intoxicating drinks, like that of drugs, should only be in the hands of authorized or licensed dealers. As the expense to the community from drinking habits is enor-mous, and as alcoholic drinks are not a necessity, but a luxury, the license to sell should require a special fee or tax. The higher this license tax is made, the smaller the number of drinking-places will be, and the more careful the licensed dealers will be to obey the laws. It is also for their interest to aid the police to close unlicensed places. License laws are favored by those who hold that there is a proper use of the lighter alcoholic beverages, as well as a danger of abuse. There are many, also, who, believing such beverages to be injurious, yet favor license laws; partly because they do not think it possible to prevent people by law from using these drinks, and partly because, as long as men use them, it seems just that the dealers should be made to bear the public loss which results from their business.

On the other hand, if the liquor traffic on the whole works evil, the State ought not to sanction it by granting licenses, as it is not willing to license lotteries. Moreover, it is thought to be undemocratic to permit the rich to sell liquors, but to forbid the poor, who cannot afford to pay the license fee.

The drinking-saloon. — The saloon is a place where almost nothing is sold except intoxicating drinks. It is well known that these drinks have their most injurious effect when taken without food. The saloons naturally become the resort of the most idle and worthless. There is a strong feeling in the United States that they are a public nuisance and ought somehow to be abolished. It has not been found easy, however, to make a law to close the drinking-saloons while restaurants and hotels are still permitted to sell liquors.

Prohibition. — Many persons who see the great harm in the alcoholic drinks hold that laws ought to be made to prevent their sale, except strictly for mechanical or medicinal purposes. They would not only have all drinking-saloons closed; no hotels should furnish wine to their guests; no grocers should sell it to their customers. In some States, as Maine and Kansas, laws have been passed to this effect. The same States have also made amendments to their constitutions, forbidding the manufacture or sale of intoxicating drinks. Many citizens aim at a similar amendment to the Constitution of the United States.

It is always unfortunate, however, when any new law touching men's customs and habits has to be passed over the protest of a large minority of the people, who have not been persuaded of the merits of the law. It is specially unfortunate if many of those who vote for the law do not actually keep it themselves. For these reasons the prohibitory laws have largely failed so far of enforcement,

except in communities where public opinion already con-
demns drinking-habits.

Public control of the liquor traffic. — The wish to
make money tempts the liquor-dealers to try to sell as
much liquor as they can, and to sell to persons who ought
not to touch it. A plan has therefore been proposed to
put this dangerous traffic entirely into the hands of the
government, so that it shall not be for any one's interest to
get profit from it. The truth is, that there is always some
need of alcohol for science, and in the arts, and for the alcoholic drinks as medicine, and for the aged. As long, also,
as many individuals conscientiously hold the old-fashioned
ideas about the use of wine and beer, they are likely to insist upon some way of procuring their drinks, and will even
be tempted to break and evade the laws, if the laws shut
up all legitimate ways of obtaining them. The plan, therefore, is that the government shall provide or license certain
places where the alcoholic drinks may be purchased under
certain strict rules. They would be refused altogether to
children and drunken persons. Otherwise their use would
be left to every one's judgment and conscience, with which
the state would not venture to meddle. Harmless drinks
should be also for sale at the same places. It should be
for the interest of the person or company in charge of the
store to sell these other drinks, while there could be no
private profit from the sale of any intoxicating beverage.
This plan is called the Gothenburg system, from the
Swedish city, where it was first adopted, and where it is
thought to have done much good in diminishing intemperance. Another form of this system is in successful operation in Norway.

Local option. — In some States the experiment has been
tried of permitting each town or city, or county, to de-

termine for itself whether it will license or prohibit the sale of intoxicating drinks. Thus where public opinion is already strong against drinking-habits, the people can vote to shut up the saloons and can require their officers to enforce the law. But where public opinion still runs in the other direction, in great towns crowded with ignorant persons or with immigrants accustomed to foreign habits, and where, therefore, the will to enforce a prohibitory law is lacking, it is permitted to regulate and license the sale of liquors; if, meanwhile, any city becomes at last tired of its liquor saloons, it can vote to try the other method. Thus by various experiments, the people can learn which method is best for the public safety and happiness.

Moral education. — Besides the change in the drinking-habits which laws aim to effect, there is a slow growth of public opinion which works to make people temperate. The evil physical effects of alcohol are coming to be better known. Drunkenness, which was once respectable, is now a disgrace. Large numbers of persons practise total abstinence and, like Benjamin Franklin, find themselves stronger, more prosperous, and happier in consequence. Generous young men see that it is a poor habit for the individual which is bad for the nation. "That cannot be good for the bee which is bad for the hive."

PART FIFTH.

INTERNATIONAL DUTIES; OR, THE RIGHTS AND DUTIES OF NATIONS.

PART FIFTH.

INTERNATIONAL DUTIES; OR, THE RIGHTS AND DUTIES OF NATIONS.

CHAPTER XLII.

INTERNATIONAL LAW, AND HOW IT GROWS.

Ancient warfare. — In early times war was the common condition in which people lived. It was thought right to do as much harm as possible to a foreign country. A weak nation was regarded as fair prey for a stronger nation. Quarrels were always breaking out between neighboring peoples. Prisoners taken in war, if not butchered, were held as slaves. Private property was the booty of the victors. On the sea, men were even more inhumane than on the land. Ships driven on shore or wrecked were, even to a quite recent period, the plunder of the people of the country on whose shores they were driven. The foreign sailors who escaped the storm were liable to be killed if they went on shore.

International jealousy. — War was not the only evil which kept neighboring nations apart. Men used also to be very jealous and suspicious of foreigners, as well as of their customs and religion: they did not welcome foreign immigration. It was thought necessary to put heavy and costly restrictions on foreign trade. It was believed that money ought not, under any circumstances, to be sent out of the country. It used to be thought desirable to have other countries poor.

The dawn of international rights. — There were a few circumstances which mitigated the horrors of ancient war. It was early held that the persons of heralds or ambassadors were sacred. Though the dead were liable to be stripped of their clothing and ornaments, their burial was generally permitted. Sometimes a truce was agreed upon for this purpose. The oppression of stronger tribes or nations led the weaker to combine in confederations and alliances. These alliances were celebrated by solemn religious oaths. The Greeks, for instance, united against the Persians, and for a while almost stopped fighting among themselves. The vast empires of the Assyrians and the Persians compelled a degree of peace between the subject nations; and increasing travel and commerce brought about the acquaintance of people of different languages. It was found to be more profitable to the conquerors to spare the conquered than to destroy them. Thus the power of Rome was built up by a wise system of tolerating the customs and the religion of her subjects.

Christianity. — When Christianity was established there was a new bond among different nations; for everywhere there were Christians pledged to befriend each other. Christianity, however, in spite of its benevolent principles, did not succeed in making nations live together peaceably. On the contrary, some of the most terrible wars came about between Christian nations and over religious quarrels.

Popular government. — At last in certain countries, and especially in England, the people came to have political power. While before, war had been carried on merely for the benefit of the rulers, or at least of the soldiers, now the rulers were obliged to have some form of consent from the people.

Popular intelligence. — Meanwhile, the people, having learned to read and to think, had become more intelligent, and therefore averse to war. They had also become better acquainted with the people of other nations, and had found out their good qualities. They discovered that they were richer by trading than by fighting. Moreover, the fact that war had become very expensive and terribly destructive worked to abate its horrors, since even bad rulers feared to ask their people to pay its cost or run the risk of failing in it. The growing humanity of our modern times also insisted that respect should be paid, in case of war, to the property, as well as to the lives, of non-combatants and private citizens.

Reciprocity of interests. — People are also slowly learning that it is for their own advantage that their foreign customers should be prosperous, and therefore able to buy more goods and to pay their debts. As it is desirable to have one's fellow-citizens well off, so it is desirable to have all the different families of nations prosper together.

Thus religion and self-interest, as well as the general humanizing influence of travel and commerce, have slowly tended to bring nations to a more friendly feeling towards each other, and even when war arises, to preserve some measure of respect and sympathy towards foes, in place of the ancient hate and cruelty.

The new sentiment. — The change which has come to pass in the relation of states to each other may be briefly expressed as follows: Once different peoples regarded each other as enemies, and the prosperity of one was thought to be the injury of another. Now they regard each other as neighbors, and the harm of one nation is believed to be a loss to all the others.

International law. — There have gradually been established, partly through treaties, partly by the precedents of usage, certain rules or laws governing the behavior of nations towards each other, exactly as the laws of a state regulate the behavior of citizens. International law is the working out of the principles of justice and humanity among neighboring nations. There are courts in each nation which have the important duty of deciding questions of international law. The United States courts have this jurisdiction.

CHAPTER XLIII.

THE RIGHTS OF NATIONS.

The three purposes of international law. — We learned that there were three purposes of government, — protection from enemies abroad, protection from the injustice of fellow-citizens, and public convenience. International law follows three similar purposes.

In the first place, it unites different nations against common enemies. Thus it aims to suppress piracy and the slave-trade. It has rules for giving up dangerous criminals to justice.

In the second place, international law aims to secure fair dealing among neighboring nations. There are certain important mutual rights and duties between nations which international law aims to define. Thus treaties and usage fix and preserve the sacredness of boundary lines, upon which no foreign nation has a right to trespass.

Thirdly, international law aims at the general convenience. There are certain objects — for example, a universal postal service — which many governments unite to secure. Treaties and usage also serve to protect travellers and foreign residents, as well as the goods of foreign merchants, in all civilized countries. Lighthouses and coast surveys are maintained for the interest of the commerce of the world.

The diplomatic service. — Ambassadors, consuls, and other public agents, with certain powers and privileges attached to their office, are recognized by foreign governments as representing the rights and interests of their countrymen.

Domestic affairs. — Every nation has a right to manage its affairs without dictation from other nations. If France, for example, wants a president, rather than a king, England and Germany have no right to interfere. Likewise, in the American Civil War, it was the right of our government to settle our difficulties without interference from other countries. This is the same kind of right which belongs to every household to make its own rules without dictation from outside.

Foreign commerce and intercourse. — On the same principle, every nation has a right, if it is judged to be best, and no treaty forbids, to exclude the people or the products of another country. China has thus the right to forbid Europeans from residing in her territory, or to shut out British opium. When we say that the Chinese have a right to exclude foreigners, we do not decide whether such action is wise or righteous. We mean that the Chinese have a right, in their own country, not to be molested by other nations. So likewise, if the safety of our institutions could be proved to require it, we should have the right to limit foreign immigration.

The custom-house. — A nation has also a right to require taxes or custom-dues upon the importation of foreign goods, and to make its own rules to govern foreign trade. Thus nearly everything which comes into our country has to pay a high duty; partly to raise the revenue for our national expenses, and partly because a majority of those who make our laws believe that it is for the interests of our people to make foreign cloth, books, iron, etc., so costly that our people will be obliged to buy the products of our own industries. This " protection," as it is called, diminishes trade with foreign nations ; but they have no right, because their trade is injured, or because they think our laws foolish, to compel us to admit their goods free.

Maritime rights. — It is the right of every nation, while at peace, that her ships should sail the seas without molestation. That is to say, the ocean is recognized as the great common highway, free to all. The fisheries also, except close to shore, are common international property. The right to the seas is limited, however, by certain conditions of international law. A ship has no right, for instance, to be engaged in the slave-trade, or to carry material of war to belligerent nations. As soon as a ship leaves the open sea and comes to land or into a harbor, she must regard the rules of the country.

Rights of travel and of foreign residence. — It is the right of every nation that her citizens, so far as they are allowed to travel or to reside in other countries, should have as ample protection of life and property as is afforded to the citizens of those countries. If an American resides in Germany or Japan, he is entitled, like a guest in a house, to the same care which the German or Japanese government gives any of its own people.

Authors' and inventors' rights. — It is generally held that writers and inventors are entitled to some compensation for their work from the public, which they instruct, entertain, or profit. This compensation is given in the form of copyrights upon books or patents upon inventions. If such compensation is justly due from the country in which the author or inventor lives, there is no reason why it should not also be due from any other country which uses the inventions or reads the books. The proposed system of international patents and copyrights has its rise in this principle.

CHAPTER XLIV.

THE DUTIES OF NATIONS.

Obvious or recognized duties. — There are certain obvious duties which nations owe each other, such as keeping treaties and observing the usages and forms which, like good manners among neighbors, promote convenience and friendly feeling. It follows that each government ought to forbid its people to do harm to the persons or property of another nation. Thus in our Civil War it was the duty of the British government to forbid shipbuilders to fit out privateers, like the " Alabama," to prey on our commerce.

Duties of honor. — Besides duties already recognized by treaty and custom, there are further duties, which grow out of the principle that all nations are neighbors. The barbarous way was to make laws against foreigners as enemies. A nation did right, therefore, it was thought, to rob them if it could, through its laws and taxes, of their share in trade. On the contrary, the laws of a nation ought not only to secure the rights of its own citizens, but also to regard the interests of foreigners.

As laws ought not to be designed to interfere to give any class or individual more than a fair share, so they ought not to be designed to interfere with the natural working of the law of supply and demand, in order to give a nation more than its share as compared with its neighbors. This is not only justice; it is for the interest of a nation to deal fairly with its neighbors; for, as we have seen, the wealth of one nation is not gained out of the losses of its neighbors, but out of their wealth. It is therefore desirable, so far as laws and taxes can be so arranged, to increase the prosperity of neighboring nations rather than to diminish it.

The duties of nations towards their colonies. — Certain races, as the Greeks in old times, and the Anglo-Saxons in modern times, have spread over the world by planting colonies. Thus the United States were first settled by colonies; and our Western Territories to-day may be considered as colonies from the older parts of the country. It is the duty of a nation to protect its colonists from foreign enemies and savages, and to establish as rapidly as possible settled government. It should be the aim of the parent state to raise the colony to self-support and self government. If the colony, when established, remains a part of the older nation, it is entitled to fair representation in the general government. It ought then to meet its proportionate share of the general expense.

The duties of civilized nations to the less civilized. — The duties of nations to each other are complicated by the fact that large parts of the world are still possessed by barbarous or half-civilized people. Such nations either do not recognize international obligations at all, or could not be depended upon to keep them.

Among so-called civilized nations, moreover, conduct is still often dictated by jealousy or enmity of other nations. There is thus a vast difference of level between the ideas, the customs, and the prosperity of different nations. It is therefore claimed by some that certain temporary guards and defences may have to be put up by the laws of a country against the operation of bad laws and customs elsewhere. Thus ignorant foreign immigrants, like the Chinese, it is said, might come to this country in such numbers as to endanger our institutions, and might therefore need to be restricted. Or the cheap labor of underpaid foreign workmen, it is claimed, might threaten to lower the wages and prosperity of our working people. So, too, the serious misgovernment or anarchy of a half-civilized state, some think, may call for intervention from outside, not only for the interests of foreign residents, but also for the sake of the oppressed native people.

To these things it may be answered that, as a rule, it is better to trust men than to be afraid of them; that the more intelligent need least to fear the power or competition of the ignorant; and that it is even more dangerous for nations than for neighbors to meddle and interfere with each other's affairs.

The duties of nations towards tribes of savages. — Most of the great nations of the world have, either in their own territory or among their coloniés, various barbarous tribes. Such tribes cannot justly be said to own the land over which they only roam and hunt. They have no right, therefore, to prevent settlers who will use the land from coming to it. On the other hand, the savages have certain rights which deserve consideration. The proper treatment of these rights is one of the most difficult problems.

It is the duty of a nation to give the same treatment to the savages within its borders that it gives to other men. Its duty is to protect them in the rights which they have in common with all men; as, for instance, in ownership of the lands which they actually occupy or cultivate. It is a duty to afford suitable education to the children of the savage people, that they may adapt themselves to the change of life which civilization brings. The savages ought to be allowed to acquire independent property, as others do; and upon proper qualification they ought to be given a share in the government. On the contrary, it is not a duty to recognize savage tribes as sovereign nations, and it is wrong to give them rations and presents, which degrade and pauperize them.

Our Indian wards. — There are more than a quarter of a million of Indians, mostly in the Western States, the Indian and other Territories, and in Alaska, with whom our government has had peculiar relations.

Most of these Indians have had assigned to them *reservations*, or great tracts of land. Sometimes they have been removed to these reservations by our armies after a war; or the reservations have been secured by peaceful treaty on the part of our government. Frequently the government has also promised money or rations to support the Indians, or to pay them for giving up lands which the white people wanted to settle upon. Thus the Indians have been pushed further west, and have been confined within narrower limits, while the buffaloes and game or which they once subsisted have disappeared.

The government has appointed, through the office of the Secretary of the Interior, agents for the reservations, to furnish supplies and to look after the interests of the Indians, as if they were wards of the nation. White persons were forbidden to settle upon the reservations or to trade with the Indians.

Our government meant to do justly and to make the Indians comfortable. But the reservation system made them miserable .paupers. They came to depend upon the rations of the government. They were often given very poor land, which they could not cultivate; and no individual had any land of his own. If they had anything to sell, they were shut away by the boundary of the reservation from bringing it to market. If they were wronged, they could not go to court to obtain justice as citizens, or even as foreigners may. Often, too, the agent was a bad man who used his office to make himself rich by stealing from the supplies meant for the Indians. Thus millions of dollars have been benevolently expended in doing more harm than good.

New methods of treating the Indians. — The policy of the government is now being changed in several directions. Many schools have been established in which to educate the Indian children in various industries. Plans have been made to divide their land and to give them land "in severalty"; that is, private ownership of their farms, such as white men enjoy. As fast as this is done there will be no need of the reservations, or the agents, but the Indians can go with their products to market, and can buy and sell like others. They can also go to the courts to get justice. They can have a vote and be citizens on the same conditions as others. There will not be tribes any longer or chiefs, but the Indians, like the negroes in the South, will become a part of the nation.

CHAPTER XLV.

WAR AND ARBITRATION; PATRIOTISM.

War establishments. — In barbarous countries every free man is supposed to be a soldier; in civilized nations there is a standing army even in times of peace. In several countries the army is numbered by hundreds of thousands of men. Besides the enormous cost of supporting armies and their equipments, most nations also maintain expensive fortifications and ships of war. Hardly a year passes in which, in some part of the world, there is not a war. The preparation for war is thought to be one of the chief duties of a government in time of peace. In fact, the larger part of the taxes of the nations, to the amount of more than two thousand millions of dollars a year, goes for war expenses and to pay the interest of war debts.

The reason for war. — When one man injures another, or a difference arises between them, there are courts which will give justice. When, however, a difference arises between nations, or one nation injures another, there are no courts, and the injured nation must suffer, unless it is strong enough to enforce its rights. There are also no police among nations to prevent one people from attacking another. The necessity of war, therefore, grows out of the fact that a nation cannot call upon any higher power to protect it, but must defend itself. Thus nations have to deal with their quarrels and disputes as individuals used to do before there were courts or police.

Just and unjust war. — A just war is one in which a nation defends itself, or protects the rights of its people or of its allies. A just war must be for necessity, liberty, or principle. It was a just war when England beat off the great Spanish Armada in the reign of Queen Elizabeth. An unjust war is one in which a nation engages for plunder, or to increase its territory, or for national glory, or for any other reason than necessity, liberty, or principle.

The laws of war. — As a man, if obliged to defend himself against a quarrelsome neighbor, is not justified in doing unnecessary injury to life or property, or in showing malice and rancor, so when nations are drawn into war, it is not only cruel to do needless violence to the lives and property of the people, but it is also for the interest of the nations at war that nothing shall be done to prevent friendly intercourse from being resumed as soon as possible. Policy and humanity, therefore, alike forbid malevolent or needlessly destructive methods of war. The international laws of war, sanctioned partly by usage and partly by treaties, and still imperfect, may be considered an attempt to restrain the evils of war. These laws, for example, forbid the use of poison against an enemy, or of assassination, or of banditti, or of guerillas, or of savage allies. They forbid prisoners to be put to death, and require care for the wounded. They respect private property and the persons of non-combatants, as well as public buildings, libraries, and works of art. They forbid the wanton destruction of towns. So on the seas, international law respects the right of neutral vessels, except when carrying "contraband of war." Certain nations already have agreed among themselves to abolish privateering. There is a strong feeling also against the injustice of annexing foreign territory in war without the consent of the inhabitants.

Thus while in old times it used to be thought right to do the utmost possible harm to an enemy, modern warfare aims to do the least harm compatible with securing a just and permanent peace.

Arbitration. — Ignorant or barbarous people fight; intelligent people settle their differences peaceably. Thus neighbors often agree to settle a dispute by reference to a committee of their friends. So nations, instead of going to war, sometimes agree to leave a question to the decision of umpires. Thus the question of the Alabama Claims was amicably settled between Great Britain and the United States.

An international court of appeal. — There is no reason why all questions between civilized nations should not be settled without the barbarous method of war. There might be a permanent international court of appeal, to which all differences among nations should be referred. All civilized governments would bind themselves to abide by the decision of this court, as civilized men are now bound by the laws of the land. The power of all nations would be pledged, if necessary, to enforce international law. The great war establishments would be mostly abolished, and nations would adopt the higher law of treating each other as neighbors.

Patriotism and the national flag. — It is natural that every person should have a special feeling towards his own country. If his forefathers have lived there, if the nation has had a memorable history, if the laws and institutions have helped to secure freedom and prosperity, he may be expected to have a sense of affection and loyalty to his native land. This feeling is patriotism. It leads one to prefer the good of the whole country to the good of only one State. It removes the lines of north or south, and east or west, since all sections belong to the common country.

Patriotism also leads a citizen to wish to see his nation strong, prosperous, and honored among the family of nations. The national flag is the emblem of the common government, and with Americans, of the union of all the States. The patriot loves to see it flying over the public buildings and on ships in distant ports.

A citizen's duty and responsibility bind him to his own country, as family ties bind him to be faithful to his own relatives. But while patriotism urges us to seek the interest of our own country, it never requires us to serve our own country to the injury or loss of other nations. It is not patriotism to cry, " My country, right or wrong," or to help and uphold one's government in doing injustice to another country. Thus it was patriotism in the famous Englishman, John Bright, when he resigned his place in the government because he was unwilling to help carry on an unrighteous war in Egypt. Patriotism makes us wish to see our nation strong, but it ought not to make us wish to see other nations poor and unhappy; as it would be mean in a boat-race to wish for the victory of one's own crew through accident or sickness in the other crews.

Citizens by adoption. — Patriotism does not always require a citizen to be a native of his country. Thus millions of people have emigrated to America, as the fathers of all the rest once came, choosing to make this land their home. Many of these people have been poor or oppressed in their native land, and have come here to seek equal rights. These citizens of foreign birth may feel a peculiar patriotism towards the new land, which has given them a home and the privileges of citizenship on easy-terms. They have repeatedly proved their loyalty to the land of their adoption, and their willingness to die in following its flag. Neither need a man cease to love his·

old home and the fatherland because he makes a new home across the sea. Thus English, and Irish, and German Americans continue after coming here to interest themselves in the welfare of their native country, as well as in the good of America.

The common humanity. — Civilization means that men like each other more, the better they are acquainted. Religion means the same. While the ignorant and bad distrust or fear each other, the intelligent and noble see the good in strangers and foreigners. To use a fine old Roman saying, they deem that *nothing human is foreign*. As we find out, therefore, that no State in America can suffer without the other States suffering also, since all are bound up together, so we learn that no country in the world can be poor or wretched alone, for the interests of all men are alike.

Summary. — We have seen that all matters of business or government are interwoven with questions of right and wrong. No one can even make a mistake or blunder, much less do an injustice, in the conduct of his affairs, without spreading harm or loss to others. On the other hand, no one conquers honest success for himself alone. Much more in politics the wrong-doing or negligence of a single individual reacts against the welfare of the whole state, as the public spirit of one or a few keeps the state safe. But it is often costly to do right, and the gain seems far away or likely to come to others, but not to one's self; while the wrong promises for the present to be more easy and convenient; as when one is building a house, if he thinks only of the present labor and expense, it is cheaper not to put in an honest foundation and sound timber. But if he thinks of others, foresees the coming storms, and understands the laws of architecture, the right way to build seems then the only possible one.

A bit of philosophy. — There are various reasons given why we ought to do right. Some of them are long and difficult to understand; but one thing is quite certain and simple, although very wonderful. There is in every right-minded person a conscience, or sense of duty, which urges us, as soon as we are shown what is right, to do it; or, when a thing seems wrong, to refuse it. If, then, we disobey conscience and do selfish, unjust, disgraceful, or base things, we presently lose the power and will to do right; as the tree that is bent loses the power of growing straight. It is as though a disease had seized upon us, bringing pain and disquiet, or blindness and decay. Whereas, if we follow the bidding of conscience, strength, restfulness, and gladness attend us. It is as if conscience was the organ of moral health and soundness, as the heart governs the circulation of the blood.

Conscience also binds us, through just and friendly acts, to cordial, generous, and helpful relations with our fellow-men. It will not let us hate, despise, or desert them. Thus, as each man's conscience has free course, human society works together in health and happiness. But disobedience to conscience represses sympathy, separates us from each other, and locks us up each one by himself, like criminals in their solitary cells. When, therefore, any one's conscience is repressed, it is as if one of the little valves of a great engine failed to work.

This is not all. Duty is one of the great and constant forces of the universe. It is stronger than any man, or all the men who live. Whoever obeys, though no one else is with him, is sustained, as if the universe were on his side. For we know that whatever is right, or ought to be, must come in the end: those who help it will succeed; those who resist it will fail and be forgotten. For justice and right are at the foundation of the world. We must do right, then, if we want to go with the victorious forces that make life and health both for each individual and for all mankind.

The higher conscience. — There are two kinds of conscience in men. One kind is like an engine built to draw a train on a level track. It simply keeps one up to the duties which habit, custom, convenience, or expediency requires. The man with this lower power of conscience is apt to ask at every question or crisis: What will other men say or do?

The higher kind of conscience is like the powerful engine which can lift its load up a steep grade. It does not go by convenience, but by the standard of right. It does not ask what the custom is, but what it ought to be; not what others do, but what is right. The men and women who have this kind of conscience are those who help make the nation strong: out of their list come the heroes, reformers, and statesmen.

BOOKS FOR REFERENCE.

Congressional Government. By WOODROW WILSON. Houghton, Mifflin & Co.

*The State. By WOODROW WILSON. D. C. Heath & Co.

*The American Commonwealth. By JAMES BRYCE. 2 volumes. Macmillan & Co.
This is a most comprehensive and sympathetic account of our institutions.

The Nation. By ELISHA MULFORD, LL.D. Houghton, Mifflin & Co.

*Our Government: How it grew, What it does, and How it does it. By JESSE MACY. Ginn & Co.

*Civil Government in the United States. By JOHN FISKE. Houghton, Mifflin & Co.
Mr. Fiske's book gives a very clear view of the origin and growth of American institutions.

Analysis of Civil Government. By CALVIN TOWNSEND.

Shorter Course in Civil Government. By the same author. American Book Co.

*How We are governed. By ANNA LAURENS DAWES. D. Lothrop Co.

Politics, an Introduction to the Study of Comparative Constitutional Law. By W. W. CRANE and BERNARD MOSES. Putnam's Sons.

A Short History of Anglo-Saxon Freedom. By JAMES K. HOSMER. Charles Scribner's Sons.

The Ancient City. By DE COULANGES. Lee & Shepard.

The American Statesmen Series. Houghton, Mifflin & Co.

More's Utopia. Edited by J. RAWSON LUMBY. Cambridge (Eng.) University Press.

The Statesman's Year Book. Macmillan & Co.

Whittaker's Almanac.

***Political Economy.** By FRANCIS A. WALKER. Henry Holt & Co.

Either the larger book by General Walker, president of the Institute of Technology in Boston, or the more elementary work, makes an excellent introduction to the study of Political Economy.

An Introduction to Political Economy. By Prof. RICHARD T. ELY, of the Johns Hopkins University. Chautauqua Press.

***Principles of Political Economy.** GIDE. D. C. Heath & Co.

Political Economy. An elementary text-book of the economics of commerce. By E. C. K. GONNER. R. Sutton & Co., London.

***Political Economy.** By J. E. SYMES. Rivingtons, London.

Elementary Politics. By THOMAS RALEIGH. Henry Frowde, London.

These last three are little books, but thoughtful, simple in style, and inexpensive.

Problems in Political Economy. By Prof. W. G. SUMNER, of Yale College.

Manual of Political Economy. By HENRY FAWCETT.

Business. By JAMES PLATT.

Money. By the same author. Putnam's Sons.

Natural Law in the Business World. By HENRY WOOD. Lee & Shepard.

Work and Wages. By THOROLD ROGERS. Putnam's Sons.

This book gives a very interesting account of the industrial history of England.

Recent Economic Changes. By DAVID A. WELLS. Putnam's Sons.

Economics of Industry. By A. and M. P. MARSHALL. Macmillan & Co.

Social Problems. By HENRY GEORGE. Kegan Paul, Trench & Co.

Mr. George's books are from the point of view of one who believes that he has a cure for many social and political evils through "the single tax" upon land.

Economic and Social History of New England. 2 volumes. By WM. B. WEEDEN. Houghton, Mifflin & Co.

The Publications of the American Economic Association.

The Quarterly Journal of Economics. Published at Cambridge.

Everyday Business. By M. S. EMERY. Lee & Shepard.

*****A Plain Man's Talk on the Labor Question.** By SIMON NEWCOMB. Harpers.

Socialism, New and Old. By WM. GRAHAM. D. Appleton & Co.

French and German Socialism. By RICHARD T. ELY. Harpers.

Profit-Sharing between Employer and Employee. By N. P. GILMAN. Houghton, Mifflin & Co.

Mr. Gilman's book gives a clear and interesting account of the history and working of this method.

Co-operative Savings and Loan Associations. By SEYMOUR DEXTER. D. Appleton & Co.

This book is an authority upon the Co-operative Banks.

Trades Unions: their Origin and Objects, Influence and Efficacy. By WM. TRANT. Kegan Paul, Trench & Co.

*****How to Help the Poor.** By Mrs. JAMES T. FIELDS. Houghton, Mifflin & Co.

Pauperism, Its Causes and Remedies. By HENRY FAWCETT. Macmillan & Co.

Crime, Its Causes and Remedy. By GORDON RYLANDS. T. Fisher Unwin, London.

The Publications of the National Prison Association.

Notes of Lessons on Moral Subjects. By FREDERICK W. HOCKWOOD. T. Nelson & Sons, London and New York.

Lessons on Manners. By EDITH E. WIGGIN. Lee & Shepard.

***Politics for Young Americans.** By CHARLES NORDHOFF. Harpers.

This is a very useful book in the form of letters from a father to his son.

Talks about Law. By E. P. DOLE. Houghton, Mifflin & Co.

Introduction to the Study of International Law. By THEODORE D. WOOLSEY.

The Readers' Guide to Economic, Social and Political Subjects. Published for the Society for Political Education.

This last work will enable one to find the authorities upon any subject which he wishes to pursue thoroughly.

Mr. JOHN FISKE's "Civil Government" contains a useful list of books. So also does WOODROW WILSON's little book, "State and Federal Government." The Massachusetts Society for Promoting Good Citizenship, Dr. C. F. Crehore, Secretary, publishes a list of works on Civil Government, upon the recommendation of one of their committees.

The Constitution

of the

United States.

WE, the people of the United States, in order to form a more perfect union, establish justice, insure domestic tranquillity, provide for the common defense, promote the general welfare, and secure the blessings of liberty to ourselves and our posterity, do ordain and establish this Constitution for the United States of America.

ARTICLE I.

SECTION I.

All legislative powers herein granted shall be vested in a Congress of the United States, which shall consist of a Senate and House of Representatives.

SECTION II.

The House of Representatives shall be composed of members chosen every second year by the people of the several States, and the electors in each State shall have the qualifications requisite for electors of the most numerous branch of the State legislature.

No person shall be a Representative who shall not have attained the age of twenty-five years, and been seven years a citizen of the United States, and who shall not, when elected, be an inhabitant of that State in which he shall be chosen.

Representatives and direct taxes shall be apportioned among the several States which may be included within this Union, according to their respective numbers, which shall be determined by adding to the whole number of free persons, including those bound to service for a term of years, and excluding Indians not taxed, three fifths of all other persons. The actual enumeration shall be made within three years after the first meeting of the Congress of the United States, and within every subsequent term of ten years, in such manner as they shall by law direct. The number of Representatives shall not exceed one for every thirty thousand, but each State shall have at least one Representative; and until such enumeration shall be made, the State of *New Hampshire* shall be entitled to choose three, *Massachusetts* eight, *Rhode Island and Providence Plantations* one, *Connecticut* five, *New York* six, *New Jersey* four, *Pennsylvania* eight, *Delaware* one, *Maryland* six, *Virginia* ten, *North Carolina* five, *South Carolina* five, and *Georgia* three.

When vacancies happen in the representation from any State, the executive authority thereof shall issue writs of election to fill such vacancies.

The House of Representatives shall choose their Speaker and other officers, and shall have the sole power of impeachment.

SECTION III.

The Senate of the United States shall be composed of two Senators from each State, chosen by the legislature thereof, for six years; and each Senator shall have one vote.

Immediately after they shall be assembled in consequence of the first election, they shall be divided as equally as may be into three classes. The seats of the Senators of the first class shall be vacated at the expiration of the second year; of the second class, at the expiration of the fourth year, and of the third class, at the expiration of the sixth year, so that one-third may be chosen every second year; and if vacancies happen by resignation or otherwise during the recess of the legislature of any State, the executive thereof may make temporary appointments until the next meeting of the legislature, which shall then fill such vacancies.

No person shall be a Senator who shall not have attained to the age of thirty years, and been nine years a citizen of the United States, and who shall not, when elected, be an inhabitant of that State for which he shall be chosen.

The Vice-President of the United States shall be President of the Senate, but shall have no vote, unless they be equally divided.

The Senate shall choose their other officers, and also a President *pro tempore* in the absence of the Vice-President, or when he shall exercise the office of President of the United States.

The Senate shall have the sole power to try all impeachments. When sitting for that purpose, they shall be on oath or affirmation. When the President of the United States is tried, the Chief Justice shall preside : and no person shall be convicted without the concurrence of two thirds of the members present.

Judgment in cases of impeachment shall not extend further than to removal from office, and disqualification to hold and enjoy any office of honor, trust, or profit under the United States; but the party convicted shall, nevertheless, be liable and subject to indictment, trial, judgment, and punishment, according to law.

SECTION IV.

The times, places, and manner of holding elections for Senators and Representatives shall be prescribed in each State by the legislature thereof; but the Congress may at any time by law make or alter such regulations, except as to the places of choosing Senators.

The Congress shall assemble at least once in every year, and such meeting shall be on the first Monday in December, unless they shall by law appoint a different day.

SECTION V.

Each house shall be the judge of the elections, returns, and qualifications of its own members, and a majority of each shall constitute a quorum to do business; but a smaller number may adjourn from day to day, and may be authorized to compel the attendance of absent members, in such manner, and under such penalties, as each house may provide.

Each house may determine the rules of its proceedings, punish its members for disorderly behavior, and with the concurrence of two thirds, expel a member.

Each house shall keep a journal of its proceedings, and from time to time publish the same, excepting such parts as may in their judgment require secrecy, and the yeas and nays of the members of either house on any question shall, at the desire of one fifth of those present, be entered on the journal.

Neither house, during the session of Congress, shall, without the consent of the other, adjourn for more than three days, nor to any other place than that in which the two houses shall be sitting.

SECTION VI.

The Senators and Representatives shall receive a compensation for their services, to be ascertained by law and paid out of the Treasury of the United States. They shall, in all cases except treason, felony, and breach of the peace, be privileged from arrest during their attendance at the session of their respective houses, and in going to and returning from the same; and for any speech or debate in either house they shall not be questioned in any other place.

No Senator or Representative shall, during the time for which he was elected, be appointed to any civil office under the authority of the United States, which shall have been created, or the emoluments whereof shall have been increased during such time; and no person holding any office under the United States shall be a member of either house during his continuance in office.

SECTION VII.

All bills for raising revenue shall originate in the House of Representatives; but the Senate may propose or concur with amendments as on other bills.

Every bill which shall have passed the House of Representatives and the Senate shall, before it become a law, be presented to the President of the United States; if he approve he shall sign it, but if not he shall return it, with his objections, to that house in which it shall have originated, who shall enter the objections at large on their journal and proceed to reconsider it. If after such reconsideration two thirds of that house shall agree to pass the bill, it shall be sent, together with the objections, to the other house, by which it shall likewise be reconsidered, and if approved by two thirds of that house it shall become a law. But in all such cases the votes of both houses shall be determined by yeas and nays, and the names of the persons voting for and against the bill shall be entered on the journal of each house respectively. If any bill shall not be returned by the President within ten days (Sundays excepted) after it shall have been presented to him, the same shall be a law, in like manner as if he had signed it, unless the Congress by their adjournment prevent its return, in which case it shall not be a law.

Every order, resolution, or vote to which the concurrence of the Senate and House of Representatives may be necessary (except on a question of adjournment) shall be presented to the President of the United States; and before the same shall take effect, shall be approved by him, or being disapproved by him, shall be repassed by two thirds of the Senate and House of Representatives, according to the rules and limitations prescribed in the case of a bill.

SECTION VIII.

The Congress shall have power to lay and collect taxes, duties, imposts, and excises, to pay the debts and provide for the common defense and general welfare of the United States; but all duties, imposts, and excises shall be uniform throughout the United States;

To borrow money on the credit of the United States;

To regulate commerce with foreign nations and among the several States, and with the Indian tribes;

To establish an uniform rule of naturalization, and uniform laws on the subject of bankruptcies throughout the United States;

To coin money, regulate the value thereof, and of foreign coin, and fix the standard of weights and measures;

To provide for the punishment of counterfeiting the securities and current coin of the United States;

To establish post-offices and post-roads;

To promote the progress of science and useful arts by securing for limited times to authors and inventors the exclusive right to their respective writings and discoveries;

To constitute tribunals inferior to the Supreme Court;

To define and punish piracies and felonies committed on the high seas and offenses against the law of nations;

To declare war, grant letters of marque and reprisal, and make rules concerning captures on land and water;

To raise and support armies, but no appropriation of money to that use shall be for a longer term than two years;

To provide and maintain a navy;

To make rules for the government and regulation of the land and naval forces;

To provide for calling forth the militia to execute the laws of the Union, suppress insurrections, and repel invasions;

To provide for organizing, arming, and disciplining the militia, and for governing such part of them as may be employed in the service of the United States, reserving to the States respectively the appointment of the officers, and the authority of training the militia according to the discipline prescribed by Congress;

To exercise exclusive legislation in all cases whatsoever over such district (not exceeding ten miles square) as may, by cession of particular States and the acceptance of Congress, become the seat of the Government of the United States, and to exercise like authority over all places purchased by the consent of the legislature of the State in which the same shall be, for the erection of forts, magazines, arsenals, dockyards, and other needful buildings; and

To make all laws which shall be necessary and proper for carrying into execution the foregoing powers, and all other powers vested by this Constitution in the Government of the United States, or in any department or officer thereof.

SECTION IX.

The migration or importation of such persons as any of the States now existing shall think proper to admit shall not be prohibited by the Congress prior to the year one thousand eight hundred and eight, but a tax or duty may be imposed on such importation, not exceeding ten dollars for each person.

The privilege of the writ of habeas corpus shall not be suspended, unless when in cases of rebellion or invasion the public safety may require it.

No bill of attainder or ex post facto law shall be passed.

No capitation or other direct tax shall be laid, unless in proportion to the census or enumeration hereinbefore directed to be taken.

No tax or duty shall be laid on articles exported from any State.

No preference shall be given by any regulation of commerce or revenue to the ports of one State over those of another; nor shall vessels bound to or from one State be obliged to enter, clear, or pay duties in another.

No money shall be drawn from the Treasury but in con sequence of appropriations made by law; and a regular statement and account of the receipts and expenditures of all public money shall be published from time to time.

No title of nobility shall be granted by the United States; and no person holding any office of profit or trust under them shall, without the consent of the Congress, accept of any present, emolument, office, or title, of any kind whatever, from any king, prince, or foreign State.

SECTION X.

No State shall enter into any treaty, alliance, or confederation; grant letters of marque and reprisal; coin money; emit bills of credit; make anything but gold and silver coin a tender in payment of debts; pass any bill of attainder, ex post facto law, or law impairing the obligation of contracts, or grant any title of nobility.

No State shall, without the consent of Congress, lay any imposts or duties on imports or exports, except what may be absolutely necessary for executing its inspection laws; and the net produce of all duties and imposts, laid by any State on imports or exports, shall be for the use of the Treasury of the United States; and all such laws shall be subject to the revision and control of the Congress.

No State shall, without the consent of Congress, lay any duty of tonnage, keep troops or ships of war in time of peace, enter into any agreement or compact with another State or with a foreign power, or engage in war, unless actually invaded or in such imminent danger as will not admit of delay.

ARTICLE II.

SECTION I.

The executive power shall be vested in a President of the United States of America. He shall hold his office during the term of four years, and together with the Vice-President, chosen for the same term, be elected as follows:

Each State shall appoint, in such manner as the legislature thereof may direct, a number of electors, equal to the whole number of Senators and Representatives to which the State may be entitled in the Congress; but no Senator or Representative, or person holding an office of trust or profit under the United States, shall be appointed an elector.

[The electors shall meet in their respective States and vote by ballot for two persons, of whom one at least shall not be an inhabitant of the same State with themselves. And they shall make a list of all the persons voted for, and of the number of votes for each; which list they shall sign and certify, and transmit sealed to the seat of government of the United States, directed to the President of the Senate. The President of the Senate shall, in the presence of the Senate and House of Representatives, open all the certificates, and the votes shall then be counted. The person having the greatest number of votes shall be the President, if such number be a majority of the whole number of electors appointed; and if there be more than one who have such majority, and have an equal number of votes, then the House of Representatives shall immediately choose by ballot one of them for President; and if no person have a majority, then from the five highest on the list the said House shall in like manner choose the President. But in choosing the President the votes shall be taken by States, the representation from each State having one vote ; a quorum for this purpose shall consist of a member or members from two thirds of the States, and a majority of all the States shall be necessary to a choice. In every case, after the choice of the President, the person having the greatest number of votes of the electors shall be the Vice-President. But if there should remain two or more who have equal votes, the Senate shall choose from them by ballot the Vice-President.] *

The Congress may determine the time of choosing the electors and the day on which they shall give their votes, which day shall be the same throughout the United States.

No person except a natural-born citizen, or a citizen of the United States at the time of the adoption of this Constitution, shall be eligible to the office of President; neither shall any person be eligible to that office who shall not have attained to the age of thirty-five years, and been fourteen years a resident within the United States.

In case of the removal of the President from office, or of his death, resignation, or inability to discharge the powers and duties of the said office, the same shall devolve on the Vice-President, and the Congress may by law provide for the case of removal, death, resignation, or inability, both of the President and Vice-President, declaring what officer shall then act as President, and such officer shall act accordingly until the disability be removed or a President shall be elected.

The President shall, at stated times, receive for his services a compensation, which shall neither be increased nor diminished during the period for which he may have been elected, and he shall not receive within that period any other emolument from the United States or any of them.

Before he enter on the execution of his office he shall take the following oath or affirmation :

" I do solemnly swear (or affirm) that I will faithfully execute the office of President of the United States, and will to the best of my ability preserve, protect, and defend the Constitution of the United States."

SECTION II.

The President shall be Commander-in-chief of the Army and Navy of the United States, and of the militia of the several States when called into the actual service of the United States;

---

* This clause of the Constitution has been amended. See twelfth article of the amendments.

he may require the opinion, in writing, of the principal officer in each of the executive departments, upon any subject relating to the duties of their respective offices, and he shall have power to grant reprieves and pardons for offenses against the United States, except in cases of impeachment.

He shall have power, by and with the advice and consent of the Senate, to make treaties, provided two thirds of the Senators present concur; and he shall nominate, and, by and with the advice and consent of the Senate, shall appoint ambassadors, other public ministers and consuls, judges of the Supreme Court, and all other officers of the United States, whose appointments are not herein otherwise provided for, and which shall be established by law; but the Congress may by law vest the appointment of such inferior officers, as they think proper, in the President alone, in the courts of law, or in the heads of departments.

The President shall have power to fill up all vacancies that may happen during the recess of the Senate, by granting commissions which shall expire at the end of their next session.

SECTION III.

He shall from time to time give to the Congress information of the state of the Union, and recommend to their consideration such measures as he shall judge necessary and expedient; he may, on extraordinary occasions, convene both houses, or either of them, and in case of disagreement between them with respect to the time of adjournment, he may adjourn them to such time as he shall think proper; he shall receive ambassadors and other public ministers; he shall take care that the laws be faithfully executed, and shall commission all the officers of the United States.

SECTION IV.

The President, Vice-President, and all civil officers of the United States shall be removed from office on impeachment for and conviction of treason, bribery, or other high crimes and misdemeanors.

ARTICLE III.

SECTION I.

The judicial power of the United States shall be vested in one Supreme Court, and in such inferior courts as the Congress may from time to time ordain and establish. The judges, both of the supreme and inferior courts, shall hold their offices during good behavior, and shall, at stated times, receive for their services a compensation which shall not be diminished during their continuance in office.

SECTION II.

The judicial power shall extend to all cases, in law and equity, arising under this Constitution, the laws of the United States, and treaties made, or which shall be made, under their authority; to all cases affecting ambassadors, other public ministers, and consuls; to all cases of admiralty and maritime jurisdiction; to controversies to which the United States shall be a party; to controversies between two or more States; between a State and citizens of another State; between citizens of different States; between citizens of the same State claiming lands under grants of different States, and between a State, or the citizens thereof, and foreign States, citizens, or subjects.

In all cases affecting ambassadors, other public ministers and consuls, and those in which a State shall be a party, the Supreme Court shall have original jurisdiction. In all the other cases before mentioned the Supreme Court shall have appellate jurisdiction, both as to law and fact, with such exceptions and under such regulations as the Congress shall make.

The trial of all crimes, except in cases of impeachment, shall be by jury; and such trial shall be held in the State where the said crimes shall have been committed; but when not committed within any State, the trial shall be at such place or places as the Congress may by law have directed.

SECTION III.

Treason against the United States shall consist only in levying war against them, or in adhering to their enemies, giving them aid and comfort. No person shall be convicted of treason unless on the testimony of two witnesses to the same overt act, or on confession in open court.

The Congress shall have power to declare the punishment of treason, but no attainder of treason shall work corruption of blood or forfeiture except during the life of the person attainted.

ARTICLE IV.

SECTION I.

Full faith and credit shall be given in each State to the

public acts, records, and judicial proceedings of every other State. And the Congress may by general laws prescribe the manner in which such acts, records, and proceedings shall be proved, and the effect thereof.

SECTION II.

The citizens of each State shall be entitled to all privileges and immunities of citizens in the several States.

A person charged in any State with treason, felony, or other crime, who shall flee from justice, and be found in another State, shall, on demand of the executive authority of the State from which he fled, be delivered up, to be removed to the State having jurisdiction of the crime.

No person held to service or labor in one State, under the laws thereof, escaping into another, shall, in consequence of any law or regulation therein, be discharged from such service or labor, but shall be delivered up on claim of the party to whom such service or labor may be due.

SECTION III.

New States may be admitted by the Congress into this Union ; but no new State shall be formed or erected within the jurisdiction of any other State ; nor any State be formed by the junction of two or more States or parts of States, without the consent of the legislatures of the States concerned as well as of the Congress.

The Congress shall have power to dispose of and make all needful rules and regulations respecting the territory or other property belonging to the United States ; and nothing in this Constitution shall be so construed as to prejudice any claims of the United States or of any particular State.

SECTION IV.

The United States shall guarantee to every State in this Union a republican form of government, and shall protect each of them against invasion, and on application of the legislature, or of the executive (when the legislature cannot be convened), against domestic violence.

ARTICLE V.

The Congress, whenever two thirds of both houses shall deem it necessary, shall propose amendments to this Constitution, or, on the application of the legislatures of two thirds of the several States, shall call a convention for proposing amendments, which in either case shall be valid to all intents and purposes as part of this Constitution, when ratified by the legislatures of three fourths of the several States, or by conventions in three fourths thereof, as the one or the other mode of ratification may be proposed by the Congress, provided that no amendments which may be made prior to the year one thousand eight hundred and eight shall in any manner affect the first and fourth clauses in the ninth section of the first article; and that no State, without its consent, shall be deprived of its equal suffrage in the Senate.

ARTICLE VI.

All debts contracted and engagements entered into, before the adoption of this Constitution, shall be as valid against the United States under this Constitution as under the confederation.

This Constitution, and the laws of the United States which shall be made in pursuance thereof, and all treaties made, or which shall be made, under the authority of the United States, shall be the supreme law of the land; and the judges in every State shall be bound thereby, anything in the Constitution or laws of any State to the contrary notwithstanding.

The Senators and Representatives before mentioned, and the members of the several State legislatures, and all executive and judicial officers both of the United States and of the several States, shall be bound by oath or affirmation to support this Constitution; but no religious test shall ever be required as a qualification to any office or public trust under the United States.

ARTICLE VII.

The ratification of the conventions of nine States shall be sufficient for the establishment of this Constitution between the States so ratifying the same.

Done in convention by the unanimous consent of the States present, the seventeenth day of September, in the year of our Lord one thousand seven hundred and eighty-seven, and of the independence of the United States of America the twelfth. In witness whereof, we have hereunto subscribed our names.

George Washington, President, and Deputy from VIRGINIA.
NEW HAMPSHIRE — John Langdon, Nicholas Gilman.
MASSACHUSETTS — Nathaniel Gorham, Rufus King.
CONNECTICUT — William Samuel Johnson, Roger Sherman.
NEW YORK — Alexander Hamilton.
NEW JERSEY — William Livingston, David Brearly, William Patterson, Jonathan Dayton.
PENNSYLVANIA — Benjamin Franklin, Thomas Mifflin, Robert Morris, George Clymer, Thomas Fitzsimons, Jared Ingersoll, James Wilson, Gouverneur Morris.
DELAWARE — George Read, Gunning Bedford, Jr., John Dickinson, Richard Bassett, Jacob Broom.
MARYLAND — James McHenry, Daniel of St. Thomas Jenifer, Daniel Carroll.
VIRGINIA — John Blair, James Madison, Jr.
NORTH CAROLINA — William Blount, Richard Dobbs Spaight, Hugh Williamson.
SOUTH CAROLINA — John Rutledge, Charles Cotesworth Pinckney, Charles Pinckney, Pierce Butler.
GEORGIA — William Few, Abraham Baldwin.

Attest : William Jackson, *Secretary.*

AMENDMENTS.

ARTICLE I.

Congress shall make no law respecting an establishment of religion, or prohibiting the free exercise thereof; or abridging the freedom of speech or of the press; or the right of the people peaceably to assemble, and to petition the government for a redress of grievances.

ARTICLE II.

A well-regulated militia being necessary to the security of a free State, the right of the people to keep and bear arms shall not be infringed.

ARTICLE III.

No soldier shall, in time of peace, be quartered in any house without the consent of the owner, nor in time of war, but in a manner to be prescribed by law.

ARTICLE IV.

The right of the people to be secure in their persons, houses, papers, and effects, against unreasonable searches and seizures, shall not be violated, and no warrants shall issue but upon probable cause, supported by oath or affirmation, and particularly describing the place to be searched, and the person or things to be seized.

ARTICLE V.

No person shall be held to answer for a capital or otherwise infamous crime, unless on a presentment or indictment of a grand jury, except in cases arising in the land or naval forces, or in the militia, when in actual service in time of war or public danger; nor shall any person be subject for the same offense to be twice put in jeopardy of life or limb; nor shall be compelled in any criminal case to be a witness against himself, nor be deprived of life, liberty, or property, without due process of law; nor shall private property be taken for public use without just compensation.

ARTICLE VI.

In all criminal prosecutions the accused shall enjoy the right to a speedy and public trial, by an impartial jury of the State and district wherein the crime shall have been committed, which district shall have been previously ascertained by law, and to be informed of the nature and cause of the accusation ; to be confronted with the witnesses against him; to have compulsory process for obtaining witnesses in his favor, and to have the assistance of counsel for his defense.

ARTICLE VII.

In suits at common law, where the value in controversy shall exceed twenty dollars, the right of trial by jury shall be preserved, and no fact tried by a jury shall be otherwise re-examined in any court of the United States, than according to the rules of the common law.

ARTICLE VIII.

Excessive bail shall not be required, nor excessive fines imposed, nor cruel and unusual punishments inflicted.

ARTICLE IX..

The enumeration in the Constitution of certain rights shall not be construed to deny or disparage others retained by the people.

ARTICLE X.

The powers not delegated to the United States by the Constitution, nor prohibited by it to the States, are reserved to the States respectively or to the people.

ARTICLE XI.

The judicial power of the United States shall not be construed to extend to any suit in law or equity, commenced or prosecuted against one of the United States by citizens of another State, or by citizens or subjects of any foreign State.

ARTICLE XII.

The electors shall meet in their respective States and vote by ballot for President and Vice-President, one of whom, at least, shall not be an inhabitant of the same State with themselves; they shall name in their ballots the person voted for as President, and in distinct ballots the person voted for as Vice-President, and they shall make distinct lists of all persons voted for as President and of all persons voted for as Vice-President, and of the number of votes for each; which lists they shall sign and certify, and transmit sealed to the seat of the government of the United States, directed to the President of the Senate. The President of the Senate shall, in the presence of the Senate and House of Representatives, open all the certificates and the votes shall then be counted. The person having the greatest number of votes for President shall be the President, if such number be a majority of the whole number of electors appointed; and if no person have such majority, then from the persons having the highest numbers not exceeding three on the list of those voted for as President, the House of Representatives shall choose immediately, by ballot, the President. But in choosing the President the votes shall be taken by States, the representation from each State having one vote; a quorum for this purpose shall consist of a member or members from two thirds of the States, and a majority of all the States shall be necessary to a choice. And if the House of Representatives shall not choose a President whenever the right of choice shall devolve upon them, before the fourth day of March next following, then the Vice-President shall act as President, as in the case of the death or other constitutional disability of the President.

The person having the greatest number of votes as Vice-President shall be the Vice-President, if such number be a majority of the whole number of electors appointed; and if no person have a majority, then from the two highest numbers on the list the Senate shall choose the Vice-President; a quorum for the purpose shall consist of two thirds of the whole number of Senators, and a majority of the whole number shall be necessary to a choice. But no person constitutionally ineligible to the office of President shall be eligible to that of Vice-President of the United States.

ARTICLE XIII.

SECTION 1. Neither slavery nor involuntary servitude, except as a punishment for crime whereof the party shall have been duly convicted, shall exist within the United States or any place subject to their jurisdiction.

SECTION 2. Congress shall have power to enforce this article by appropriate legislation.

ARTICLE XIV.

SECTION 1. All persons born or naturalized in the United States, and subject to the jurisdiction thereof, are citizens of the United States and of the State wherein they reside. No State shall make or enforce any law which shall abridge the privileges or immunities of citizens of the United States; nor shall any State deprive any person of life, liberty, or property, without due process of law; nor deny to any person within its jurisdiction the equal protection of the laws.

SECTION 2. Representatives shall be apportioned among the several States according to their respective numbers, counting the whole number of persons in each State, excluding Indians not taxed. But when the right to vote at any election for the choice of electors for President and Vice-President of the United States, Representatives in Congress, the executive and judicial officers of a State, or the members of the legislature thereof, is denied to any of the male inhabitants of such State, being twenty-one years of age, and citizens of the United States, or in any way abridged, except for participation in rebellion, or other crime, the basis of representation therein shall be reduced in the proportion which the number of such male citizens shall bear to the whole number of male citizens twenty-one years of age in such State.

SECTION 3. No person shall be a Senator or Representative in Congress, or elector of President and Vice-President, or hold any office, civil or military, under the United States or under any State, who, having previously taken an oath as a member of Congress, or as an officer of the United States, or as a member of any State legislature, or as an executive or judicial officer of any State, to support the Constitution of the United States, shall have engaged in insurrection or rebellion against the same, or given aid or comfort to the enemies thereof. But Congress may, by a vote of two thirds of each house, remove such disability.

SECTION 4. The validity of the public debt of the United States, authorized by law, including debts incurred for payment of pensions and bounties for services in suppressing insurrection or rebellion, shall not be questioned. But neither the United States nor any State shall assume or pay any debt or obligation incurred in aid of insurrection or rebellion against the United States, or any claim for the loss or emancipation of any slave; but all such debts, obligations, and claims shall be held illegal and void.

SECTION 5. The Congress shall have power to enforce, by appropriate legislation, the provisions of this article.

ARTICLE XV.

SECTION 1. The right of citizens of the United States to vote shall not be denied or abridged by the United States or by any State on account of race, color, or previous condition of servitude.

SECTION 2. The Congress shall have power to enforce this article by appropriate legislation.

FRANKLIN'S SPEECH ON THE LAST DAY OF THE CON-STITUTIONAL CONVENTION.

From Madison's Journal.

MONDAY, September 17. *In Convention* — The engrossed Constitution being read, Doctor Franklin rose with a speech in his hand, which he had reduced to writing for his own convenience, and which Mr. Wilson read in the words following:

" MR. PRESIDENT : I confess that there are several parts of this Constitution which I do not at present approve, but I am not sure I shall never approve them. For, having lived long, I have experienced many instances of being obliged by better information, or fuller consideration, to change opinions even on important subjects which I once thought right, but found to be otherwise. It is therefore that, the older I grow, the more apt I am to doubt my own judgment, and to pay more respect to the judgment of others. Most men, indeed, as well as most sects in religion, think themselves in possession of all truth, and that wherever others differ from them it is so far error. Steele, a Protestant, in a dedication tells the Pope that the only difference between our churches, in their opinions of the certainty of their doctrines, is, 'the Church of Rome is infallible, and the Church of England is never in the wrong.' But though many private persons think almost as highly of their own infallibility as of that of their sect, few express it so naturally as a certain French lady who, in a dispute with her sister, said, 'I don't know how it happens, sister, but I meet with nobody but myself that is always in the right — *il n'y a que moi a toujours raison.*' In these sentiments, sir, I agree to this Constitution, with all its faults, if they are such, because I think a General Government necessary for us, and there is no form of government but what may be a blessing to the people if well administered: and believe further, that this is likely to be well administered for a course of years, and can only end in despotism, as other forms have done before it, when the people shall become so corrupted as to need despotic government, being incapable of any other. I doubt, too, whether any other Convention we can obtain may be able to make a better Constitution. For when you assemble a number of men to have the advantage of their joint wisdom, you inevitably assemble with those men all their prejudices, their passions, their errors of opinion, their local interests, and their selfish views. From such an assembly can a perfect production be expected? It, therefore, astonishes me, sir, to find this system approaching so near to perfection as it does: and I think it will astonish our enemies, who are waiting with confidence to hear that our councils are confounded, like those of the builders of Babel, and that our States are on the point of separation, only to meet hereafter for the purpose of cutting one another's throats. Thus I consent, sir, to this Constitution because I expect no better, and because I am not sure that it is not the best. The opinions I have had of its errors I sacrifice to the public good. I have never whispered a syllable of them abroad. Within these walls they were born and here they shall die. If every one of us, in returning to our constituents, were to report the objections he has had to it, and endeavor to gain partisans in support of them, we might prevent its being generally received, and thereby lose all the salutary effects and great advantages resulting naturally in our favor among foreign nations as well as among ourselves, from our real or apparent unanimity. Much of the strength and efficiency of any government, in procuring and securing happiness to the people, depends on opinion — on the general opinion of the goodness of the government as well as of the wisdom and integrity of its governors. I hope, therefore, that for our own sakes, as a part of the people, and for the sake of posterity, we shall act heartily and unanimously in recommending this Constitution (if approved by Congress and confirmed by the Conventions) wherever our influence may extend, and turn our future thoughts and endeavors to the means of having it well administered. On the whole, sir, I cannot help expressing a wish that every member of the Convention who

may still have objections to it would, with me, on this occasion doubt
a little of his own infallibility, and, to make manifest our unanimity,
put his name to this instrument."

He then moved that the Constitution be signed by the members,
and offered the following as a convenient form, viz.: "Done in
Convention by the unanimous consent of *the States* present the
seventeenth of September, etc. In witness whereof we have hereunto subscribed our names." This ambiguous form had been drawn
up by Mr. Gouverneur Morris, in order to gain the dissenting members, and put into the hands of Doctor Franklin, that it might have
the better chance of success. [Considerable discussion followed,
Randolph and Gerry stating their reasons for refusing to sign the
Constitution. Mr. Hamilton expressed his anxiety that every member should sign. A few characters of consequence, he said, by
opposing or even refusing to sign the Constitution, might do infinite
mischief by kindling the latent sparks that lurk under an enthusiasm
in favor of the Convention which may soon subside. No man's ideas
were more remote from the plan than his own were known to be; but
is it possible to deliberate between anarchy and convulsion on one
side, and the chance of good to be expected from the plan on the
other? This discussion concluded, the Convention voted that its
journal and other papers should be retained by the President, subject
to the order of Congress.] The members then proceeded to sign the
Constitution as finally amended. The Constitution being signed by
all the members except Mr. Randolph, Mr. Mason, and Mr. Gerry,
who declined giving it the sanction of their names, the Convention dis-
solved itself by an adjournment sine die.

Whilst the last members were signing, Doctor Franklin, looking
towards the President's chair, at the back of which a rising sun happened to be painted, observed to a few members near him that painters had found it difficult to distinguish in their art a rising from a
setting sun. I have, said he, often and often, in the course of the
session, and the vicissitudes of my hopes and fears as to its issue,
looked at that behind the President without being able to tell whether
it was rising or setting; but now, at length, I have the happiness to
know that it is a rising, and not a setting, sun.

The Federal Convention which framed the Constitution met at Philadelphia in May, 1787, and completed its work September 17. The number of
delegates chosen to the convention was sixty-five; ten did not attend; six-
teen declined signing the Constitution, or left the convention before it was
ready to be signed; thirty-nine signed.

The States ratified the Constitution in the following order:

Delaware	December 7, 1787	Maryland	April 28, 1788
Pennsylvania	December 12, 1787	South Carolina	May 23, 1788
New Jersey	December 18, 1787	New Hampshire	June 21, 1788
Georgia	January 2, 1788	Virginia	June 25, 1788
Connecticut	January 9, 1788	New York	July 26, 1788
Massachusetts	February 6, 1788	North Carolina	November 21, 1789
	Rhode Island	May 29, 1790	

The first ten amendments were proposed in 1789, and declared adopted in 1791.

The eleventh amendment was proposed in 1794, and declared adopted in 1798.

The twelfth amendment was proposed in 1803, and declared adopted in 1804.

The thirteenth amendment was proposed and adopted in 1865.

The fourteenth amendment was proposed in 1866, and adopted in 1868

The fifteenth amendment was proposed in 1869, and adopted in 1870

THE CONSTITUTION OF THE UNITED STATES.

With Bibliographical and Historical Notes and Outlines for Study

PREPARED BY EDWIN D. MEAD.

This Manual is published by the Directors of the Old South Studies in History and Politics, for the use of schools and of such clubs, classes and individual students as may wish to make a careful study of the Constitution and its history. The societies of young men and women now happily being organized everywhere in America for historical and political study can do nothing better to begin with than to make themselves thoroughly familiar with the Constitution. It is especially with such societies in view that the table of topics for study, which follows the very full bibliographical notes in this manual, has been prepared. A copy of the manual will be sent to any address on receipt of twenty-five cents; one hundred copies, fifteen dollars. Address *Directors of Old South Studies, Old South Meeting House*, or *D. C. Heath & Co., 5 Somerset street, Boston.*

OLD SOUTH LEAFLETS, GENERAL SERIES.

No. 1. Constitution of the United States 2. Articles of Confederation. 3. Declaration of Independence. 4. Washington's Farewell Address. 5. Magna Charta. 6. Vane's "Healing Question." 7. Charter of Massachusetts Bay, 1629. 8. Fundamental Orders of Connecticut, 1638. 9. Franklin's Plan of Union, 1754. 10. Washington's Inaugurals. 11. Lincoln's Inaugurals and Emancipation Proclamation. 12. The Federalist, Nos. 1, 2 and 3—etc. Price, five cents per copy; one hundred copies, three dollars. *Directors of Old South Studies, Old South Meeting House, Boston.*

PUBLISHED FOR SCHOOLS AND THE TRADE BY

D. C. HEATH & CO., 5 Somerset St., Boston.